MARK TWA

NO. 44,
THE
MYSTERIOUS
STRANGER

THE MARK TWAIN LIBRARY

The Library offers for the first time popular editions of Mark Twain's best works just as he wanted them to be read. These moderately priced volumes, faithfully reproduced from the California scholarly editions and printed on acid-free paper, are sparingly annotated and include all the original illustrations that Mark Twain commissioned and enjoyed.

"Huck waited for no particulars. He sprang away
and sped down the hill as fast as his
legs could carry him."

—THE ADVENTURES OF TOM SAWYER

Mark Twain's manuscript for the title page

MARK TWAIN

NO. 44,
THE
MYSTERIOUS
STRANGER

BEING AN ANCIENT TALE FOUND IN A JUG,
AND FREELY TRANSLATED FROM THE JUG

Foreword and Notes by
John S. Tuckey

Text established by
William M. Gibson
and the staff of the Mark Twain Project

University of California Press

Berkeley   Los Angeles   London

This Mark Twain Library text of *No. 44* is a photographic reproduction of the text published in *Mark Twain's Mysterious Stranger Manuscripts,* ed. William M. Gibson (University of California Press, 1969), which was approved by the Center for Editions of American Authors (CEAA). Editorial work on that text was made possible by a generous grant, administered through the CEAA, from the Research Materials Program of the National Endowment for the Humanities.

University of California Press
Berkeley and Los Angeles
University of California Press, Ltd.
London

Manufactured in the United States of America

1 2 3 4 5 6 7 8 9 0

Twain, Mark, 1835–1910.
   No. 44, The Mysterious Stranger (The Mark Twain Library)
   Originally published as part of Mark Twain's Mysterious Stranger Manuscripts: Berkeley: University of California Press, 1969.
   Includes bibliographical references.
   I. Twain, Mark, 1835–1910. Mysterious stranger. II. Title. III. Series: Twain, Mark, 1835–1910. Mark Twain Library.
PS1322.M97 1982 813'.4 81–40326
ISBN 0–520–04544–0
ISBN 0–520–04545–9 (pbk.)

Discounts are available for large quantity purchases by groups or schools. Write the Sales Department, University of California Press, Berkeley, CA 94720.

The Mark Twain Library is designed by Steve Renick.

CONTENTS

FOREWORD

This fantasy-rich last novel by Mark Twain was written during his late sixties and early seventies. It is his final version of a story that survives in three distinct drafts, all of which he left unpublished at the time of his death in 1910. By 1908 he had carried this version to novel length and had written the remarkable, indeed uncanny, final chapter, but he had not taken steps to publish his work. The reader now has in his hands the only story Mark Twain himself ever called "The Mysterious Stranger." But a quite different, editorially fabricated tale, partly based on an earlier, incomplete draft, has long borne that title as a purported work by Mark Twain. A false "Stranger" has thus been parading before the world while the real one has remained hidden and unknown. If Mark Twain's surviving spirit has the human scene in view, the prank-loving humorist is probably enjoying the resulting confusion.

The setting of the story is medieval Austria, and the prevailing tone might be fairly described as gothic. Mark Twain had been fascinated by medieval settings as early as 1859, when as a young man of twenty-four he had written "The Mysterious Murders in Risse," and as late as 1889 and 1896, when he had published *A Connecticut Yankee in King Arthur's Court* and *Joan of Arc*. Although he took some pains to use authentic details in all these works, Mark Twain habitually imbued the narrative with his more intimate, firsthand knowledge of his own home town, Hannibal, Missouri.

In *No. 44, The Mysterious Stranger* he drew heavily on his early recollections of his own midwestern boyhood. He did so not to write again about adventures along the Mississippi, as he had done in *Tom Sawyer* (1876) and *Huckleberry Finn* (1885), but to bring the special magic of those memories into a scene laid in an imaginary European village in 1490. He also made use of his more recent impressions of the Swiss town of Weggis, by Lake Lucerne, where he had lived while making notes for this story.

Psychologically considered, Eseldorf (German for "Assville") is, however, the world—complacent in its drowsiness, populated with unawakened minds. The main action of the novel takes place, by contrast, in a printshop—a potentially subversive center of enlightenment. The printshop is hidden within the labyrinthine expanses of a vast, mouldering castle with hundreds of empty rooms, suggestive of the unused capacities of the human brain. In writing of the printshop, Mark Twain was again recalling early experiences in Hannibal, where he had in his twelfth year been apprenticed to the printing trade. Starting as a printer's devil, even as the character he curiously calls "44," the young Sam Clemens had been required to do the dirtiest work of the shop—such as washing type, inking forms, and cleaning out the receptacle for broken type metal known as the hellbox. Also, like 44, he had creative powers that were to lift him immensely above such a lowly station: printer's devil, yes, but possessed of a powerful dæmon.

First appearing at the castle as a penniless lad seeking work, 44 quickly shows himself to be no ordinary human being. To August Feldner, the young printshop worker who tells the story, he displays an ability to do miracles. Mysterious and incredible things begin to happen around the castle. August is guided by 44 in exploring unknown possibilities of life that may be attained through the higher powers of mind.

This long overlooked last novel by Mark Twain, rich in fantasy and full of magical events, is a psychic adventure, a journey into the deeper mind and beyond—into the realm of the unconscious and of dream ex periences, and on at last to that appalling void which one must brave in order to become whole. The phantasmagoric effects, the sudden shifts in time, place, scene, and mood, are fitting aspects of this tale spun out of dream-stuff.

John S. Tuckey

MARK TWAIN

NO. 44,
THE
MYSTERIOUS
STRANGER

Chapter 1

It was in 1490—winter. Austria was far away from the world, and asleep; it was still the Middle Ages in Austria, and promised to remain so forever. Some even set it away back centuries upon centuries and said that by the mental and spiritual clock it was still the Age of Faith in Austria. But they meant it as a compliment, not a slur, and it was so taken, and we were all proud of it. I remember it well, although I was only a boy; and I remember, too, the pleasure it gave me.

Yes, Austria was far from the world, and asleep, and our village was in the middle of that sleep, being in the middle of Austria. It drowsed in peace in the deep privacy of a hilly and woodsy solitude where news from the world hardly ever came to disturb its dreams, and was infinitely content. At its front flowed the tranquil river, its surface painted with cloud-forms and the reflections of drifting arks and stone-boats; behind it rose the woody steeps to the base of the lofty precipice; from the top of the precipice frowned the vast castle of Rosenfeld, its long stretch of towers and bastions mailed in vines; beyond the river, a league to the left, was a tumbled expanse of forest-clothed hills cloven by winding gorges where the sun never penetrated; and to the right, a precipice overlooked the river, and

3

between it and the hills just spoken of lay a far-reaching plain dotted with little homesteads nested among orchards and shade-trees.

The whole region for leagues around was the hereditary property of prince Rosenfeld, whose servants kept the castle always in perfect condition for occupancy, but neither he nor his family came there oftener than once in five years. When they came it was as if the lord of the world had arrived, and had brought all the glories of its kingdoms along; and when they went they left a calm behind which was like the deep sleep which follows an orgy.

Eseldorf was a paradise for us boys. We were not overmuch pestered with schooling. Mainly we were trained to be good Catholics; to revere the Virgin, the Church and the saints above everything; to hold the Monarch in awful reverence, speak of him with bated breath, uncover before his picture, regard him as the gracious provider of our daily bread and of all our earthly blessings, and ourselves as being sent into the world with the one only mission, to labor for him, bleed for him, die for him, when necessary. Beyond these matters we were not required to know much; and in fact, not allowed to. The priests said that knowledge was not good for the common people, and could make them discontented with the lot which God had appointed for them, and God would not endure discontentment with His plans. This was true, for the priests got it of the Bishop.

It was discontentment that came so near to being the ruin of Gretel Marx the dairyman's widow, who had two horses and a cart, and carried milk to the market town. A Hussite woman named Adler came to Eseldorf and went slyly about, and began to persuade some of the ignorant and foolish to come privately by night to her house and hear "God's *real* message," as she called it. She was a cunning woman, and sought out only those few who could read— flattering them by saying it showed their intelligence, and that only the intelligent could understand her doctrine. She gradually got ten together, and these she poisoned nightly with her heresies in her house. And she gave them Hussite sermons, all written out, to keep for their own, and persuaded them that it was no sin to read them.

One day Father Adolf came along and found the widow sitting in the shade of the horse-chestnut that stood by her house, reading these iniquities. He was a very loud and zealous and strenuous priest, and was always working to get more reputation, hoping to be a Bishop some day; and he was always spying around and keeping a sharp lookout on other people's flocks as well as his own; and he was dissolute and profane and malicious, but otherwise a good enough man, it was generally thought. And he certainly had talent; he was a most fluent and chirpy speaker, and could say the cuttingest things and the wittiest, though a little coarse, maybe—however it was only his enemies who said that, and it really wasn't any truer of him than of others; but he belonged to the village council, and lorded it there, and played smart dodges that carried his projects through, and of course that nettled the others; and in their resentment they gave him nicknames privately, and called him the "Town Bull," and "Hell's Delight," and all sorts of things; which was natural, for when you are in politics you are in the wasp's nest with a short shirt-tail, as the saying is.

He was rolling along down the road, pretty full and feeling good, and braying "We'll sing the wine-cup and the lass" in his thundering bass, when he caught sight of the widow reading her book. He came to a stop before her and stood swaying there, leering down at her with his fishy eyes, and his purple fat face working and grimacing, and said—

"What is it you've got there, Frau Marx? What are you reading?"

She let him see. He bent down and took one glance, then he knocked the writings out of her hand and said angrily—

"Burn them, burn them, you fool! Don't you know it's a sin to read them? Do you want to damn your soul? Where did you get them?"

She told him, and he said—

"By God I expected it. I will attend to that woman; I will make this place sultry for her. You go to her meetings, do you? What does she teach you—to worship the Virgin?"

"No—only God."

"I thought it. You are on your road to hell. The Virgin will punish you for this—you mark my words." Frau Marx was getting frightened; and was going to try to excuse herself for her conduct, but Father Adolf shut her up and went on storming at her and telling her what the Virgin would do with her, until she was ready to swoon with fear. She went on her knees and begged him to tell her what to do to appease the Virgin. He put a heavy penance on her, scolded her some more, then took up his song where he had left off, and went rolling and zigzagging away.

But Frau Marx fell again, within the week, and went back to Frau Adler's meeting one night. Just four days afterward both of her horses died! She flew to Father Adolf, full of repentance and despair, and cried and sobbed, and said she was ruined and must starve; for how could she market her milk now? What *must* she do? tell her what to do. He said—

"I told you the Virgin would punish you—didn't I tell you that? Hell's bells! did you think I was lying? You'll pay attention next time, I reckon."

Then he told her what to do. She must have a picture of the horses painted, and walk on pilgrimage to the Church of Our Lady of the Dumb Crèatures, and hang it up there, and make her offerings; then go home and sell the skins of her horses and buy a lottery ticket bearing the number of the date of their death, and then wait in patience for the Virgin's answer. In a week it came, when Frau Marx was almost perishing with despair—her ticket drew fifteen hundred ducats!

That is the way the Virgin rewards a real repentance. Frau Marx did not fall again. In her gratitude she went to those other women and told them her experience and showed them how sinful and foolish they were and how dangerously they were acting; and they all burned their sermons and returned repentant to the bosom of the Church, and Frau Adler had to carry her poisons to some other market. It was the best lesson and the wholesomest our village ever had. It never allowed another Hussite to come there; and for reward the Virgin watched over it and took care of it personally, and made it fortunate and prosperous always.

It was in conducting funerals that Father Adolf was at his best, if he hadn't too much of a load on, but only about enough to make him properly appreciate the sacredness of his office. It was fine to see him march his procession through the village, between the kneeling ranks, keeping one eye on the candles blinking yellow in the sun to see that the acolytes walked stiff and held them straight, and the other watching out for any dull oaf that might forget himself and stand staring and covered when the Host was carried past. He would snatch that oaf's broad hat from his head, hit him a staggering whack in the face with it and growl out in a low snarl—

"Where's your manners, you beast?—and the Lord God passing by!"

Whenever there was a suicide he was active. He was on hand to see that the government did its duty and turned the family out into the road, and confiscated its small belongings and didn't smouch any of the Church's share; and he was on hand again at midnight when the corpse was buried at the cross-roads—not to do any religious office, for of course that was not allowable—but to see, for himself, that the stake was driven through the body in a right and permanent and workmanlike way.

It was grand to see him make procession through the village in plague-time, with our saint's relics in their jeweled casket, and trade prayers and candles to the Virgin for her help in abolishing the pest.

And he was always on hand at the bridge-head on the 9th of December, at the Assuaging of the Devil. Ours was a beautiful and massive stone bridge of five arches, and was seven hundred years old. It was built by the Devil in a single night. The prior of the monastery hired him to do it, and had trouble to persuade him, for the Devil said he had built bridges for priests all over Europe, and had always got cheated out of his wages; and this was the last time he would trust a Christian if he got cheated now. Always before, when he built a bridge, he was to have for his pay the first passenger that crossed it—everybody knowing he meant a Christian, of course. But no matter, he didn't *say* it, so they always sent a jackass or a chicken or some other undamnable passenger across

first, and so got the best of him. This time he *said* Christian, and
wrote it in the bond himself, so there couldn't be any misunder-
standing. And that isn't tradition, it is history, for I have seen that
bond myself, many a time; it is always brought out on Assuaging
Day, and goes to the bridge-head with the procession; and anybody
who pays ten groschen can see it and get remission of thirty-three
sins besides, times being easier for every one then than they are
now, and sins much cheaper; so much cheaper that all except the
very poorest could afford them. Those were good days, but they are
gone and will not come any more, so every one says.

Yes, he put it in the bond, and the prior said he didn't want the
bridge built yet, but would soon appoint a day—perhaps in about a
week. There was an old monk wavering along between life and
death, and the prior told the watchers to keep a sharp eye out and
let him know as soon as they saw that the monk was actually dying.
Towards midnight the 9th of December the watchers brought him
word, and he summoned the Devil and the bridge was begun. All
the rest of the night the prior and the Brotherhood sat up and
prayed that the dying one might be given strength to rise up and
walk across the bridge at dawn—strength enough, but not too
much. The prayer was heard, and it made great excitement in
heaven; insomuch that all the heavenly host got up before dawn
and came down to see; and there they were, clouds and clouds of
angels filling all the air above the bridge; and the dying monk
tottered across, and just had strength to get over; then he fell dead
just as the Devil was reaching for him, and as his soul escaped the
angels swooped down and caught it and flew up to heaven with it,
laughing and jeering, and Satan found he hadn't anything but a
useless carcase.

He was very angry, and charged the prior with cheating him, and
said "*this* isn't a Christian," but the prior said "Yes it is, it's a *dead*
one." Then the prior and all the monks went through with a great
lot of mock ceremonies, pretending it was to assuage the Devil and
reconcile him, but really it was only to make fun of him and stir up
his bile more than ever. So at last he gave them all a solid good
cursing, they laughing at him all the time. Then he raised a black

storm of thunder and lightning and wind and flew away in it; and as he went the spike on the end of his tail caught on a capstone and tore it away; and there it always lay, throughout the centuries, as proof of what he had done. I have seen it myself, a thousand times. Such things speak louder than written records; for written records can lie, unless they are set down by a priest. The mock Assuaging is repeated every 9th of December, to this day, in memory of that holy thought of the prior's which rescued an imperiled Christian soul from the odious Enemy of mankind.

There have been better priests, in some ways, than Father Adolf, for he had his failings, but there was never one in our commune who was held in more solemn and awful respect. This was because he had absolutely no fear of the Devil. He was the only Christian I have ever known of whom that could be truly said. People stood in deep dread of him, on that account; for they thought there must be something supernatural about him, else he could not be so bold and so confident. All men speak in bitter disapproval of the Devil, but they do it reverently, not flippantly; but Father Adolf's way was very different; he called him by every vile and putrid name he could lay his tongue to, and it made every one shudder that heard him; and often he would even speak of him scornfully and scoffingly; then the people crossed themselves and went quickly out of his presence, fearing that something fearful might happen; and this was natural, for after all is said and done Satan is a sacred character, being mentioned in the Bible, and it cannot be proper to utter lightly the sacred names, lest heaven itself should resent it.

Father Adolf had actually met Satan face to face, more than once, and defied him. This was known to be so. Father Adolf said it himself. He never made any secret of it, but spoke it right out. And that he was speaking true, there was proof, in at least one instance; for on that occasion he quarreled with the Enemy, and intrepidly threw his bottle at him, and there, upon the wall of his study was the ruddy splotch where it struck and broke.

The priest that we all loved best and were sorriest for, was Father Peter. But the Bishop suspended him for talking around in conversation that God was all goodness and would find a way to save *all* his poor human children. It was a horrible thing to say, but there was never any absolute proof that Father Peter said it; and it was out of character for him to say it, too, for he was always good and gentle and truthful, and a good Catholic, and always teaching in the pulpit just what the Church required, and nothing else. But there it was, you see: he wasn't charged with saying it in the pulpit, where all the congregation could hear and testify, but only outside, in talk; and it is easy for enemies to manufacture *that*. Father Peter denied it; but no matter, Father Adolf wanted his place, and he told the Bishop, and swore to it, that he overheard Father Peter say it; heard Father Peter say it to his niece, when Father Adolf was behind the door listening—for he was suspicious of Father Peter's soundness, he said, and the interests of religion required that he be watched.

The niece, Gretchen, denied it, and implored the Bishop to believe her and spare her old uncle from poverty and disgrace; but Father Adolf had been poisoning the Bishop against the old man a long time privately, and he wouldn't listen; for he had a deep admiration of Father Adolf's bravery toward the Devil, and an awe of him on account of his having met the Devil face to face; and so he was a slave to Father Adolf's influence. He suspended Father Peter, indefinitely, though he wouldn't go so far as to excommunicate him on the evidence of only one witness; and now Father Peter had been out a couple of years, and Father Adolf had his flock.

Those had been hard years for the old priest and Gretchen. They had been favorites, but of course that changed when they came under the shadow of the Bishop's frown. Many of their friends fell away entirely, and the rest became cool and distant. Gretchen was a lovely girl of eighteen, when the trouble came, and she had the best head in the village, and the most in it. She taught the harp, and earned all her clothes and pocket money by her own industry. But her scholars fell off one by one, now; she was forgotten when there were dances and parties among the youth of the village; the young fellows stopped coming to the house, all except Wilhelm Meidling —and he could have been spared; she and her uncle were sad and forlorn in their neglect and disgrace, and the sunshine was gone out of their lives. Matters went worse and worse, all through the two years. Clothes were wearing out, bread was harder and harder to get. And now at last, the very end was come. Solomon Isaacs had lent all the money he was willing to put on the house, and gave notice that to-morrow he should foreclose.

Chapter 2

I HAD BEEN familiar with that village life, but now for as much as a year I had been out of it, and was busy learning a trade. I was more curiously than pleasantly situated. I have spoken of Castle Rosenfeld; I have also mentioned a precipice which overlooked the river. Well, along this precipice stretched the towered and battlemented mass of a similar castle—prodigious, vine-clad, stately and beautiful, but mouldering to ruin. The great line that had possessed it and made it their chief home during four or five centuries was extinct, and no scion of it had lived in it now for a hundred years. It was a stanch old pile, and the greater part of it was still habitable. Inside, the ravages of time and neglect were less evident than they were outside. As a rule the spacious chambers and the vast corridors, ballrooms, banqueting halls and rooms of state were bare and melancholy and cobwebbed, it is true, but the walls and floors were in tolerable condition, and they could have been lived in. In some of the rooms the decayed and ancient furniture still remained, but if the empty ones were pathetic to the view, these were sadder still.

This old castle was not wholly destitute of life. By grace of the Prince over the river, who owned it, my master, with his little household, had for many years been occupying a small portion of it, near the centre of the mass. The castle could have housed a thousand persons; consequently, as you may say, this handful was lost in it, like a swallow's nest in a cliff.

My master was a printer. His was a new art, being only thirty or forty years old, and almost unknown in Austria. Very few persons

in our secluded region had ever seen a printed page, few had any
very clear idea about the art of printing, and perhaps still fewer had
any curiosity concerning it or felt any interest in it. Yet we had to
conduct our business with some degree of privacy, on account of
the Church. The Church was opposed to the cheapening of books
and the indiscriminate dissemination of knowledge. Our villagers
did not trouble themselves about our work, and had no commerce
in it; we published nothing there, and printed nothing that they
could have read, they being ignorant of abstruse sciences and the
dead languages.

We were a mixed family. My master, Heinrich Stein, was portly,
and of a grave and dignified carriage, with a large and benevolent
face and calm deep eyes—a patient man whose temper could stand
much before it broke. His head was bald, with a valance of silky
white hair hanging around it, his face was clean shaven, his rai-
ment was good and fine, but not rich. He was a scholar, and a
dreamer or a thinker, and loved learning and study, and would have
submerged his mind all the days and nights in his books and been
pleasantly and peacefully unconscious of his surroundings, if God
had been willing. His complexion was younger than his hair; he
was four or five years short of sixty.

A large part of his surroundings consisted of his wife. She was
well along in life, and was long and lean and flat-breasted, and had
an active and vicious tongue and a diligent and devilish spirit, and
more religion than was good for her, considering the quality of it.
She hungered for money, and believed there was a treasure hid in
the black deeps of the castle somewhere; and between fretting and
sweating about that and trying to bring sinners nearer to God when
any fell in her way she was able to fill up her time and save her life
from getting uninteresting and her soul from getting mouldy.
There was old tradition for the treasure, and the word of Balthasar
Hoffman thereto. He had come from a long way off, and had
brought a great reputation with him, which he concealed in our
family the best he could, for he had no more ambition to be burnt
by the Church than another. He lived with us on light salary and
board, and worked the constellations for the treasure. He had an

easy berth and was not likely to lose his job if the constellations held out, for it was Frau Stein that hired him; and her faith in him, as in all things she had at heart, was of the staying kind. Inside the walls, where was safety, he clothed himself as Egyptians and magicians should, and moved stately, robed in black velvet starred and mooned and cometed and sun'd with the symbols of his trade done in silver, and on his head a conical tower with like symbols glinting from it. When he at intervals went outside he left his business suit behind, with good discretion, and went dressed like anybody else and looking the Christian with such cunning art that St. Peter would have let him in quite as a matter of course, and probably asked him to take something. Very naturally we were all afraid of him—abjectly so, I suppose I may say—though Ernest Wasserman professed that he wasn't. Not that he did it publicly; no, he didn't; for, with all his talk, Ernest Wasserman had a judgment in choosing the right place for it that never forsook him. He wasn't even afraid of ghosts, if you let him tell it; and not only that but didn't believe in them. That is to say, he *said* he didn't believe in them. The truth is, he would say any foolish thing that he thought would make him conspicuous.

To return to Frau Stein. This masterly devil was the master's second wife, and before that she had been the widow Vogel. She had brought into the family a young thing by her first marriage, and this girl was now seventeen and a blister, so to speak; for she was a second edition of her mother—just plain galley-proof, neither revised nor corrected, full of turned letters, wrong fonts, outs and doubles, as we say in the printing-shop—in a word, *pi,* if you want to put it remorselessly strong and yet not strain the facts. Yet if it ever would be fair to strain facts it would be fair in her case, for she was not loath to strain them herself when so minded. Moses Haas said that whenever she took up an en-quad fact, just watch her and you would see her try to cram it in where there wasn't breathing-room for a 4-m space; and she'd do it, too, if she had to take the sheep-foot to it. Isn't it neat! Doesn't it describe it to a dot? Well, he could say such things, Moses could—as malicious a devil as we had on the place, but as bright as a lightning-bug and as sudden, when he was in the humor. He had a talent for getting himself hated, and always had it out at usury. That daughter kept the name she was born to—Maria Vogel; it was her mother's preference and her own. Both were proud of it, without any reason, except reasons which they invented, themselves, from time to time, as a market offered. Some of the Vogels may have been distinguished, by not getting hanged, Moses thought, but no one attached much importance to what the mother and daughter claimed for them. Maria had plenty of energy and vivacity and tongue, and was shapely enough but not pretty, barring her eyes, which had all kinds of fire in them, according to the mood of the moment—opal-fire, fox-fire, hell-fire, and the rest. She hadn't any fear, broadly speaking. Perhaps she had none at all, except for Satan, and ghosts, and witches and the priest and the magician, and a sort of fear of God in the dark, and of the lightning when she had been blaspheming and hadn't time to get in *aves* enough to square up and cash-in. She despised Marget Regen, the master's niece, along with Marget's mother, Frau Regen, who was the master's sister and a dependent and bedridden widow. She loved Gustav Fischer, the big and blonde and handsome and good-hearted journeyman, and detested the rest of the tribe impartially, I think. Gustav did not reciprocate.

Marget Regen was Maria's age—seventeen. She was lithe and graceful and trim-built as a fish, and she was a blue-eyed blonde, and soft and sweet and innocent and shrinking and winning and gentle and beautiful; just a vision for the eyes, worshipful, adorable, enchanting; but that wasn't the hive for her. She was a kitten in a menagerie.

She was a second edition of what her mother had been at her age; but struck from the standing forms and needing no revising, as one says in the printing-shop. That poor meek mother! yonder she had lain, partially paralysed, ever since her brother my master had brought her eagerly there a dear and lovely young widow with her little child fifteen years before; the pair had been welcome, and had forgotten their poverty and poor-relation estate and been happy during three whole years. Then came the new wife with her five-year brat, and a change began. The new wife was never able to root out the master's love for his sister, nor to drive sister and child from under the roof, but she accomplished the rest: as soon as she had gotten her lord properly trained to harness, she shortened his visits to his sister and made them infrequent. But she made up for this by going frequently herself and roasting the widow, as the saying is.

Next was old Katrina. She was cook and housekeeper; her forbears had served the master's people and none else for three or four generations; she was sixty, and had served the master all his life, from the time when she was a little girl and he was a swaddled baby. She was erect, straight, six feet high, with the port and stride of a soldier; she was independent and masterful, and her fears were limited to the supernatural. She believed she could whip anybody on the place, and would have considered an invitation a favor. As far as her allegiance stretched, she paid it with affection and reverence, but it did not extend beyond "her family"—the master, his sister, and Marget. She regarded Frau Vogel and Maria as aliens and intruders, and was frank about saying so.

She had under her two strapping young wenches—Sara and Duffles (a nickname), and a manservant, Jacob, and a porter, Fritz.

Next, we have the printing force.

Adam Binks, sixty years old, learnèd bachelor, proof-reader, poor, disappointed, surly.

Hans Katzenyammer, 36, printer, huge, strong, freckled, red-headed, rough. When drunk, quarrelsome. Drunk when opportunity offered.

Moses Haas, 28, printer; a looker-out for himself; liable to say acid things about people and to people; take him all around, not a pleasant character.

Barty Langbein, 15; cripple; general-utility lad; sunny spirit; affectionate; could play the fiddle.

Ernest Wasserman, 17, apprentice; braggart, malicious, hateful, coward, liar, cruel, underhanded, treacherous. He and Moses had a sort of half fondness for each other, which was natural, they having one or more traits in common, down among the lower grades of traits.

Gustav Fischer, 27, printer; large, well built, shapely and muscular; quiet, brave, kindly, a good disposition, just and fair; a slow temper to ignite, but a reliable burner when well going. He was about as much out of place as was Marget. He was the best man of them all, and deserved to be in better company.

Last of all comes August Feldner, 16, 'prentice. This is myself.

Chapter 3

OF SEVERAL conveniences there was no lack; among them, fire-wood and room. There was no end of room, we had it to waste. Big or little chambers for all—suit yourself, and change when you liked. For a kitchen we used a spacious room which was high up over the massive and frowning gateway of the castle and looked down the woody steeps and southward over the receding plain.

It opened into a great room with the same outlook, and this we used as dining room, drinking room, quarreling room—in a word, family room. Above its vast fire-place, which was flanked with fluted columns, rose the wide granite mantel, heavily carved, to the high ceiling. With a cart-load of logs blazing here within and a snow-tempest howling and whirling outside, it was a heaven of a place for comfort and contentment and cosiness, and the exchange of injurious personalities. Especially after supper, with the lamps going and the day's work done. It was not the tribe's custom to hurry to bed.

The apartments occupied by the Steins were beyond this room to the east, on the same front; those occupied by Frau Regen and Marget were on the same front also, but to the west, beyond the kitchen. The rooms of the rest of the herd were on the same floor, but on the other side of the principal great interior court—away over in the north front, which rose high in air above precipice and river.

The printing-shop was remote, and hidden in an upper section of a round tower. Visitors were not wanted there; and if they had tried

to hunt their way to it without a guide they would have concluded
to give it up and call another time before they got through.

One cold day, when the noon meal was about finished, a most
forlorn looking youth, apparently sixteen or seventeen years old,
appeared in the door, and stopped there, timid and humble, ventur-
ing no further. His clothes were coarse and old, ragged, and lightly
powdered with snow, and for shoes he had nothing but some old
serge remnants wrapped about his feet and ancles and tied with
strings. The war of talk stopped at once and all eyes were turned
upon the apparition; those of the master, and Marget, and Gustav
Fischer, and Barty Langbein, in pity and kindness, those of Frau
Stein and the rest in varying shades of contempt and hostility.

"What do you want here?" said the Frau, sharply.

The youth seemed to wince under that. He did not raise his
head, but with eyes still bent upon the floor and shyly fumbling his
ruin of a cap which he had removed from his head, answered
meekly—

"I am friendless, gracious lady, and am so—*so* hungry!"

"*So* hungry, are you?"—mimicking him. "Who invited you?
How did you get in? Take yourself out of this!"

She half rose, as if minded to help him out with her hands.
Marget started to rise at the same moment, with her plate in her
hands and an appeal on her lips: "May I, madam?"

"No! Sit down!" commanded the Frau. The master, his face all
pity, had opened his lips—no doubt to say the kind word—but he
closed them now, discouraged. Old Katrina emerged from the
kitchen, and stood towering in the door. She took in the situation,
and just as the boy was turning sorrowfully away, she hailed him:

"Come back, child, there's room in my kitchen, and plenty to eat,
too!"

"Shut your mouth you hussy, and mind your own affairs and
keep to your own place!" screamed the Frau, rising and turning
toward Katrina, who, seeing that the boy was afraid to move, was
coming to fetch him. Katrina, answering no word, came striding on.
"Command her, Heinrich Stein! will you allow your own wife to be
defied by a servant?"

The master said "It isn't the first time," and did not seem ungratified.

Katrina came on, undisturbed; she swung unheeding past her mistress, took the boy by the hand, and led him back to her fortress, saying, as she crossed its threshold,

"If any of you wants this boy, you come and get him, that's all!"

Apparently no one wanted him at that expense, so no one followed. The talk opened up briskly, straightway. Frau Stein wanted the boy turned out as soon as might be; she was willing he should be fed, if he was so hungry as he had said he was, which was probably a lie, for he had the look of a liar, she said, but shelter he could have none, for in her opinion he had the look of a murderer and a thief; and she asked Maria if it wasn't so. Maria confirmed it, and then the Frau asked for the general table's judgment. Opinions came freely: negatives from the master and from Marget and Fischer, affirmatives from the rest; and then war broke out. Presently, as one could easily see, the master was beginning to lose patience. He was likely to assert himself when that sign appeared. He suddenly broke in upon the wrangle, and said,

"Stop! This is a great to-do about nothing. The boy is not necessarily *bad* because he is unfortunate. And if he *is* bad, what of it? A bad person can be as hungry as a good one, and hunger is always respectable. And so is weariness. The boy is worn and tired, any one can see it. If he wants rest and shelter, *that* is no crime; let him say it and have it, be he bad or good—there's room enough."

That settled it. Frau Stein was opening her mouth to try and unsettle it again when Katrina brought the boy in and stood him before the master and said, encouragingly,

"Don't be afraid, the master's a just man. Master, he's a plenty good enough boy, for all he looks such a singed cat. He's out of luck, there's nothing else the matter with him. Look at his face, look at his eye. He's not a beggar for love of it. He wants work."

"*Work!*" scoffed Frau Stein; "that tramp?" And "work!" sneered this and that and the other one. But the master looked interested, and not unpleased. He said,

"Work, is it? What kind of work are you willing to do, lad?"

"He's willing to do any kind, sir," interrupted Katrina, eagerly, "and he don't want any pay."

"What, no pay?"

"No sir, nothing but food to eat and shelter for his head, poor lad."

"Not even clothes?"

"He shan't go naked, sir, if you'll keep him, my wage is bail for that."

There was an affectionate light in the boy's eye as he glanced gratefully up at his majestic new friend—a light which the master noted.

"Do you think you could do rough work—rough, hard drudgery?"

"Yes, sir, I could, if you will try me; I am strong."

"Carry fire-logs up these long stairways?"

"Yes, sir."

"And scrub, like the maids; and build fires in the rooms; and carry up water to the chambers; and split wood; and help in the laundry and the kitchen; and take care of the dog?"

"Yes, sir, all those things, if you will let me try."

"All for food and shelter? Well, I don't see how a body is going to refu—"

"Heinrich Stein, wait! If you think you are going to nest this vermin in this place without ever so much as a by-your-leave to me, I can tell you you are very much mis—"

"Be quiet!" said the husband, sternly. "Now, then, you have all expressed your opinions about this boy, but there is one vote which you have not counted. I value that one above some of the others— above any of the others, in fact. On that vote by itself I would give him a trial. That is my decision. You can discuss some other subject, now—this one is finished. Take him along, Katrina, and give him a room and let him get some rest."

Katrina stiffened with pride and satisfaction in her triumph. The boy's eyes looked his gratitude, and he said,

"I would like to go to work *now*, if I may, sir."

Before an answer could come, Frau Stein interrupted:

"I want to *know*. Whose vote was it that wasn't counted? I'm not hard of hearing, and I don't know of any."

"The dog's."

Everybody showed surprise. But there it was: the dog hadn't made a motion when the boy came in. Nobody but the master had noticed it, but it was the fact. It was the first time that that demon had ever treated a stranger with civil indifference. He was chained in the corner, and had a bone between his paws and was gnawing it; and not even growling, which was not his usual way. Frau Stein's eyes beamed with a vicious pleasure, and she called out,

"You want work, do you? Well, there it is, cut out for you. Take the dog out and give him an airing!"

Even some of the hardest hearts there felt the cruelty of it, and their horror showed in their faces when the boy stepped innocently forward to obey.

"Stop!" shouted the master, and Katrina, flushing with anger, sprang after the youth and halted him.

"Shame!" she said; and the master turned his indignation loose and gave his wife a dressing down that astonished her. Then he said to the stranger,

"You are free to rest, lad, if you like, but if you would rather work, Katrina will see what she can find for you. What is your name?"

The boy answered, quietly,

"Number 44, New Series 864,962."

Everybody's eyes came open in a stare. Of course. The master thought perhaps he hadn't heard aright; so he asked again, and the boy answered the same as before,

"Number 44, New Series 864,962."

"What a hell of a name!" ejaculated Hans Katzenyammer, piously.

"Jail-number, likely," suggested Moses Haas, searchingly examining the boy with his rat eyes, and unconsciously twisting and stroking his silky and scanty moustache with his fingers, a way he had when his cogitations were concentrated upon a thing.

"It's a strange name," said the master, with a barely noticeable touch of suspicion in his tone, "where did you get it?"

"I don't know, sir," said No. 44, tranquilly, "I've always had it."

The master forbore to pursue the matter further, probably fearing that the ice was thin, but Maria Vogel chirped up and asked,

"Have you ever been in jail?"

The master burst in with—

"There, that's enough of that! You needn't answer, my boy, unless you want to." He paused—hopeful, maybe—but 44 did not seize the opportunity to testify for himself. He stood still and said nothing. Satirical smiles flitted here and there, down the table, and the master looked annoyed and disappointed, though he tried to conceal it. "Take him along, Katrina." He said it as kindly as he could, but there was just a trifle of a chill in his manner, and it delighted those creatures.

Katrina marched out with 44.

Out of a wise respect for the temper the master was in, there was no outspoken comment, but a low buzz skimmed along down the table, whose burden was, "That silence was a confession—the chap's a Jail-Bird."

It was a bad start for 44. Everybody recognized it. Marget was troubled, and asked Gustav Fischer if he believed the boy was what these people were calling him. Fischer replied, with regret in his tone,

"Well, you know, Fräulein, he could have denied it, and he didn't do it."

"Yes, I know, but think what a good face he has. And pure, too; and beautiful."

"True, quite true. And it's astonishing. But there it is, you see—he didn't deny it. In fact he didn't even seem greatly interested in the matter."

"I know it. It is unaccountable. What do you make out of it?"

"The fact that he didn't see the gravity of the situation marks him for a fool. But it isn't the face of a fool. That he could be silent at such a time is constructive evidence that he is a Jail-Bird—with

that face! which is impossible. I can't solve you that riddle, Fräulein
—it's beyond my depth."

Forty-Four entered, straining under a heavy load of logs, which
he dumped into a great locker and went briskly out again. He was
quickly back with a similar load; and another, and still another.

"There," said the master, rising and starting away, "that will do;
you are not required to kill yourself."

"One more—just one more," said the boy, as if asking a favor.

"Very well, but let that be the last," said the master, as if
granting one; and he left the room.

Forty-Four brought the final load, then stood, apparently waiting
for orders. None coming, he asked for them. It was Frau Stein's
chance. She gave him a joyfully malicious glance out of her yellow
eyes, and snapped out—

"Take the dog for an airing!"

Outraged, friend and foe alike rose at her! They surged forward to
save the boy, but they were too late; he was already on his knees
loosing the chain, his face and the dog's almost in contact. And now
the people surged back to save themselves; but the boy rose and
went, with the chain in his hand, and the dog trotted after him
happy and content.

Chapter 4

D ID IT make a stir? Oh, on your life! For nearly two minutes
the herd were speechless; and if I may judge by myself, they
quaked, and felt pale; then they all broke out at once, and discussed
it with animation and most of them said what an astonishing thing
it was—and unbelievable, too, if they hadn't seen it with their own
eyes. With Marget and Fischer and Barty the note was admiration.
With Frau Stein, Maria, Katzenyammer and Binks it was wonder,
but wonder mixed with maledictions—maledictions upon the devil
that possessed the Jail-Bird—they averring that no stranger unpro-
tected by a familiar spirit could touch that dog and come away but

in fragments; and so, in their opinion the house was in a much more serious plight, now, than it was before when it only had a thief in it. Then there were three silent ones: Ernest and Moses indicated by their cynical manner and mocking smiles that they had but a small opinion of the exploit, it wasn't a matter to make such a fuss about; the other silent one—the magician—was so massively silent, so weightily silent, that it presently attracted attention. Then a light began to dawn upon some of the tribe; they turned reverent and marveling eyes upon the great man, and Maria Vogel said with the happy exultation of a discoverer—

"There he stands, and let him deny it if he can! He put power upon that boy with his magic. I just suspected it, and now I know it! Ah, you are caught, you can't escape—own up, you wonder of the ages!"

The magician smiled a simpering smile, a detected and convicted smile, and several cried out—

"There, he *is* caught—he's trying to deny it, and he can't! Come, be fair, be good, confess!" and Frau Stein and Maria took hold of his great sleeves, peering worshipingly up in his face and tried to detain him; but he gently disengaged himself and fled from the room, apparently vastly embarrassed. So that settled the matter. It was such a manifest confession that not a doubter was left, every individual was convinced; and the praises that that man got would have gone far to satisfy a god. He was great before, he was held in awe before, but that was as nothing to the towering repute to which he had soared now. Frau Stein was in the clouds. She said that this was the most astonishing exhibition of magic power Europe had ever seen, and that the person who could doubt, after this, that he could work any miracle he wanted to would justly take rank as a fool. They all agreed that that was so, none denying it or doubting; and Frau Stein, taking her departure with the other ladies, declared that hereafter the magician should occupy her end of the table and she would move to a humbler place at his right, where she belonged.

All this was gall and vinegar to that jealous reptile Ernest Wasserman, who could not endure to hear anybody praised, and he began to cast about to turn the subject. Just then Fischer opened the way by remarking upon the Jail-Bird's strength, as shown in the wood-carrying. He said he judged that the Jail-Bird would be an ugly customer in a rough stand-up fight with a youth of his own age.

"*Him!*" scoffed Ernest, "I'm of his age, and I'll bet I'd make him sorry if he was to tackle me!"

This was Moses's chance. He said, with mock solicitude,

"Don't. Think of your mother. Don't make trouble with him, he might hurt you badly."

"Never you mind worrying about me, Moses Haas. Let him look out for himself if he meddles with me, that's all."

"Oh," said Moses, apparently relieved, "I was afraid you were going to meddle with *him*. I see he is not in any danger." After a pause, "Nor you," he added carelessly.

The taunt had the intended effect.

"Do you think I'm afraid to meddle with him? I'm not afraid of fifty of him. *I'll* show him!"

Forty-Four entered with the dog, and while he was chaining him Ernest began to edge toward the door.

"Oh," simpered Moses, "good-bye, ta-ta, I thought you were going to meddle with the Jail-Bird."

"What, to-day—and him all tired out and not at his best? I'd be ashamed of myself."

"Haw-haw-haw!" guffawed that lumbering ox, Hans Katzenyammer, "hear the noble-hearted poltroon!"

A whirlwind of derisive laughter and sarcastic remarks followed, and Ernest, stung to the quick, threw discretion to the winds and marched upon the Jail-Bird, and planted himself in front of him, crying out,

"Square off! Stand up like a man, and defend yourself."

"Defend myself?" said the boy, seeming not to understand. "From what?"

"From me—do you hear?"

"From you? I have not injured you; why should you wish to hurt me?"

The spectators were disgusted—and disappointed. Ernest's courage came up with a bound. He said fiercely,

"Haven't you any sense? Don't you know anything? You've got to fight me—do you understand that?"

"But I cannot fight you; I have nothing against you."

Ernest, mocking: "Afraid of *hurting* me, I suppose."

The Jail-Bird answered quite simply,

"No, there is no danger of that. I have nothing to hurt you for, and I shall not hurt you."

"Oh, thanks—how kind. Take that!"

But the blow did not arrive. The stranger caught both of Ernest's wrists and held them fast. Our apprentice tugged and struggled and perspired and swore, while the men stood around in a ring and laughed, and shouted, and made fun of Ernest and called him all sorts of outrageous pet names; and still the stranger held him in that grip, and did it quite easily and without puffing or blowing, whereas Ernest was gasping like a fish; and at last, when he was worn out and couldn't struggle any more, he snarled out,

"I give in—let go!" and 44 let go and said gently, "if you will let me I will stroke your arms for you and get the stiffness and the pain out;" but Ernest said "You go to hell," and went grumbling away and shaking his head and saying what he would do to the Jail-Bird one of these days, he needn't think it's over yet, he'd better look out or he'll find he's been fooling with the wrong customer; and so flourished out of the place and left the men jeering and yelling, and the Jail-Bird standing there looking as if it was all a puzzle to him and he couldn't make it out.

Chapter 5

THINGS were against that poor waif. He had maintained silence when he had had an opportunity to deny that he was a Jail-Bird, and that was bad for him. It got him that name, and he was likely to keep it. The men considered him a milksop because he spared

Ernest Wasserman when it was evident that he could have
whipped him. Privately my heart bled for the boy, and I wanted to
be his friend, and longed to tell him so, but I had not the courage,
for I was made as most people are made, and was afraid to follow
my own instincts when they ran counter to other people's. The best
of us would rather be popular than right. I found that out a good
while ago. Katrina remained the boy's fearless friend, but she was
alone in this. The master used him kindly, and protected him when
he saw him ill treated, but further than this it was not in his nature
to go except when he was roused, the current being so strong
against him.

As to the clothes, Katrina kept her word. She sat up late, that
very first night, and made him a coarse and cheap, but neat and
serviceable doublet and hose with her own old hands; and she
properly shod him, too. And she had her reward, for he was a
graceful and beautiful creature, with the most wonderful eyes, and
these facts all showed up, now, and filled her with pride. Daily he
grew in her favor. Her old hungry heart was fed, she was a mother
at last, with a child to love,—a child who returned her love in full
measure, and to whom she was the salt of the earth.

As the days went along, everybody talked about 44, everybody
observed him, everybody puzzled over him and his ways; but it was
not discoverable that he ever concerned himself in the least degree
about this or was in any way interested in what people thought of
him or said about him. This indifference irritated the herd, but the
boy did not seem aware of it.

The most ingenious and promising attempts to ruffle his temper
and break up his calm went for nothing. Things flung at him struck
him on the head or the back, and fell at his feet unnoticed; now and
then a leg was shoved out and he tripped over it and went heavily
down amid delighted laughter, but he picked himself up and went
on without remark; often when he had brought a couple of twenty-
pound cans of water up two long flights of stairs from the well in
the court, they were seized and their winter-cold contents poured
over him, but he went back unmurmuring for more; more than
once, when the master was not present, Frau Stein made him share

the dog's dinner in the corner, but he was content and offered no protest. The most of these persecutions were devised by Moses and Katzenyammer, but as a rule were carried out by that shabby poor coward, Ernest.

You see, now, how I was situated. I should have been despised if I had befriended him; and I should have been treated as he was, too. It is not everybody that can be as brave as Katrina was. More than once she caught Moses devising those tricks and Ernest carrying them out, and gave both of them an awful hiding; and once when Hans Katzenyammer interfered she beat that big ruffian till he went on his knees and begged.

What a devil to work the boy was! The earliest person up found him at it by lantern-light, the latest person up found him still at it long past midnight. It was the heaviest manual labor, but if he was ever tired it was not perceptible. He always moved with energy, and seemed to find a high joy in putting forth his strange and enduring strength.

He made reputation for the magician right along; no matter what unusual thing he did, the magician got the credit of it; at first the magician was cautious, when accused, and contented himself with silences which rather confessed than denied the soft impeachment, but he soon felt safe to throw that policy aside and frankly take the credit, and he did it. One day 44 unchained the dog and said "Now behave yourself, Felix, and don't hurt any one," and turned him loose, to the consternation of the herd, but the magician sweetly smiled and said,

"Do not fear. It is a little caprice of mine. My spirit is upon him, he cannot hurt you."

They were filled with adoring wonder and admiration, those people. They kissed the hem of the magician's robe, and beamed unutterable things upon him. Then the boy said to the dog,

"Go and thank your master for this great favor which he has granted you."

Well, it was an astonishing thing that happened, then. That ignorant and malignant vast animal, which had never been taught language or manners or religion or any other valuable thing, and could not be expected to understand a dandy speech like that, went and stood straight up on its hind feet before the magician, with its nose on a level with his face, and curved its paws and ducked its head piously, and said

"Yap-yap!—yap-yap!—yap-yap!" most reverently, and just as a Christian might at prayers.

Then it got down on all fours, and the boy said,

"Salute the master, and retire as from the presence of royalty."

The dog bowed very solemnly, then backed away stern-first to his corner—not with grace it is true, but well enough for a dog that hadn't had any practice of that kind and had never heard of royalty before nor its customs and etiquettes.

Did that episode take those people's breath away? You will not doubt it. They actually went on their knees to the magician, Frau Stein leading, the rest following. I know, for I was there and saw it. I was amazed at such degraded idolatry and hypocrisy—at least servility—but I knelt, too, to avert remark.

Life was become very interesting. Every few days there was a fresh novelty, some strange new thing done by the boy, something to wonder at; and so the magician's reputation was augmenting all the time. To be envied is the secret longing of pretty much all human beings—let us say *all*; to be envied makes them happy. The magician was happy, for never was a man so envied; he lived in the clouds.

I passionately longed to know 44, now. The truth is, he was being envied himself! Spite of all his shames and insults and persecutions. For, there is no denying it, it was an enviable conspicuousness and glory to be the instrument of such a dreaded and extraordinary magician as that and have people staring at you and holding their breath with awe while you did the miracles he devised. It is not for me to deny that I was one of 44's enviers. If I hadn't been, I should have been no natural boy. But I *was* a natural boy, and I longed to be conspicuous, and wondered at and talked about. Of course the case was the same with Ernest and Barty, though they did as I did—concealed it. I was always throwing myself in the magician's way whenever I could, in the hope that he would do miracles through me, too, but I could not get his attention. He never seemed to see me when he was preparing a prodigy.

At last I thought of a plan that I hoped might work. I would seek 44 privately and tell him how I was feeling and see if he would help me attain my desire. So I hunted up his room, and slipped up there clandestinely one night after the herd were in bed, and waited. After midnight an hour or two he came, and when the light of his lantern fell upon me he set it quickly down, and took me by both of my hands and beamed his gladness from his eyes, and there was no need to say a word.

Chapter 6

He closed the door, and we sat down and began to talk, and he said it was good and generous of me to come and see him, and he hoped I would be his friend, for he was lonely and so wanted companionship. His words made me ashamed—so ashamed, and I felt so shabby and mean, that I almost had courage enough to come out and tell him how ignoble my errand was and how selfish. He smiled most kindly and winningly, and put out his hand and patted me on the knee, and said,

"Don't mind it."

I did not know what he was referring to, but the remark puzzled me, and so, in order not to let on, I thought I would throw out an observation—anything that came into my head; but nothing came but the weather, so I was dumb. He said,

"Do you care for it?"

"Care for what?"

"The weather."

I was puzzled again; in fact astonished; and said to myself "This is uncanny; I'm afraid of him."

He said cheerfully,

"Oh, you needn't be. Don't you be uneasy on my account."

I got up trembling, and said,

"I—I am not feeling well, and if you don't mind, I think I will excuse myself, and—"

"Oh, don't," he said, appealingly, "don't go. Stay with me a little. Let me do something to relieve you—I shall be so glad."

"You are so kind, so good," I said, "and I wish I could stay, but I will come another time. I—well, I—you see, it is cold, and I seem to have caught a little chill, and I think it will soon pass if I go down and cover up warm in bed—"

"Oh, a hot drink is a hundred times better, a hundred times!—that is what you really want. Now isn't it so?"

"Why yes; but in the circumstances—"

"Name it!" he said, all eager to help me. "Mulled claret, blazing hot—isn't that it?"

"Yes, indeed; but as we haven't any way to—"

"Here—take it as hot as you can bear it. You'll soon be all right."

He was holding a tumbler to me—fine, heavy cut-glass, and the steam was rising from it. I took it, and dropped into my chair again, for I was faint with fright, and the glass trembled in my hand. I drank. It was delicious; yes, and a surprise to my ignorant palate.

"Drink!" he said. "Go on—drain it. It will set you right, never fear. But this is unsociable; I'll drink with you."

A smoking glass was in his hand; I was not quick enough to see where it came from. Before my glass was empty he gave me a full one in its place and said heartily,

"Go right on, it will do you good. You are feeling better already, now aren't you?"

"Better?" said I to myself; "as to temperature, yes, but I'm scared to rags."

He laughed a pleasant little laugh and said,

"Oh, I give you my word there's no occasion for that. You couldn't be safer in my good old Mother Katrina's protection. Come, drink another."

I couldn't resist; it was nectar. I indulged myself. But I was miserably frightened and uneasy, and I couldn't stay; I didn't know what might happen next. So I said I must go. He wanted me to sleep in his bed, and said he didn't need it, he should be going to work pretty soon; but I shuddered at the idea, and got out of it by saying I should rest better in my own, because I was accustomed to it. So then he stepped outside the door with me, earnestly thanking me over and over again for coming to see him, and generously forbearing to notice how pale I was and how I was quaking; and he made me promise to come again the next night, I saying to myself that I should break that promise if I died for it. Then he said good-bye, with a most cordial shake of the hand, and I stepped feebly into the black gloom—and found myself in my own bed, with my door closed, my candle blinking on the table, and a welcome great fire flaming up the throat of the chimney!

It made me gasp! But no matter, I presently sank deliciously off to sleep, with that noble wine weltering in my head, and my last expiring effort at cerebration hit me with a cold shock:

"Did he *overhear* that thought when it passed through my mind—when I said I would break that promise if I died for it?"

Chapter 7

To my astonishment I got up thoroughly refreshed when called at sunrise. There was not a suggestion of wine or its effects in my head.

"It was all a dream," I said, gratefully. "I can get along without the mate to it."

By and by, on a stairway I met 44 coming up with a great load of wood, and he said, beseechingly,

"You *will* come again to-night, won't you?"

"Lord! I thought it was a dream," I said, startled.

"Oh, no, it was not a dream. I should be sorry, for it was a pleasant night for me, and I was *so* grateful."

There was something so pathetic in his way of saying it that a great pity rose up in me and I said impulsively,

"I'll come if I die for it!"

He looked as pleased as a child, and said,

"It's the same phrase, but I like it better this time." Then he said, with delicate consideration for me, "Treat me just as usual when others are around; it would injure you to befriend me in public, and I shall understand and not feel hurt."

"You are just lovely!" I said, "and I honor you, and would brave them all if I had been born with any spirit—which I wasn't."

He opened his big wondering eyes upon me and said,

"Why do you reproach yourself? You did not make yourself; how then are you to blame?"

How perfectly sane and sensible that was—yet I had never thought of it before, nor had ever heard even the wisest of the professionally wise people say it—nor anything half so intelligent and unassailable, for that matter. It seemed an odd thing to get it from a boy, and he a vagabond landstreicher at that. At this juncture a proposition framed itself in my head, but I suppressed it, judging that there could be no impropriety in my acting upon it without permission if I chose. He gave me a bright glance and said,

"Ah, you couldn't if you tried!"

"Couldn't what?"

"Tell what happened last night."

"Couldn't I?"

"No. Because I don't wish it. What I don't wish, doesn't happen. I'm going to tell you various secrets by and by, one of these days. You'll keep them."

"I'm sure I'll try to."

"Oh, tell them if you think you *can!* Mind, I don't say you shan't, I only say you can't."

"Well, then, I shan't try."

Then Ernest came whistling gaily along, and when he saw 44 he cried out,

"Come, hump yourself with that wood, you lazy beggar!"

I opened my mouth to call him the hardest name in my stock, but nothing would come. I said to myself, jokingly, "Maybe it's because 44 disapproves."

Forty-Four looked back at me over his shoulder and said,

"Yes, that is it."

These things were dreadfully uncanny, but interesting. I went musing away, saying to myself, "he must have read my thoughts when I was minded to ask him if I might tell what happened last night." He called back from far up the stairs,

"I did!"

Breakfast was nearing a finish. The master had been silent all through it. There was something on his mind; all could see it. When he looked like that, it meant that he was putting the sections of an important and perhaps risky resolution together, and bracing up to pull it off and stand by it. Conversation had died out; everybody was curious, everybody was waiting for the outcome.

Forty-Four was putting a log on the fire. The master called him. The general curiosity rose higher still, now. The boy came and stood respectfully before the master, who said,

"Forty-Four, I have noticed—Forty-Four is correct, I believe?—"

The boy inclined his head and added gravely,

"New Series 864,962."

"We will not go into that," said the master with delicacy, "that is your affair and I conceive that into it charity forbids us to pry. I have noticed, as I was saying, that you are diligent and willing, and have borne a hard lot these several weeks with exemplary patience. There is much to your credit, nothing to your discredit."

The boy bent his head respectfully, the master glanced down the table, noted the displeasure along the line, then went on.

"You have earned friends, and it is not your fault that you haven't them. You haven't one in the castle, except Katrina. It is not fair. I am going to be your friend myself."

The boy's eyes glowed with happiness, Maria and her mother tossed their heads and sniffed, but there was no other applause. The master continued.

"You deserve promotion, and you shall have it. Here and now I raise you to the honorable rank of apprentice to the printer's art, which is the noblest and the most puissant of all arts, and destined in the ages to come to promote the others and preserve them."

And he rose and solemnly laid his hand upon the lad's shoulder like a king delivering the accolade. Every man jumped to his feet excited and affronted, to protest against this outrage, this admission of a pauper and tramp without name or family to the gate leading to the proud privileges and distinctions and immunities of their great order; but the master's temper was up, and he said he would turn adrift any man that opened his mouth; and he commanded them to sit down, and they obeyed, grumbling, and pretty nearly strangled with wrath. Then the master sat down himself, and began to question the new dignitary.

"This is one of the learned professions. Have you studied the Latin, Forty-Four?"

"No, sir."

Everybody laughed, but not aloud.

"The Greek?"

"No, sir."

Another clandestine laugh; and this same attention greeted all the answers, one after the other. But the boy did not blush, nor look confused or embarrassed; on the contrary he looked provokingly contented and happy and innocent. I was ashamed of him, and felt for him; and that showed me that I was liking him very deeply.

"The Hebrew?"

"No, sir."

"Any of the sciences?—the mathematics? astrology? astronomy? chemistry? medicine? geography?"

As each in turn was mentioned, the youth shook his untroubled head and answered "No, sir," and at the end said,

"None of them, sir."

The amusement of the herd was almost irrepressible by this time; and on his side the master's annoyance had risen very nearly to the bursting point. He put in a moment or two crowding it down, then asked,

"Have you ever studied *anything?*"

"No, sir," replied the boy, as innocently and idiotically as ever.

The master's project stood defeated all along the line! It was a critical moment. Everybody's mouth flew open to let go a triumphant shout; but the master, choking with rage, rose to the emergency, and it was his voice that got the innings:

"By the splendor of God I'll teach you myself!"

It was just grand! But it was a mistake. It was all I could do to keep from raising a hurrah for the generous old chief. But I held in. From the apprentices' table in the corner I could see every face, and I knew the master had made a mistake. I knew those men. They could stand a good deal, but the master had played the limit, as the saying is, and I knew it. He had struck at their order, the apple of their eye, their pride, the darling of their hearts, their dearest possession, their nobility—as they ranked it and regarded it—and had degraded it. They would not forgive that. They would seek revenge, and find it. This thing that we had witnessed, and which had had the form and aspect of a comedy, was a tragedy. It was a turning point. There would be consequences. In ordinary cases where there was matter for contention and dispute, there had always been chatter and noise and jaw, and a general row; but now the faces were black and ugly, and not a word was said. It was an omen.

We three humble ones sat at our small table staring; and thinking thoughts. Barty looked pale and sick. Ernest searched my face with his evil eyes, and said,

"I caught you talking with the Jail-Bird on the stairs. You needn't try to lie out of it, I saw you."

All the blood seemed to sink out of my veins, and a cold terror crept through me. In my heart I cursed the luck that had brought upon me that exposure. What should I do? What could I do? What could I say in my defence? I could think of nothing; I had no words, I was dumb—and that creature's merciless eyes still boring into me. He said,

"Say—you are that animal's *friend*. Now deny it if you can."

I was in a bad scrape. He would tell the men, and I should be an outcast, and they would make my life a misery to me. I was afraid enough of the men, and wished there was a way out, but I saw there was none, and that if I did not want to complete my disaster I must pluck up some heart and not let this brute put me under his feet. I wasn't afraid of *him,* at any rate; even *my* timidity had its limitations. So I pulled myself together and said,

"It's a lie. I did talk with him, and I'll do it again if I want to, but that's no proof that I'm his friend."

"Oho, so you don't deny it! That's enough. I wouldn't be in your shoes for a good deal. When the men find it out you'll catch it, I can tell you that."

That distressed Barty, and he begged Ernest not to tell on me, and tried his best to persuade him; but it was of no use. He said he would tell if he died for it.

"Well, then," I said, "go ahead and do it; it's just like your sort, anyway. Who cares?"

"Oh, you don't care, don't you? Well, we'll see if you won't. And I'll tell them you're his friend, too."

If that should happen! The terror of it roused me up, and I said, "Take that back, or I'll stick this dirk into you!"

He was badly scared, but pretended he wasn't, and laughed a sickly laugh and said he was only funning. That ended the discussion, for just then the master rose to go, and we had to rise, too, and look to our etiquette. I was sufficiently depressed and unhappy, for I knew there was sorrow in store for me. Still, there was one comfort: I should not be charged with being poor 44's friend, I hoped and believed; so matters were not quite so calamitous for me as they might have been.

We filed up to the printing rooms in the usual order of precedence, I following after the last man, Ernest following after me, and Barty after him. Then came 44.

Forty-Four would have to do his studying after hours. During hours he would now fill Barty's former place and put in a good deal of his time in drudgery and dirty work; and snatch such chances as he could, in the intervals, to learn the first steps of the divine art—composition, distribution and the like.

Certain ceremonies were Forty-Four's due when as an accredited apprentice he crossed the printing-shop's threshold for the first time. He should have been invested with a dagger, for he was now privileged to bear minor arms—foretaste and reminder of the future still prouder day when as a journeyman he would take the rank of a gentleman and be entitled to wear a sword. And a red chevron should have been placed upon his left sleeve to certify to the world his honorable new dignity of printer's apprentice. These courtesies were denied him, and omitted. He entered unaccosted and unwelcomed.

The youngest apprentice should now have taken him in charge and begun to instruct him in the rudimentary duties of his position. Honest little Barty was commencing this service, but Katzenyammer the foreman stopped him, and said roughly,

"Get to your case!"

So 44 was left standing alone in the middle of the place. He looked about him wistfully, mutely appealing to all faces but mine, but no one noticed him, no one glanced in his direction, or seemed aware that he was there. In the corner old Binks was bowed over a proof-slip; Katzenyammer was bending over the imposing-stone making up a form; Ernest, with ink-ball and coarse brush was proving a galley; I was overrunning a page of Haas's to correct an out; Fischer, with paste-pot and brown linen, was new-covering the tympan; Moses was setting type, pulling down his guide for every line, weaving right and left, bobbing over his case with every type he picked up, fetching the box-partition a wipe with it as he brought it away, making two false motions before he put it in the stick and a third one with a click on his rule, justifying like a rail fence, spacing like an old witch's teeth—hair-spaces and m-quads turn about—just a living allegory of falseness and pretence from his green silk eye-shade down to his lifting and sinking heels, making show and bustle enough for 3,000 an hour, yet never good for 600 on a fat take and double-leaded at that. It was inscrutable that God would endure a comp like that, and lightning so cheap.

It was pitiful to see that friendless boy standing there forlorn in that hostile stillness. I did wish somebody would relent and say a kind word and tell him something to do. But it could not happen; they were all waiting to see trouble come to him, all expecting it, all tremulously alert for it, all knowing it was preparing for him, and wondering whence it would come, and in what form, and who would invent the occasion. Presently they knew. Katzenyammer had placed his pages, separated them with reglets, removed the strings from around them, arranged his bearers; the chase was on, the sheep-foot was in his hand, he was ready to lock up. He slowly turned his head and fixed an inquiring scowl upon the boy. He stood so, several seconds, then he stormed out,

"Well, are you going to fetch me some quoins, or *not?*"

Cruel! How could *he* know what the strange word meant? He begged for the needed information with his eloquent eyes—the men were watching and exulting—Katzenyammer began to move toward him with his big hand spread for cuffing—ah, my God, I mustn't venture to speak, was there no way to save him? Then I had a lightning thought; would he gather it from my brain?— *"Forty-Four, that's the quoin-box, under the stone table!"*

In an instant he had it out and on the imposing-stone! He was saved. Katzenyammer and everybody looked amazed. And deeply disappointed.

For a while Katzenyammer seemed to be puzzling over it and trying to understand it; then he turned slowly to his work and selected some quoins and drove them home. The form was ready. He set that inquiring gaze upon the boy again. Forty-Four was watching with all his eyes, but it wasn't any use; how was he to guess what was wanted of him? Katzenyammer's face began to work, and he spat dry a couple of times, spitefully; then he shouted,

"Am *I* to do it—or *who?*"

I was ready this time. I said to myself, "Forty-Four, raise it carefully on its edge, get it under your right arm, carry it to that machine yonder, which is the press, and lay it gently down flat on that stone, which is called the bed of the press."

He went tranquilly to work, and did the whole thing as right as nails—did it like an old hand! It was just astonishing. There wasn't another untaught and unpractised person in all Europe who could have carried that great and delicate feat half-way through without piing the form. I was so carried away that I wanted to shout. But I held in.

Of course the thing happened, now, that was to be expected. The men took Forty-Four for an old apprentice, a refugee flying from a hard master. They could not ask him, as to that, custom prohibiting it; but they could ask him other questions which could be awkward. They could be depended upon to do that. The men all left their work and gathered around him, and their ugly looks promised trouble. They looked him over silently—arranging their game, no doubt—he standing in the midst, waiting, with his eyes cast down. I was dreadfully sorry for him. I knew what was coming, and I saw no possibility of his getting out of the hole he was in. The very first question would be unanswerable, and quite out of range of help from me. Presently that sneering Moses Haas asked it:

"So you are an experienced apprentice to this art, and yet don't know the Latin!"

There it was! I knew it. But—oh, well, the boy was just an ever-fresh and competent mystery! He raised his innocent eyes and placidly replied,

"Who—I? Why yes, I know it."

They gazed at him puzzled—stupefied, as you might say. Then Katzenyammer said,

"Then what did you tell the master that lie for?"

"I? I didn't know I told him a lie; I didn't mean to."

"Didn't mean to? Idiot! he asked you if you knew the Latin, and you said no."

"Oh, no," said the youth, earnestly, "it was quite different. He asked me if I had *studied* it—meaning in a school or with a teacher, as I judged. Of course I said no, for I had only picked it up—from books—by myself."

"Well, upon my soul, you *are* a purist, when it comes to cast-iron exactness of statement," said Katzenyammer, exasperated. "Nobody knows how to take you or what to make of you; every time a person puts his finger on you you're not there. Can't you do *anything* but the unexpected? If you belonged to me, damned if I wouldn't drown you."

"Look here, my boy," said Fischer, not unkindly, "do you know

—as required—the rudiments of all those things the master asked you about?"

"Yes, sir."

"Picked them up?"

"Yes, sir."

I wished he hadn't made that confession. Moses saw a chance straightway:

"Honest people don't get into this profession on picked-up culture; they don't get in on odds and ends, they have to *know* the initial stages of the sciences and things. You sneaked in without an examination, but you'll pass one now, or out you go."

It was a lucky idea, and they all applauded. I felt more comfortable, now, for if he could take the answers from my head I could send him through safe. Adam Binks was appointed inquisitor, but I soon saw that 44 had no use for me. He was away up. I would have shown off if I had been in his place and equipped as he was. But he didn't. In knowledge Binks was a child to him—that was soon apparent. He wasn't competent to examine 44; 44 took him out of his depth on every language and art and science, and if erudition had been water he would have been drowned. The men had to laugh, they couldn't help it; and if they had been manly men they would have softened toward their prey, but they weren't and they didn't. Their laughter made Binks ridiculous, and he lost his temper; but instead of venting it on the laughers he let drive at the boy, the shameless creature, and would have felled him if Fischer hadn't caught his arm. Fischer got no thanks for that, and the men would have resented his interference, only it was not quite safe and they didn't want to drive him from their clique, anyway. They could see that he was at best only lukewarm on their side, and they didn't want to cool his temperature any more.

The examination-scheme was a bad failure—a regular collapse, in fact,—and the men hated the boy for being the cause of it, whereas they had brought it upon themselves. That is just like human beings. The foreman spoke up sharply, now, and told them to get to work; and said that if they fooled away any more of the shop's time he would dock them. Then he ordered 44 to stop idling around and get about his business. No one watched 44 now; they all thought he knew his duties, and where to begin. But it was plain to me that he didn't; so I prompted him out of my mind, and couldn't keep my attention on my work, it was so interesting and so wonderful to see him perform.

Under my unspoken instructions he picked up all the good type and broken type from about the men's feet and put the one sort in the pi pile and the other in the hell-box; turpentined the inking-balls and cleaned them; started up the ley-hopper; washed a form in the sink, and did it well; removed last week's stiff black towel from the roller and put a clean one in its place; made paste; dusted out several cases with a bellows; made glue for the bindery; oiled the platen-springs and the countersunk rails of the press; put on a paper apron and inked the form while Katzenyammer worked off a token of signature 16 of a Latin Bible, and came out of the job as black as a chimney-sweep from hair to heels; set up pi; struck galley-proofs; tied up dead matter like an artist, and set it away on the standing galley without an accident; brought the quads when the men jeff'd for takes, and restored them whence they came when the lucky comps were done chuckling over their fat and the others done damning their lean; and would have gone innocently to the village saddler's after strap-oil and *got* it—on his rear—if it had occurred to the men to start him on the errand—a thing they didn't think of, they supposing he knew that sell by memorable experience; and so they lost the best chance they had in the whole day to expose him as an impostor who had never seen a printing-outfit before.

A marvelous creature; and he went through without a break; but by consequence of my having to watch over him so persistently I set a proof that had the smallpox, and the foreman made me distribute his case for him after hours as a "lesson" to me. He was not a stingy man with that kind of tuition.

I had saved 44, unsuspected and without damage or danger to myself, and it made me lean toward him more than ever. That was natural.

Then, when the day was finished, and the men were washing up and I was feeling good and fine and proud, Ernest Wasserman came out and told on me!

Chapter 8

I SLIPPED out and fled. It was wise, for in this way I escaped the first heat of their passion, or I should have gotten not merely insults but kicks and cuffs added. I hid deep down and far away, in an unvisited part of the castle among a maze of dark passages and corridors. Of course I had no thought of keeping my promise to visit 44; but in the circumstances he would not expect it—I knew that. I had to lose my supper, and that was hard lines for a growing lad. And I was like to freeze, too, in that damp and frosty place. Of sleep little was to be had, because of the cold and the rats and the ghosts. Not that I saw any ghosts, but I was expecting them all the time, and quite naturally, too, for that historic old ruin was lousy with them, so to speak, for it had had a tough career through all the centuries of its youth and manhood—a career filled with romance and sodden with crime—and it is my experience that between the misery of watching and listening for ghosts and the fright of seeing them there is not much choice. In truth I was not sorry sleep was chary, for I did not wish to sleep. I was in trouble, and more was preparing for me, and I wanted to pray for help, for therein lay my best hope and my surest. I had moments of sleep now and then, being a young creature and full of warm blood, but in the long intervals I prayed persistently and fervently and sincerely. But I knew I needed more powerful prayers than my own—prayers of the pure and the holy—prayers of the consecrated—prayers certain to be heard, whereas mine might not be. I wanted the prayers of the Sisters of Perpetual Adoration. They could be had for 50 silver groschen. In time of threatened and imminent trouble, trouble which promised to be continuous, one valued their championship far above that of any priest, for his prayers would ascend at regularly appointed times only, with nothing to protect you in the exposed intervals between, but theirs were perpetual—hence their name—there were no intervals, night or day: when two of the Sisters rose from before the altar two others knelt at once in their place and the supplications went on unbroken. Their convent was on the other side of the river, beyond the village, but Katrina would get the money to them for me. They would take special pains for any of us in the castle, too, for our Prince had been doing them a valuable favor lately, to appease God on account of a murder he had done on an elder brother of his, a great Prince in Bohemia and head of the house. He had repaired and renovated and sumptuously fitted up the ancient chapel of our castle, to be used by them while their convent, which had been struck by lightning again and much damaged, was undergoing reparations. They would be coming over for Sunday, and the usual service would be greatly augmented, in fact doubled: the Sacred Host would be exposed in the monstrance, and four Sisters instead of two would hold the hours of adoration; yet if you sent your 50 groschen in time you would be entitled to the advantage of this, which is getting in on the ground floor, as the saying is.

Our Prince not only did for them what I have mentioned, but was paying for one-third of those repairs on their convent besides. Hence we were in great favor. That dear and honest old Father Peter would conduct the service for them. Father Adolf was not willing, for there was no money in it for the priest, the money all going to the support of a little house of homeless orphans whom the good Sisters took care of.

At last the rats stopped scampering over me, and I knew the long night was about at an end; so I groped my way out of my refuge. When I reached Katrina's kitchen she was at work by candle-light, and when she heard my tale she was full of pity for me and maledictions for Ernest, and promised him a piece of her mind, with foot-notes and illustrations; and she bustled around and hurried up a hot breakfast for me, and sat down and talked and gossiped, and enjoyed my voracity, as a good cook naturally would, and indeed I was fairly famished. And it was good to hear her rage at those rascals for persecuting her boy, and scoff at them for that they couldn't produce one individual manly enough to stand up for him and the master. And she burst out and said she wished to God Doangivadam was here, and I just jumped up and flung my arms around her old neck and hugged her for the thought! Then she went gently down on her knees before the little shrine of the Blessed Virgin, I doing the same of course, and she prayed for help for us all out of her fervent and faithful heart, and rose up refreshed and strengthened and gave our enemies as red-hot and competent a damning as ever came by natural gift from uncultured lips in my experience.

The dawn was breaking, now, and I told her my project concerning the Sisters of the Perpetual Adoration, and she praised me and blest me for my piety and right-heartedness, and said she would send the money for me and have it arranged. I had to ask would she lend me two groschen, for my savings lacked that much of being fifty, and she said promptly—

"Will I? and you in this trouble for being good to my boy? That I will; and I'd do it if it was five you wanted!"

And the tears came in her eyes and she gave me a hug; then I hasted to my room and shut the door and locked it, and fished my hoard out of its hiding-place and counted the coins, and there were *fifty*. I couldn't understand it. I counted them again—twice; but there was no error, there were two there that didn't belong. So I didn't have to go into debt, after all. I gave the money to Katrina and told her the marvel, and she counted it herself and was astonished, and couldn't understand it any more than I could. Then came sudden comprehension! and she sank down on her knees before the shrine and poured out her thanks to the Blessed Virgin for this swift and miraculous answer.

She rose up the proudest woman in all that region; and she was justified in feeling so. She said—and tried to say it humbly—

"To think She would do it for me, a poor lowly servant, dust of the earth: There's crowned monarchs She wouldn't do it for!" and her eyes blazed up in spite of her.

It was all over the castle in an hour, and wheresoever she went, there they made reverence and gave her honor as she passed by.

It was a bad day that had dawned for 44 and me, this wretched Tuesday. The men were sour and ugly. They snarled at me whenever they could find so much as half an occasion, they sneered at me and made jokes about me; and when Katzenyammer wittily called me by an unprintable name they shouted with laughter, and sawed their boxes with their composing-rules, which is a comp's way of expressing sarcastic applause. The laughter was praise of the foreman's wit, the sarcasm was for me. You must choose your man when you saw your box; not every man will put up with it. It is the most capable and eloquent expression of derision that human beings have ever invented. It is an urgent and strenuous and hideous sound, and when an expert makes it it shrieks out like the braying of a jackass. I have seen a comp draw his sword for that. As for that name the foreman gave me, it stung me and embittered me more than any of the other hurts and humiliations that were put upon me; and I was girl-boy enough to cry about it, which delighted the men beyond belief, and they rubbed their hands and shrieked with delight. Yet there was no point in that name when applied to a person of my shape, therefore it was entirely witless. It was the slang name (imported from England), used by printers to describe a certain kind of type. All types taper slightly, and are narrower at the letter than at the base of the shank; but in some fonts this spread is so pronounced that you can almost detect it with the eye, loose and exaggerative talkers asserting that it was exactly the taper of a leather bottle. Hence that odious name: and now they had fastened it upon me. If I knew anything about printers, it would stick. Within the hour they had added it to my slug! Think of that. Added it to my number, by initials, and there you could read it in the list above the take-file: "*Slug 4, B.-A.*" It may seem a small thing; but I can tell you that not all seemingly small things are small to a boy. That one shamed me as few things have done since.

The men were persistently hard on poor unmurmuring 44.

Every time he had to turn his back and cross the room they rained quoins and 3-m quads after him, which struck his head and bounded off in a kind of fountain-shower. Whenever he was bending down at any kind of work that required that attitude, the nearest man would hit him a blistering whack on his southern elevation with the flat of a galley, and then apologise and say,

"Oh, was it you? I'm sorry; I thought it was the master."

Then they would all shriek again.

And so on and so on. They insulted and afflicted him in every way they could think of—and did it far more for the master's sake than for his own. It was their purpose to provoke a retort out of 44, then they would thrash him. But they failed, and considered the day lost.

Wednesday they came loaded with new inventions, and expected to have better luck. They crept behind him and slipped cakes of ice down his back; they started a fire under the sink, and when he discovered it and ran to put it out they swarmed there in artificial excitement with buckets of water and emptied them on him instead of on the fire, and abused him for getting in the way and defeating their efforts; while he was inking for Katzenyammer, this creature continually tried to catch him on the head with the frisket before he could get out of the way, and at last fetched it down so prematurely that it failed to get home, but struck the bearers and got itself bent like a bow—and he got a cursing for it, as if it had been his fault.

They led him a dog's life all the forenoon—but they failed again. In the afternoon they gave him a Latin Bible-take that took him till evening to set up; and after he had proved it and was carrying away the galley, Moses tripped him and he fell sprawling, galley and all. The foreman raged and fumed over his clumsiness, putting all the blame on him and none on Moses, and finished with a peculiarly mean piece of cruelty: ordering him to come back after supper and set up the take again, by candle-light, if it took him all night.

This was a little too much for Fischer's stomach, and he began to remonstrate; but Katzenyammer told him to mind his own business;

and the others moved up with threatenings in their eyes, and so Fischer had to stand down and close his mouth. He had occasion to be sorry he had tried to do the boy a kindness, for it gave the foreman an excuse to double-up the punishment. He turned on Fischer and said,

"You think you've got some influence here, don't you? I'll give you a little lesson that'll teach you that the best way for you to get this Jail-Bird into trouble is to come meddling around here trying to get him out of it."

Then he told 44 he must set up the pi'd matter and distribute it before he began on the take!

An all-night job!—and that poor friendless creature hadn't done a thing to deserve it. Did the master know of these outrages? Yes, and was privately boiling over them; but he had to swallow his wrath, and not let on. The men had him in their power, and knew it. He was under heavy bonds to finish a formidable piece of work for the University of Prague—it was almost done, a few days more would finish it, to fall short of completion would mean ruin. He must see nothing, hear nothing, of these wickednesses: if his men should strike—and they only wanted an excuse and were playing for it—where would he get others? Venice? Frankfort? Paris? London? Why, these places were weeks away!

The men went to bed exultant that Wednesday night, and I sore-hearted.

But lord, how premature we were: the boy's little job was all right in the morning! Ah, he *was* the most astonishing creature!

Then the disaster fell: the men gave it up and struck! The poor master, when he heard the news, staggered to his bed, worn out with worry and wounded pride and despair, to toss there in fever and delirium and gabble distressful incoherencies to his grieving nurses, Marget and Katrina. The men struck in the forenoon of Thursday, and sent the master word. Then they discussed and discussed—trying to frame their grounds. Finally the document was ready, and they sent it to the master. He was in no condition to read it, and Marget laid it away. It was very simple and direct. It said that the Jail-Bird was a trial to them, and an unendurable aggravation; and that they would not go back to work again until he was sent away.

They knew the master couldn't send the lad away. It would break his sword and degrade him from his guild, for he could prove no offence against the apprentice. If he did not send 44 away work would stand still, he would fail to complete his costly printing-contract and be ruined.

So the men were happy; the master was their meat, as they expressed it, no matter which move he made, and he had but the two.

Chapter 9

I T WAS a black and mournful time, that Friday morning that the works stood idle for the first time in their history. There was no hope. As usual the men went over to early mass in the village, like the rest of us, but they did not come back for breakfast—naturally. They came an hour later, and idled about and put in the dull time the best they could, with dreary chat, and gossip, and prophecies, and cards. They were holding the fort, you see; a quite unnecessary service, since there was none to take it. It would not have been safe for any one to set a type there.

No, there was no hope. By and by Katrina was passing by a group of the strikers, when Moses, observing the sadness in her face, could not forbear a gibe:

"I wouldn't look so disconsolate, Katrina, prayer can pull off anything, you know. Toss up a hint to your friend the Virgin."

You would have thought, by the sudden and happy change in her aspect, that he had uttered something very much pleasanter than a coarse blasphemy. She retorted,

"Thanky, dog, for the idea. I'll do it!" and she picked up her feet and moved off briskly.

I followed her, for that remark had given me an idea, too. It was this: to cheer up, on our side, and stop despairing and get down to work—bring to our help every supernatural force that could be had for love or money: the Blessed Mother, Balthasar the magician, and the Sisters of the Perpetual Adoration. It was a splendid inspiration, and she was astonished at my smartness in thinking of it. She was electrified with hope and she praised me till I blushed; and indeed I was worthy of some praise, on another count: for I told her to withdraw my former "intention," (you have to name your desire—called "intention"—when you apply to the P. A.,) and tell the Sisters not to pray for my relief, but leave me quite out and throw all their strength into praying that Doangivadam might come to the master's rescue—an exhibition of self-sacrifice on my part which Katrina said was noble and beautiful and God would remember it and requite it to me; and indeed I had thought of that already, for it would be but right and customary.

At my suggestion she said she would get 44 to implore his overlord the magician to exert his dread powers in the master's favor. So now our spirits had a great uplift; our clouds began to pass, and the sun to shine for us again. Nothing could be more judicious than the arrangement we had arrived at; by it we were pooling our stock, not scattering it; by it we had our money on three cards instead of one, and stood to win on one turn or another. Katrina said she would have all these great forces at work within the hour, and keep them at it without intermission until the winner's flag went up.

I went from Katrina's presence walking on air, as the saying is. Privately I was afraid we had one card that was doubtful—the magician. I was entirely certain that he could bring victory to our flag if he chose, but would he choose? He probably would if Maria and her mother asked him, but who was to ask them to ask him? Katrina? They would not want the master ruined, since that would be their own ruin; but they were in the dark, by persuasion of the strikers, who had made them believe that no one's ruin was really going to result except 44's. As for 44 having any influence with his mighty master, I did not take much stock in that; one might as well expect a poor lackey to have the ear and favor of a sovereign.

I expected a good deal of Katrina's card, and as to my own I hadn't the least doubt. It would fetch Doangivadam, let him be where he might; of that I felt quite sure. What he might be able to accomplish when he arrived—well, that was another matter. One thing could be depended upon, anyway—he would take the side of the under dog in the fight, be that dog in the right or in the wrong, and what man could do he would do—and up to the limit, too.

He was a wandering comp. Nobody knew his name, it had long ago sunk into oblivion under that nickname, which described him to a dot. Hamper him as you might, obstruct him as you might, make things as desperate for him as you pleased, he didn't give a damn, and said so. He was always gay and breezy and cheerful, always kind and good and generous and friendly and careless and wasteful, and couldn't keep a copper, and never tried. But let his fortune be up or down you never could catch him other than handsomely dressed, for he was a dandy from the cradle, and a flirt. He was a beauty, trim and graceful as Satan, and was a born masher and knew it. He was not afraid of anything or anybody, and was a fighter by instinct and partiality. All printers were pretty good swordsmen, but he was a past master in the art, and as agile as a cat and as quick. He was very learned, and could have occupied with credit the sanctum sanctorum, as the den of a book-editor was called, in the irreverent slang of the profession. He had a baritone voice of great power and richness, he had a scientific knowledge of music, was a capable player upon instruments, was possessed of a wide knowledge of the arts in general, and could swear in nine languages. He was a good son of the Church, faithful to his religious duties, and the most pleasant and companionable friend and comrade a person could have.

But you never could get him to stay in a place, he was always wandering, always drifting about Europe. If ever there was a perpetual sub, he was the one. He could have had a case anywhere for the asking, but if he had ever had one, the fact had passed from the memory of man. He was sure to turn up with us several times a year, and the same in Frankfort, Venice, Paris, London, and so on, but he was as sure to flit again after a week or two or three—that is to say, as soon as he had earned enough to give the boys a rouse and have enough left over to carry him to the next front-stoop on his milk-route, as the saying is.

Here we were, standing still, and so much to do! So much to do, and so little time to do it in: it must be finished by next Monday; those commissioners from Prague would arrive then, and demand their two hundred Bibles—the sheets, that is, we were not to bind them. Half of our force had been drudging away on that great job for eight months; 30,000 ems would finish the composition; but for our trouble, we could turn on our whole strength and do it in a day of 14 hours, then print the final couple of signatures in a couple of hours more and be far within contract-time—and here we were, idle, and ruin coming on!

All Friday and Saturday I stumped nervously back and forth between the Owl Tower and the kitchen—watching from the one, in hope of seeing Doangivadam come climbing up the winding road; seeking Katrina in the other for consultation and news. But when night shut down, Saturday, nothing definite had happened, uncertainty was still our portion, and we did not know where we were at, as the saying is. The magician had treated 44 to an exceedingly prompt snub and closed out his usefulness as an ambassador; then Katrina had scared Maria and her mother into a realization of their danger and they had tried *their* hands with Balthasar. He was very gracious, very sympathetic, quite willing to oblige, but pretty non-committal. He said that these printers were not the originators of this trouble, and were acting in opposition to their own volition; they were only unwitting tools—tools of three of the most malignant and powerful demons in hell, demons whom he named, and whom he had battled with once before, overcoming them, but at cost of his life almost. They were not conspiring against the master, that was only a blind—he, the magician, was the prey they were after, and he could not as yet foresee how the struggle would come out; but he was consulting the stars, and should do his best. He believed that three other strong demons were in the conspiracy, and he was working spells to find out as to this; if it should turn out to be so, he should have to command the presence and aid of the very Prince of Darkness himself! The result would necessarily be terrible, for many innocent persons would be frightened to death by his thunders and lightnings and his awful aspect; still, if the ladies desired it—

But the ladies didn't! nor any one else, for that matter. So there it stood. If the three extra fiends didn't join the game, we might expect Balthasar to go in and win it and make everything comfortable again for the master; but if they joined, the game was blocked, of course, since no one was willing to have Lucifer go to the bat. It was a momentous uncertainty; there was nothing for it but to wait and see what those extras would elect to do.

Meantime Balthasar was doing his possible—we could see that. He was working his incantations right along, and sprinkling powders, and lizards, and newts, and human fat, and all sorts of puissant things into his caldron, and enveloping himself in clouds of smoke and raising a composite stink that made the castle next to unendurable, and could be smelt in heaven.

I clung to my hope, and stuck to the Owl Tower till night closed down and veiled the road and the valley in a silvery mist of moonlight, but Doangivadam did not come, and my heart was very heavy.

But in the morrow was promise; the service in our chapel would have double strength, because four Sisters would be on duty before the altar, whereas two was the custom. That thought lifted my hope again.

Apparently all times are meet for love, sad ones as well as bright and cheerful ones. Down on the castle roof I could see two couples doing overtime—Fischer and Marget, and Moses and Maria. I did not care for Maria, but if I had been older, and Fischer had wanted to put on a sub—but it was long ago, long ago, and such things do not interest me now. She was a beautiful girl, Marget.

Chapter 10

It was a lovely Sunday, calm and peaceful and holy, and bright with sunshine. It seemed strange that there could be jarrings and enmities in so beautiful a world. As the forenoon advanced the household began to appear, one after another, and all in their best; the women in their comeliest gowns, the men in velvets and laces, with snug-fitting hose that gave the tendons and muscles of their legs a chance to show their quality. The master and his sister were brought to the chapel on couches, that they might have the benefit of the prayers—he pale and drowsing and not yet really at himself; then the rest of us (except 44 and the magician) followed and took our places. It was not a proper place for sorcerers and their tools. The villagers had come over, and the seats were full.

The chapel was fine and sumptuous in its new paint and gilding; and there was the organ, in full view, an invention of recent date, and hardly any in the congregation had ever seen one before. Presently it began to softly rumble and moan, and the people held their breath for wonder at the adorable sounds, and their faces were alight with ecstasy. And I—I had never heard anything so plaintive, so sweet, so charged with the deep and consoling spirit of religion. And oh, so dreamily it moaned, and wept, and sighed and sang, on and on, gently rising, gently falling, fading and fainting, retreating to dim distances and reviving and returning, healing our hurts, soothing our griefs, steeping us deeper and deeper in its unutterable peace—then suddenly it burst into breath-taking rich thunders of triumph and rejoicing, and the consecrated ones came filing in! You will believe that all worldly thoughts, all ungentle thoughts, were gone from that place, now; you will believe that these uplifted and yearning souls were as a garden thirsting for the fructifying dew of truth, and prepared to receive it and hold it precious and give it husbandry.

Father Peter's face seemed to deliver hope and blessing and grace upon us just by the benignity and love that was in it and beaming from it. It was good to look at him, that true man. He described to us the origin of the Perpetual Adoration, which was a seed planted in the heart of the Blessed Margaret Alacoque by Our Lord himself, what time he complained to her of the neglect of his worship by the people, after all he had done for men. And Father Peter said,

"The aim of the Perpetual Adoration is to give joy to Our Lord, and to make at least some compensation by its atonement for the ingratitude of mankind. It keeps guard day and night before the Most Holy, to render to the forgotten and unknown Eucharistic God acts of praise and thanksgiving, of adoration and reparation. It is not deterred by the summer's heat nor the winter's cold. It knows no rest, no ceasing, night or day. What a sublime vocation! After the sacerdotal dignity, one more sublime can hardly be imagined. A priestly virgin should the adorer be, who raises her spotless hands and pure heart in supplication toward heaven imploring mercy, who continually prays for the welfare of her fellow creatures, and in particular for those who have recommended themselves to her prayers."

Father Peter spoke of the blessings both material and spiritual that would descend upon all who gave of their substance toward the repairing of the convent of the Sisters of the Adoration and its new chapel, and said,

"In our new chapel the Blessed Sacrament will be solemnly exposed for adoration during the greater part of the year. It is our hearts' desire to erect for Our Lord and Savior a beautiful altar, to place Him on a magnificent throne, to surround Him with splendor and a sea of light; for," continued he, "Our Lord said again to his servant Margaret Alacoque: 'I have a burning thirst to be honored by men, in the Blessed Sacrament—I wish to be treated as king in a royal palace.' You have therefore His own warrant and word: it is Our Lord's desire to dwell in a royal palace and to be treated as a king."

Many among us, recognizing the reasonableness of this ambition, rose and went forward and contributed money, and I would have done likewise, and gladly, but I had already given all I possessed. Continuing, Father Peter said, referring to testimonies of the supernatural origin and manifold endorsements of the Adoration,

"Miracles not contained in Holy Scripture are not articles of faith, and are only to be believed when proved by trustworthy witnesses."

"But," he added, "God permits such miracles from time to time, in order to strengthen our faith or to convert sinners." Then most earnestly he warned us to be on our guard against accepting miracles, or what seemed to be miracles, upon our own judgment and without the educated and penetrating help of a priest or a bishop. He said that an occurrence could be extraordinary without necessarily being miraculous; that indeed a true miracle was usually not merely extraordinary, it was also a thing likely to happen. Likely, for the reason that it happened in circumstances where it manifestly had a service to perform—circumstances which showed that it was not idly sent, but for a solemn and sufficient purpose. He illustrated this with several most interesting instances where both the likelihood of the events and their unusual nature were strikingly perceptible; and not to cultured perceptions alone perhaps, but possibly to even untrained intelligences. One of these he called "The miracle of Turin," and this he told in these words:

"In the year 1453 a church in Isiglo was robbed and among other things a precious monstrance was stolen which still contained the Sacred Host. The monstrance was put in a large sack and a beast of burden carried the booty of the robbers. On the 6th of June the thieves were passing through the streets of Turin with their spoil, when suddenly the animal became furious and no matter how much it was beaten could not be forced from the spot. At once the cords with which the burden was fastened to the ass's back broke, the sack opened of itself, the monstrance appeared, rose on high, and miraculously remained standing in the air to the astonishment of the many spectators. The news of this wonderful event was quickly spread through the city. Bishop Louis appeared with the chapter of his cathedral and the clergy of the city. But behold, a new prodigy! The Sacred Host leaves the case in which it was enclosed, the monstrance lowers itself to the ground, but the Sacred Host remains immovable and majestic in the air, shining like the sun and sending forth in all directions rays of dazzling splendor.

The astonished multitude loudly expressed its joy and admiration, and prostrated itself weeping and adoring before the divine Savior, who displayed His glory here in such a visible manner. The bishop too on his knees implored our Lord to descend into the chalice which he raised up to Him. Thereupon the Sacred Host slowly descended and was carried to the church of St. John amid the inexpressible exultation of the people. The city of Turin had a grand basilica built on the spot where the miracle took place."

He observed that here we had two unchallengeable testimonies to the genuineness of the miracle: that of the bishop, who would not deceive, and that of the ass, who could not. Many in the congregation who had thitherto been able to restrain themselves, now went forward and contributed. Continuing, Father Peter said,

"But now let us hear how our dear Lord, in order to call His people to repentance, once showed something of His majesty in the city of Marseilles, in France. It was A.D. 1218 that the Blessed Sacrament was exposed for adoration in the convent church of the Cordeliers for the forty hours devotion. Many devout persons were assisting at the divine service, when suddenly the sacramental species disappeared and the people beheld the King of Glory in person. His countenance shone with brightness, His look was at once severe and mild, so that no one could bear His gaze. The faithful were motionless with fear, for they soon comprehended what this august apparition meant. Bishop Belsune had more than sixty persons witness to this fact, upon oath."

Yet notwithstanding this the people continued in sin, and had to be again admonished. As Father Peter pointed out:

"At the same time it was revealed to two saintly persons that our Lord would soon visit the city with a terrible punishment if it would not be converted. After two years a pestilence really came and carried off a great part of the inhabitants."

Father Peter told how, two centuries before, in France, Beelzebub and another devil had occupied a woman, and refused to come forth at the command of the bishop, but fled from her, blaspheming, when the Sacred Host was exposed, "this being witnessed by more than 150,000 persons;" he also told how a picture of the

Sacred Host, being painted in the great window of a church that was habitually being struck by lightning, protected it afterward; then he used that opportunity to explain that churches are not struck by lightning by accident, but for a worthy and intelligent purpose:

"Four times our chapel has been struck by lightning. Now some might ask: why did God not turn away the lightning? God has in all things his most wise design, and we are not permitted to search into it. But certain it is, that if our chapel had not been visited in this way, we would not have called on the kindness and charity of the devout lovers of the Holy Eucharist. We would have remained hidden and would have been happy in our obscurity. Perhaps just *this* was His loving design."

Some who had never contributed since the chapel was first struck, on account of not understanding the idea of it before, went forward cheerfully, now, and gave money; but others, like the brewer Hummel, ever hard-headed and without sentiment, said it was an extravagant way to advertise, and God the Father would do well to leave such things to persons in the business, practical persons who had had experience; so Hummel and his like gave nothing. Father Peter told one more miracle, and all were sorry it was the last, for we could have listened hours, with profit, to these moving and convincing wonders:

"On the afternoon of February 3d, 1322, the following incident took place in the Loretto Chapel at Bordeaux. The learned priest, Dr. Delort, professor of theology in Bordeaux, exposed the Blessed Sacrament for adoration. After the Pange lingua had been chanted the sacristan suddenly arises, taps the priest on the shoulder and says: 'God appears in the Sacred Host.' Dr. Delort raises his eyes, looks at the Sacred Host and perceives the apparition. Thinking it might be a mere effect of the light he changes his position in order to be able to see better. He now sees that the Sacred Host had, so to say, separated into two parts, in order to make room in the middle for the form of a young man of wondrous beauty. The breast of Jesus projected beyond the circle of the monstrance, and He graciously moved His head whilst with His right hand He blessed the assembly.

His left hand rested on His heart. The sacristan, several children, and many adults saw the apparition, which lasted during the entire time of the exposition. With superhuman strength the priest then took the monstrance—and constantly gazing at the divine countenance—he gave the final benediction. The commemoration of this apparition is celebrated every year in this convent."

There was not a dry eye in the house.

At this moment the lightning struck the chapel once more and emptied it in a moment, everybody fleeing from it in a frenzy of terror.

This was clearly another miracle, for there was not a cloud in the sky. Proof being afterward collected and avouched by Father Peter, it was accepted and consecrated at Rome, and our chapel became celebrated by reason of it, and a resort for pilgrims.

Chapter 11

To katrina and me the miracle meant that my card had turned up, and we were full of joy and confidence. Doangivadam was coming, we were sure of it. I hurried to the Owl Tower and resumed my watch.

But it was another disappointment. The day wasted away, hour by hour, the night closed down, the moon rose, and still he did not come. At eleven I gave it up and came down heavy-hearted and stiff with the cold. We could not understand it. We talked it over, we turned it this way and that, it was of no use, the thing was incomprehensible. At last Katrina had a thought that seemed to throw light, and she uttered it, saying,

"Sometimes such things are delayed, for a wise purpose, a purpose hidden from us, and which it is not meet for us to inquire into: to punish Marseilles and convert it, the cholera was promised, by a revelation—but it did not come for two years."

"Ah, dear, that is it," I said, "I see it now. He will come in two years, but then it will be too late. The poor master! nothing can save him, he is lost. Before sunset to-morrow the strikers will have triumphed, and he will be a ruined man. I will go to bed; I wish I might never wake again."

About nine the next morning, Doangivadam arrived! Ah, if he could only have come a few short days before! I was all girl-boy again, I couldn't keep the tears back. At his leisure he had strolled over from the village inn, and he marched in among us, gay and jovial, plumed and gorgeous, and took everybody by surprise. Here he was in the midst, scattering salutations all around. He chucked old Frau Stein under the chin and said,

"Beautiful as ever, symbol of perpetual youth!" And he called Katrina his heart's desire and snatched a kiss; and fell into raptures over Maria, and said she was just dazzling and lit up the mouldy castle like the sun; then he came flourishing in where the men were at their early beer and their rascal plans, now at the threshold of success; and he started to burst out with some more cordialities there, but not a man rose nor gave him a look of welcome, for they knew him, and that as soon as he found out how things stood he would side with the under dog in the fight, from nature and habit. He glanced about him, and his face sobered. He backed against an unoccupied table, and half-sitting upon its edge, crossed his ancles, and continued his examination of the faces. Presently he said, gravely,

"There's something the matter, here; what is it?"

The men sat glum and ugly, and no one answered. He looked toward me, and said,

"Tell me about it, lad."

I was proud of his notice, and it so lifted my poor courage that although I dreaded the men and was trembling inside, I actually opened my mouth to begin; but before I could say anything 44 interposed and said, meekly,

"If you please, sir, it would get him into trouble with the men, and he is not the cause of the difficulty, but only I. If I may be allowed to explain it—"

Everybody was astonished to see poor 44 making so hardy a

venture, but Katzenyammer glanced at him contemptuously and
cut him short:

"Shut your mouth, if you please, and look to it that you don't
open it again."

"Suppose *I* ask him to open it," said Doangivadam; "what will
you do about it?"

"*Close* it for him—that's what."

A steely light began to play in Doangivadam's eyes, and he called
44 to his side and said,

"Stand there. I'll take care of you. Now go on."

The men stirred in their chairs and straightened up, their faces
hardening—a sort of suggestion of preparation, of clearing for
action, so to speak. There was a moment's pause, then the boy said
in a level and colorless voice, like one who is not aware of the
weight of his words,

"I am the new apprentice. Out of unmerited disapproval of me,
and for no other or honorable reason, these cowardly men conspired
to ruin the master."

The astonished men, their indignant eyes fixed upon the boy,
began slowly to rise; said Doangivadam,

"They did, did they?"

"Yes," said the boy.

"The—*sons* of bitches!" and every sword was out of its sheath in
an instant, and the men on their feet.

"Come on!" shouted Doangivadam, fetching his long rapier up
with a whiz and falling into position.

But the men hesitated, wavered, gave back, and that was the
friend of the under dog's opportunity—he was on them like a cat.
They recovered, and braced up for a moment, but they could not
stand against the man's impetuous assault, and had to give way
before it and fall back, one sword after another parting from their
hands with a wrench and flying, till only two of the enemy remained armed—Katzenyammer and Binks—then the champion
slipped and fell, and they jumped for him to impale him, and I
turned sick at the sight; but 44 sprang forward and gripped their
necks with his small hands and they sank to the floor limp and
gasping. Doangivadam was up and on guard in a moment, but the

battle was over. The men formally surrendered—except the two that lay there. It was as much as ten minutes before they recovered; then they sat up, looking weak and dazed and uncertain, and maybe thinking the lightning had struck again; but the fight was all out of them and they did not need to surrender; they only felt of their necks and reflected.

We victors stood looking down upon them, the prisoners of war stood grouped apart and sullen.

"How was that done?" said Doangivadam, wondering; "what was it done with?"

"He did it with his hands," I said.

"With his hands? Let me see them, lad . . . . Why, they are soft and plump—just a girl's. Come, there's no strength in these paddies; what is the secret of this thing?"

So I explained:

"It isn't his own strength, sir; his master gives it him by magic— Balthasar the enchanter."

So then he understood it.

He noticed that the men had fallen apart and were picking up their swords, and he ordered 44 to take the swords away from them and bring them to him. And he chuckled at the thought of what the boy had done, and said,

"If they resist, try those persuaders of yours again."

But they did not resist. When 44 brought him the swords he piled them on the table and said,

"Boy, you were not in the conspiracy; with that talent of yours, why didn't you make a stand?"

"There was no one to back me, sir."

"There's something in that. But I'm here, now. It's backing enough, isn't it? You'll enlist for the war?"

"Yes, sir."

"That settles it. I'll be the right wing of the army, and you'll be the left. We will concentrate on the conspiracy here and now. What is your name?"

The boy replied with his customary simplicity,

"No. 44, New Series 864,962."

Doangivadam, who was inserting the point of his rapier into its sheath, suspended the operation where it was, and after a moment asked,

"What did I understand you to say?"

"No. 44, New Series 864,962."

"Is—is that your *name?*"

"Yes, sir."

"My—word, but it's a daisy! In the hurry of going to press, let's dock it to Forty-Four and put the rest on the standing-galley and let it go for left-over at half rates. Will that do?"

"Yes, sir."

"Come, now—range up, men, and plant yourselves! Forty-Four is going to resume his account of the conspiracy. Now go on, 44, and speak as frankly as you please."

Forty-Four told the story, and was not interrupted. When it was finished Doangivadam was looking sober enough, for he recognized that the situation was of a seriousness beyond anything he had guessed—in fact it had a clearly hopeless look, so far as he could at the moment see. The men had the game in their hands; how could he, or any other, save the master from the ruin they had planned? That was his thought. The men read it in his face, and they looked the taunts which they judged it injudicious to put into words while their weapons were out of their reach. Doangivadam noted the looks and felt the sting of them as he sat trying to think out a course. He finished his thinkings, then spoke:

"The case stands like this. If the master dismisses 44—but he can't lawfully do it; that way out is blocked. If 44 remains, you refuse to work, and the master cannot fulfill his contract. That is ruin for him. You hold all the cards, that is evident.

Having conceded this, he began to reason upon the matter, and to plead for the master, the just master, the kind and blameless master, the generous master, now so sorely bested, a master who had never wronged any one, a master who would be compassionate if he were in their place and they in his . . . . .

It was time to interrupt him, lest his speech begin to produce effects, presently; and Katzenyammer did it.

"That's enough of that taffy—shut it off!" he said. "We stand solid; the man that weakens—let him look to himself!"

The war-light began to rise in Doangivadam's eyes, and he said—

"You refuse to work. Very well, I can't make you, and I can't persuade you—but starvation can! I'll lock you into the shop, and put guards over you, and the man that breaks out shall have his reward."

The men realized that the tables had been turned; they knew their man—he would keep his word; he had their swords, he was master of the situation. Even Katzenyammer's face went blank with the suddenness of the checkmate, and his handy tongue found nothing at the moment to say. By order the men moved by in single file and took up their march for the shop, followed by 44 and Doangivadam, who carried swords and maintained peace and order. Presently—

"Halt!" cried the commander. "There's a man missing. Where is Ernest Wasserman?"

It was found that he had slipped out while 44 was telling his story. But all right, he was heard coming, now. He came swaying and tottering in, sank into a chair, looking snow white, and said, "O, Lord!"

Everybody forgot the march, and crowded around him, eager to find out what dreadful thing had happened. But he couldn't answer questions, he could only moan and shiver and say—

"Don't ask *me!* I've been to the shop! O, *lordy*-lord, oh, *lordy*-lord!"

They couldn't get a thing out of him but that, he was that used up and gone to pieces. Then there was a break for the shop, Doangivadam in the lead, and the rest clattering after him through the dim and musty corridors. When we arrived we saw a sight to turn a person to stone: there before our eyes the press was whirling out printed sheets faster than a person could count them—just *snowing* them onto the pile, as you may say—yet *there wasn't a human creature in sight anywhere!*

And that wasn't all, nor the half. All the *other* printing-shop work was going briskly on—yet nobody there, not a living thing to be seen! You would see a sponge get up and dip itself in a basin of water; see it sail along through the air; see it halt an inch above a galley of dead matter and squeeze itself and drench the galley, then toss itself aside; then an invisible expert would flirt the leads out of that matter so fast they fairly seemed to rain onto the imposing-stone, and you would see the matter contract and shrink together under the process; next you would see as much as five inches of that matter separate itself from the mass and rise in the air and stand upright; see it settle itself upon that invisible expert's ring-finger as upon a seat; see it move across the room and pause above a case and go to scattering itself like lightning into the boxes—raining again? yes, it was like that. And in half or three-quarters of no time you would see that five inches of matter scatter itself out and another five come and take its place; and in another minute or two there would be a mountain of wet type in every box and the job finished.

At other cases you would see "sticks" hovering in the air above the space-box; see a line set, spaced, justified and the rule slipped over in the time it takes a person to snap his fingers; next minute the stick is full! next moment it is emptied into the galley! and in ten minutes the *galley's* full and the case empty! It made you dizzy to see these incredible things, these impossible things.

Yes, all the different kinds of work were racing along like Sam Hill—*and all in a sepulchral stillness.* The way the press was carrying on, you would think it was making noise enough for an insurrection, but in a minute you would find it was only your fancy, it wasn't producing a sound—then you would have that sick and chilly feeling a person always has when he recognizes that he is in the presence of creatures and forces not of this world. The invisibles were making up forms, locking up forms, unlocking forms, carrying new signatures to the press and removing the old: abundance of movement, you see, plenty of tramping to and fro, yet you couldn't hear a footfall; there wasn't a spoken word, there wasn't a whisper, there wasn't a sigh—oh, the saddest, uncanniest silence that ever was.

But at last I noticed that there really was one industry lacking—a couple of them: no proofs were taken, no proofs were read! Oh, these *were* experts, sure enough! When *they* did a thing, they did it right, apparently, and it hadn't any occasion to be corrected.

Frightened? We were paralyzed; we couldn't move a limb to get away, we couldn't even cross ourselves, we were so nerveless. And we couldn't look away, the spectacle of those familiar objects drifting about in the air unsupported, and doing their complex and beautiful work without visible help, was so terrifyingly fascinating that we had to look and keep on looking, we couldn't help it.

At the end of half an hour the distribution stopped, and the composing. In turn, one industry after another ceased. Last of all, the churning and fluttering press's tremendous energies came to a stand-still; invisible hands removed the form and washed it, invisible hands scraped the bed and oiled it, invisible hands hung the frisket on its hook. Not anywhere in the place was any motion, any movement, now; there was nothing there but a soundless emptiness, a ghostly hush. This lasted during a few clammy moments, then came a sound from the furthest case—soft, subdued, but harsh, gritty, mocking, sarcastic: the scraping of a rule on a box-partition! and with it came half a dozen dim and muffled spectral chuckles, the dry and crackly laughter of the dead, as it seemed to me.

In about a minute something cold passed by. Not wind, just cold. I felt it on my cheek. It was one of those ghosts; I did not need any one to tell me that; it had that damp, tomby feel which you do not get from any live person. We all shrank together, so as not to obstruct the others. They straggled along by at their leisure, and we counted the frosts as they passed: eight.

Chapter 12

W̲ᴇ ᴀʀʀɪᴠᴇᴅ back to our beer-and-chess room troubled and miserable. Our adventure went the rounds of the castle, and soon the ladies and the servants came, pale and frightened, and when they heard the facts it knocked them dumb for one while, which was not a bad thing.

But the men were not dumb. They boldly proposed to denounce the magician to the Church and get him burnt, for this thing was a

little *too* much, they said. And just then the magician appeared,
and when he heard those awful words, fire and the Church, he was
that scared he couldn't stand; the bones fairly melted in his legs and
he squshed down in a chair alongside of Frau Stein and Maria, and
began to beg and beseech. His airy pride and self-sufficiency had all
gone out of him, and he pretended with all his might that he hadn't
brought those spectres and hadn't had anything to do with it. He
seemed so earnest that a body could hardly keep from believing
him, and so distressed that I had to pity him though I had no love
for him, but only admiration.

But Katzenyammer pressed him hard, and so did Binks and
Moses Haas, and when Maria and her mother tried to put in a word
for him they convinced nobody and did him no good. Doangivadam
put the climax to the poor man's trouble and hit the nail on the
head with a remark which everybody recognized as the wisest and
tellingest thing that had been said yet. He said—

"Balthasar Hoffman, such things don't happen by accident—you
know that very well, and we all do. You are the only person in the
castle that has the power to do a miracle like that. Now then—
firstly, it *happened*; secondly, it didn't happen by itself; thirdly, *you
are here*. What would anybody but a fool conclude?"

Several shouted—

"He's *got* him! got him where he can't budge!"

Another shouted—

"He doesn't answer, and he can't—the stake's the place for him!"

The poor old thing began to cry. The men rose against him in a
fury; they were going to seize him and hale him before the authori-
ties, but Doangivadam interposed some more wisdom, good and
sound. He said—

"Wait. It isn't the best way. He will leave the enchantment on,
for revenge. We want it taken off, don't we?"

Everybody agreed, by acclamation. Doangivadam certainly had a
wonderful head, and full of talent.

"Very well, then. Now Balthasar Hoffman, you've got a chance
for your life. It has suited you to deny, in the most barefaced way,
that you put that enchantment on—let that pass, it doesn't signify.

What we want to know now, is, if we let you alone, do you promise it shan't happen again?"

It brought up his spirits like raising the dead, he was so glad and grateful.

"I do, I do!" he said; "on my honor it shan't happen again."

It made the greatest change. Everybody was pleased, and the awful shadow of that fear vanished from all faces, and they were as doomed men that had been saved. Doangivadam made the magician give his honor that he would not try to leave the castle, but would stand by, and be a safeguard; and went on to say—

"That enchantment had malice back of it. It is my opinion that those invisible creatures have been setting up and printing mere rubbish, in order to use up the paper-supply and defeat the master's contract and ruin him. I want somebody to go and see. Who will volunteer?"

There was a large silence; enough of it to spread a foot deep over four acres. It spread further and further, and got thicker and thicker. Finally Moses Haas said, in his mean way—

"Why don't *you* go?"

They all had to smile at that, for it was a good hit. Doangivadam managed to work up a smile, too, but you could see it didn't taste good; then he said—

"I'll be frank about it. I don't go because I am afraid to. Who is the bravest person here?"

Nearly everybody nominated Ernest Wasserman, and laughed, and Doangivadam ordered him to go and see, but he spoke out with disgust and indignation and said—

"See you in hell, first, and *then* I wouldn't!"

Then old Katrina spoke up proud and high, and said—

"There's my boy, there. I lay he's not afraid. Go 'long and look, child."

They thought 44 wouldn't, but I thought he would, and I was right, for he started right along, and Doangivadam patted him on the head and praised his pluck as he went by. It annoyed Ernest Wasserman and made him jealous, and he pursed up his lips and said—

"I wasn't *afraid* to go, but I'm no slave and I wasn't going to do it on any random unclassified Tom-Dick-and-Harry's orders."

Not a person laughed or said a word, but every man got out his composing rule and scraped wood, and the noise of it was like a concert of jackasses. That is a thing that will take the stiffening out of the conceitedest donkey you can start, and it squelched Ernest Wasserman, and he didn't pipe up any more. Forty-Four came back with an astonisher. He said—

"The invisibles have finished the job, and it's perfect. The contract is saved."

"Carry that news to the master!" shouted Doangivadam, and Marget got right up and started on that mission; and when she delivered it and her uncle saw he was saved in purse and honor and everything, it was medicine for him, and he was a well man again or next to it before he was an hour older.

Well, the men looked that disgusted, you can't think—at least those that had gotten up the strike. It was a good deal of a pill, and Katzenyammer said so; and said—

"We've got to take it—but there'll be sugar on it. We've lost the game, but I'll not call off the strike nor let a man go to work till we've been paid *waiting*-wages."

The men applauded.

"What's waiting-wages?" inquired Doangivadam.

"Full wages for the time we've lost during the strike."

"M-y—word! Well, if that isn't cheek! You're to be paid for time lost in trying to ruin the master! Meantime, where does *he* come in? Who pays him *his* waiting-time?"

The leaders tossed their heads contemptuously, and Binks said he wasn't interested in irrelevances.

So there we were, you see—at a stand-still. There was plenty of work on hand, and the "takes" were on the hooks in the shop, but the men stood out; they said they wouldn't go near the place till their waiting-wages had been paid and the shop spiritually disinfected by the priest. The master was as firm; he said he would never submit to that extortion.

It seemed to be a sort of drawn battle, after all. The master had won the biggest end of the game, but the rest of it remained in the men's hands. This was exasperating and humiliating, but it was a fact just the same, and the men did a proper amount of crowing over it.

About this time Katzenyammer had a thought which perhaps had occurred to others, but he was the first to utter it. He said, with a sneer—

"A lot is being taken for granted—on not even respectable *evidence*, let alone proof. How do *we* know the contract has been completed and saved?"

It certainly was a hit, everybody recognized that; in fact you could call it a sockdolajer, and not be any out of the way. The prejudice against 44 was pretty strong, you know. Doangivadam was jostled—you could see it. He didn't know what to say—you could see that, too. Everybody had an expression on his face, now—a very exultant one on the rebel side, a very uncomfortable one on the other—with two exceptions: Katrina and 44; 44 hadn't any expression at all—his face was wood; but Katrina's eyes were snapping. She said—

"*I* know what you mean, you ornery beer-jug, you Katzenyammer; you mean he's a liar. Well, then, why don't you go and see for yourself? Answer me that—why *don't* you?"

"I don't *need* to, if you want to know. It's nothing to me—*I* don't care what becomes of the contract."

"Well, then, keep your mouth shut and mind your own business. You *dasn't* go, and you know it. Why, you great big mean coward, to call a poor friendless boy a liar, and then ain't man enough to go and prove it!"

"Look here, woman, if you—"

"Don't you call *me* woman, you scum of the earth!" and she strode to him and stood over him; "say it again and I'll tear you to rags!"

The bully murmured—

"I take it back," which made many laugh.

Katrina faced about and challenged the house to go and see. There was a visible shrinkage all around. No answer. Katrina looked at Doangivadam. He slowly shook his head, and said—

"I'll not deny it—I lack the grit."

Then Katrina stretched herself away up in the air and said—

"I'm under the protection of the Queen of Heaven, and I'll go myself! Come along, 44."

They were gone a considerable time. When they returned Katrina said—

"He showed me everything and explained it all, and it's just exactly as he told you." She searched the house, face by face, with her eyes, then settled them upon Katzenyammer and finished: "Is there any polecat here that's got the sand to doubt it *now?*"

Nobody showed up. Several of our side laughed, and Doangivadam he laughed too, and fetched his fist down with a bang on the table like the Lord Chief Justice delivering an opinion, and said—

"That settles it!"

Chapter 13

NEXT DAY was pretty dreary. The men wouldn't go to work, but loafed around moody and sour and uncomfortable. There was not much talk; what there was was mumbled, in the main, by pairs. There was no general conversation. At meals silence was the rule. At night there was no jollity, and before ten all had disappeared to their rooms and the castle was a dim and grim solitude.

The day after, the same. Wherever 44 came he got ugly looks, threatening looks, and I was afraid for him and wanted to show sympathy but was too timid. I tried to think I avoided him for his own good, but did not succeed to my satisfaction. As usual, he did not seem to know he was being so scowled at and hated. He certainly could be inconceivably stupid at times, for all he was so capable at others. Marget pitied him and said kind things to him, and Doangivadam was cordial and handsome to him, and whenever Doangivadam saw one of those scowls he insulted the man that exhibited it and invited him to exhibit it again, which he didn't. Of course Katrina was 44's friend right along. But the friendliness was confined to those three, at least as far as any open show of it went.

So things drifted along, till the contract-gentlemen came for the goods. They brought a freight wagon along, and it waited in the great court. There was an embarrassment, now. Who would box-up the goods? Our men? Indeed, no. They refused, and said they wouldn't allow any outsider to do it, either. And Katzenyammer said to Doangivadam, while he was pleading—

"Save your breath—the contract has failed, after all!"

It made Doangivadam mad, and he said—

"It hasn't failed, either. I'll box the things myself, and Katrina and I will load them into the wagon. Rather than see you people win, I'll chance death by ghost and fright. I reckon Katrina's Virgin can protect the two of us. Perhaps you boys will interfere. I have my doubts."

The men chuckled, furtively. They knew he had spoken rashly. They knew he had not taken into account the size and weight of those boxes.

He hurried away and had a private word with the master, saying—

"It's all arranged, sir. Now if you—"

"Excellent! and most unexpected. Are the men—"

"No, but no matter, it's arranged. If you can feed and wine and otherwise sumptuously and satisfactorily entertain your guests three hours, I'll have the goods in the wagon then."

"Oh, many, many thanks—I'll make them stay all night."

Doangivadam came to the kitchen, then, and told Katrina and 44 all this, and I was there just at that time and heard it; and Katrina said all right, she would protect him to the shop, now, and leave him in the care of the Virgin while he did the packing, and in two hours and a half dinner would be down to the wine and nuts and then she would come and help carry the boxes. Then he left with her, but I stayed, for no striker would be likely to venture into the kitchen, therefore I could be in 44's company without danger. When Katrina got back, she said—

"That Doangivadam's a gem of the ocean—he's a *man*, that's what he is, not a waxwork, like that Katzenyammer. I wasn't going to discourage him, but *we* can't carry the boxes. There's five, and each of them a barrow-load; and besides, there has to be four carriers to the barrow. And then—"

Forty-Four interrupted:

"There's two of you, and I'll be the other two. You two will carry one end, and I'll carry the other. I am plenty strong enough."

"Child, you'll just stay out of sight, that's what you'll do. Do you want to provoke the men every way you can think of, you foolish little numskull? Ain't they down on you a plenty, just the way it is?"

"But you see, you two *can't* carry the boxes, and if you'll only let me help—"

"You'll not budge a step—do you hear me?" She stood stern and resolute, with her knuckles in her hips. The boy looked disappointed and grieved, and that touched her. She dropped on her knees where he sat, and took his face between her hands, and said, "Kiss your old mother, and forgive"—which he did, and the tears came into her eyes, which a moment before were so stormy. "Ain't you all I've got in the world? and don't I love the ground you walk on, and can I bear to see you getting into more and more danger all the time, and no need of it? Here, bless your heart," and she jumped up and brought a pie, "You and August sample *that,* and be good. It ain't the kind you get outside of this kitchen, that you can't tell from plate-mail when you bite it in the dark."

We began on the pie with relish, and of course conversation failed for a time. By and by 44 said, softly—

"Mother, he gave his word, you know."

Katrina was hit. She had to suspend work and think that over. She seated herself against the kitchen table, with her legs aslant and braced, and her arms folded and her chin down, and muttered several times, "Yes, that's so, he did." Finally she unlimbered and reached for the butcher-knife, which she fell to sharpening with energy on a brick. Then she lightly tested its edge with the ball of her thumb, and said—

"I know it—we've got to have two more. Doangivadam will force one, and I bet I'll persuade the other."

"*Now* I'm content," said 44, fervently, which made Katrina beam with pleasure.

We stayed there in the comfortable kitchen and chatted and played checkers, intending to be asked by Katrina to take our dinner with her, for she was the friendliest and best table-company *we* had. As time drew on, it became jolly in the master's private dining-room where it was his custom to feed guests of honor and distinction, and whenever a waiter came in or went out we could hear the distant bursts of merriment, and by and by bursts of song, also, showing that the heavy part of the feeding had been accomplished. Then we had our dinner with Katrina, and about the time we had finished, Doangivadam arrived hungry and pretty well tired out and said he had packed every box; but he wouldn't take a bite, he said, until his job was finished up and the wagon loaded. So Katrina told him her plan for securing extra help by compulsion and persuasion, and he liked it and they started. Doangivadam said he hadn't seen any of the men in sight, therefore he judged they must be lying in wait somewhere about the great court so as to interrupt any scheme of bribing the two porters of the freight wagon to help carry the boxes; so it was his idea to go there and see.

Katrina ordered us to stay behind, which we didn't do, after they were out of sight. We went down by secret passages and reached the court ahead of them, and hid. We were near the wagon. The driver and porters had been given their supper, and had been to the stalls to feed and water the horses, and now they were walking up and down chatting and waiting to receive the freight. Our two friends arrived now, and in low voices began to ask these men if they had seen any men of the castle around about there, but before they could answer, something happened: we saw some dim big bulks emerge from our side of the court about fifty yards away and come in procession in our direction. Swiftly they grew more and more distinct under the stars and by the dim lamps, and they turned out to be men, and each of them was drooping under one of our big freight boxes. The idea—carrying it all alone! And another surprising thing was, that when the first man passed us it turned out to be Katzenyammer! Doangivadam was delighted out of his senses, almost, and said some splendid words of praise about his change of heart, but Katzenyammer could only grunt and growl, he was strained so by his burden.

And the next man was Binks! and there was more praise and more grunts. And next came Moses Haas—think of it! And then Gustav Fischer! And after him, the end of the procession—Ernest Wasserman! Why, Doangivadam could hardly believe it, and said he *didn't* believe it, and *couldn't*; and said *"Is* it you, Ernest?" and Ernest told him to go to hell, and then Doangivadam was satisfied and said "that settles it."

For that was Ernest's common word, and you could know him by it in the dark.

Katrina couldn't say a word, she just stood there dazed. She saw the boxes stowed in the wagon, she saw the gang file back and disappear, and still she couldn't get her voice till then; and even then all she could say, was—

"Well, it beats the band!"

Doangivadam followed them a little way, and wanted to have a supper and a night of it, but they answered him roughly and he had to give it up.

Chapter 14

THE FREIGHT wagon left at dawn; the honored guests had a late breakfast, paid down the money on the contract, then after a good-bye bottle they departed in their carriage. About ten the master, full of happiness and forgiveness and benevolent feeling, had the men assembled in the beer-and-chess room, and began a speech that was full of praises of the generous way they had thrown ill-will to the winds at the last moment and loaded the wagon last night and saved the honor and the life of his house—and went on and on, like that, with the water in his eyes and his voice trembling; and there the men sat and stared at one another, and at the master, with their mouths open and their breath standing still; till at last Katzenyammer burst out with—

"What in the nation *are* you mooning about? Have you lost your mind? *We've* saved you nothing; *we've* carried no boxes"—here he rose excited and banged the table—"and what's more, we've arranged that nobody *else* shall carry a box or load that wagon till our waiting-time's paid!"

Well, think of it! The master was so astonished that for a moment or two he couldn't pull his language; then he turned sadly and uncertainly to Doangivadam and said—

"I could not have dreamed it. Surely you told me that they—"

"Certainly I did. I told you they brought down the boxes—"

"*Listen* at him!" cried Binks, springing to his feet.

"—those five *there*—Katzenyammer at the head, Wasserman at the tail—"

"As sure as my name's Was—"

"—each with a box on his shoulders—"

All were on their feet, now, and they drowned out the speaker with a perfect deluge of derisive laughter, out of the midst of which burst Katzenyammer's bull-voice shouting—

"Oh, listen to the maniac! *Each* carrying a box weighing *five—hundred—pounds!*"

Everybody took up that telling refrain and screamed it and yelled it with all his might. Doangivadam saw the killing force of the argument, and began to look very foolish—which the men saw, and they roared at him, challenging him to get up and purge his soul and trim his imagination. He was caught in a difficult place, and he did not try to let on that he was in easy circumstances. He got up and said, quietly, and almost humbly—

"I don't understand it, I can't explain it. I realize that no man here could carry one of those boxes; and yet as sure as I am alive I saw it done, just as I have said. Katrina saw it too. We were awake, and not dreaming. I spoke to every one of the five. I saw them load the boxes into the wagon. I—"

Moses Haas interrupted:

"Excuse me, nobody loaded any boxes into the wagon. It wouldn't have been allowed. We've kept the wagon under watch." Then he said, ironically, "Next, the gentleman will work his imagination up to saying the wagon is gone and the master paid."

It was good sarcasm, and they all laughed; but the master said, gravely, "Yes, I have been paid," and Doangivadam said, "Certainly the wagon is gone."

"Oh, come!" said Moses, leaving his seat, "this is going a little *too* far; it's a trifle *too* brazen; come out and say it to the wagon's face. If you've got the cheek to do it, follow me."

He moved ahead, and everybody swarmed after him, eager to see what would happen. I was getting worried; nearly half convinced, too; so it was a relief to me when I saw that the court was empty. Moses said—

"Now then, what do you call *that*? Is it the wagon, or isn't it?"

Doangivadam's face took on the light of a restored confidence and a great satisfaction, and he said—

"I see no wagon."

"*What!*" in a general chorus.

"No—I don't see any wagon."

"Oh, great guns! perhaps the master will say *he* doesn't see a wagon."

"Indeed I see none," said the master.

"Wel-l, well, *well!*" said Moses, and was plumb nonplussed. Then he had an idea, and said, "Come, Doangivadam, you seem to be near-sighted—please to follow me and *touch* the wagon, and see if you'll have the hardihood to go on with this cheap comedy."

They walked briskly out a piece, then Moses turned pale and stopped.

"By God, it's gone!" he said.

There was more than one startled face in the crowd. They crept out, silent and looking scared; then they stopped, and sort of moaned—

"It *is* gone; it was a ghost-wagon."

Then they walked right over the place where it had been, and crossed themselves and muttered prayers. Next they broke into a fury, and went storming back to the chess-room, and sent for the magician, and charged him with breaking his pledge, and swore the Church should have him now; and the more he begged the more they scared him, till at last they grabbed him to carry him off—then he broke down, and said that if they would spare his life he would confess. They told him to go ahead, and said if his confession was not satisfactory it would be the worse for him. He said—

"I hate to say it—I wish I could be spared it—oh, the shame of it, the ingratitude of it! But—pity me, pity me!—I have been nourishing a viper in my bosom. That boy, that pupil whom I have so loved —in my foolish fondness I taught him several of my enchantments, and now he is using them for your hurt and my ruin!"

It turned me sick and faint, the way the men plunged at 44, crying "Kill him, kill him!" but the master and Doangivadam jumped in and stood them off and saved him. Then Doangivadam talked some wisdom and reasonableness into the gang which had good effect. He said—

"What is the use to kill the boy? He isn't the *source;* whatever power he has, he gets from his master, this magician here. Don't you believe that if the magician wants to, he can put a spell on the boy that will abolish his power and make him harmless?"

Of course that was so, and everybody saw it and said so. So then Doangivadam worked some more wisdom: instead of letting on to know it all himself, he gave the others a chance to seem to know a little of what was left. He asked them to assist him in this difficult case and suggest some wise and practical way to meet this emergency. It flattered them, and they unloaded the suggestion that the magician be put under bond to shut off the boy's enchantments, on pain of being delivered to the Church if anything happened again.

Doangivadam said it was the very thing; and praised the idea, and let on to think it was wonderfully intelligent, whereas it was only what he had suggested himself, and what anybody would have thought of and suggested, including the cat, there being no other way with any sense in it.

So they bonded the magician, and he didn't lose any time in furnishing the pledge and getting a new lease on his hide. Then he turned on the boy and reproached him for his ingratitude, and then he fired up on his subject and turned his tongue and his temper loose, and most certainly he did give him down the banks and roll Jordan roll! I never felt so sorry for a person, and I think others were sorry for him, too, though they would have said that as long as he deserved it he couldn't expect to be treated any gentler, and it would be a valuable lesson to him anyway, and save him future trouble, and worse. The way the magician finished, was awful; it made your blood run cold. He walked majestically across the room with his solemn professional stride, which meant that something was going to happen. He stopped in the door and faced around, everybody holding their breath, and said, slow and distinct, and pointing his long finger—

"Look at him, there where he sits—and remember my words, and the doom they are laden with. I have put him under my spells; if he thinks he can dissolve them and do you further harm, let him try. But I make this pledge and compact: on the day that he succeeds I will put an enchantment upon him, here in this room, which shall slowly consume him to ashes before your eyes!"

Then he departed. Dear me, but it was a startled crowd! Their faces were that white—and they couldn't seem to say a word. But there was one good thing to see—there was pity in every face of them! That was human nature, wasn't it—when your enemy is in awful trouble, to be sorry for him, even when your pride won't let you go and say it to him before company? But the master and Doangivadam went and comforted him and begged him to be careful and work no spells and run no risks; and even Gustav Fischer ventured to go by, and heave out a kindly word in passing; and pretty soon the news had gone about the castle, and Marget and Katrina came; *they* begged him, too, and both got to crying, and that made him so conspicuous and heroic, that Ernest Wasserman was bursting with jealousy, and you could see he wished *he* was advertised for roasting, too, if this was what you get for it.

Katrina had sassed the magician more than once and had not seemed to be afraid of him, but this time her heart was concerned and her pluck was all gone. She went to him, with the crowd at her heels, and went on her knees and begged him to be good to her boy, and stay his hand from practising enchantments, and be his guardian and protector and save him from the fire. Everybody was moved. Except the boy. It was one of his times to be an ass and a wooden-head. He certainly could choose them with the worst judgment I ever saw. Katrina was alarmed; she was afraid his seeming lack of interest would have a bad effect with the magician, so she did his manners for him and conveyed his homage and his pledges of good behavior, and hurried him out of the presence.

Well, to my mind there is nothing that makes a person interesting like his being about to get burnt up. We had to take 44 to the sick lady's room and let her gaze at him, and shudder, and shrivel, and wonder how he would look when he was done; she hadn't had such a stirring up for years, and it acted on her kidneys and her spine and her livers and all those things and her other works, and started up her flywheel and her circulation, and she said, herself, it had done her more good than any bucketful of medicine she had taken that week. And begged him to come again, and he promised he would if he could. Also said if he couldn't he would send her some of the ashes; for he certainly was a good boy at bottom, and thoughtful.

They all wanted to see him, even people that had taken hardly any interest in him before—like Sara and Duffles and the other maids, and Fritz and Jacob and the other men-servants. And they were all tender toward him, and ever so gentle and kind, and gave him little things out of their poverty, and were ever so sorry, and showed it by the tears in their eyes. But not a tear out of *him*, you might have squeezed him in the hydraulic press and you wouldn't have got dampness enough to cloud a razor, it being one of his blamed wooden times, you know.

Why, even Frau Stein and Maria were full of interest in him, and gazed at him, and asked him how it felt—in prospect, you know—and said a lot of things to him that came nearer being kind, than anything they were used to saying, by a good deal. It was surprising how popular he was, all of a sudden, now that he was in such awful danger if he didn't behave himself. And although I was around with him I never got a sour look from the men, and so I hadn't a twinge of fear the whole time. And then the supper we had that night in the kitchen!—Katrina laid out her whole strength on it, and cried all over it, and it was wonderfully good and salty.

Katrina told us to go and pray all night that God would not lead 44 into temptation, and she would do the same. I was ready and anxious to begin, and we went to my room.

Chapter 15

B UT WHEN we got there I saw that 44 was not minded to pray, but was full of other and temporal interests. I was shocked, and deeply concerned; for I felt rising in me with urgency a suspicion which had troubled me several times before, but which I had ungently put from me each time—that he was indifferent to religion. I questioned him—he confessed it! I leave my distress and consternation to be imagined, I cannot describe them.

In that paralysing moment my life changed, and I was a different being; I resolved to devote my life, with all the affections and forces and talents which God had given me to the rescuing of this endangered soul. Then all my spirit was invaded and suffused with a blessed feeling, a divine sensation, which I recognized as the approval of God. I knew by that sign, as surely as if He had spoken to me, that I was His appointed instrument for this great work. I knew that He would help me in it; I knew that whenever I should need light and leading I could seek it in prayer, and have it; I knew—

"I get the idea," said 44, breaking lightly in upon my thought, "it will be a Firm, with its headquarters up there and its hindquarters down here. There's a duplicate of it in every congregation—in every family, in fact. Wherever you find a warty little devotee who isn't in partnership with God—as *he* thinks—on a speculation to save some little warty soul that's no more worth saving than his own, stuff him and put him in the museum, it is where he belongs."

"Oh, don't say such things, I beseech you! They are so shocking, and so awful. And so unjust; for in the sight of God all souls are precious, there is no soul that is not worth saving."

But the words had no effect. He was in one of his frivolous moods, and when these were upon him one could not interest him in serious things. For all answer to what I had been saying, he said in a kindly but quite unconcerned way that we would discuss this trifle at another time, but not now. That was the very word he used; and plainly he used it without any sense of its gross impropriety. Then he added this strange remark—

"For the moment, I am not living in the present century, but in one which interests me more, for the time being. *You* pray, if you like—never mind me, I will amuse myself with a curious toy if it won't disturb you."

He got a little steel thing out of his pocket and set it between his teeth, remarking "it's a jew's-harp—the niggers use it"—and began to buffet out of it a most urgent and strenuous and vibrant and exceedingly gay and inspiriting kind of music, and at the same time he went violently springing and capering and swooping and swirling all up and down the room in a way to banish prayer and make a person dizzy to look at him; and now and then he would utter the excess of his joy in a wild whoop, and at other times he would leap into the air and spin there head over heels for as much as a minute like a wheel, and so frightfully fast that he was all webbed together and you could hear him buzz. And he kept perfect time to his music all the while. It was a most extravagant and stirring and heathen performance.

Instead of being fatigued by it he was only refreshed. He came and sat down by me and rested his hand on my knee in his winning way, and smiled his beautiful smile, and asked me how I liked it. It was so evident that he was expecting a compliment, that I was obliged to furnish it. I had not the heart to hurt him, and he so innocently proud of his insane exhibition. I could not expose to him how undignified it was, and how degrading, and how difficult it had been for me to stand it through; I forced myself to say it was "ideal—*more* than ideal;" which was of course a perfectly meaningless phrase, but he was just hungry enough for a compliment to

make him think this was one, and also make him overlook what was
going on in my mind; so his face was fairly radiant with thanks and
happiness, and he impulsively hugged me and said—

"It's lovely of you to like it so. I'll do it again!"

And at it he went, God assoil him, like a tempest. I couldn't say
anything, it was my own fault. Yet I was not really to blame, for I
could not foresee that he would take that uninflamed compliment
for an invitation to do the fiendish orgy over again. He kept it up
and kept it up until my heart was broken and all my body and spirit
so worn and tired and desperate that I could not hold in any longer,
I *had* to speak out and beg him to stop, and not tire himself so. It
was another mistake; damnation, he thought I was suffering on *his*
account! so he piped out cheerily, as he whizzed by—

"Don't worry about *me;* sit right where you are and enjoy it, I
can do it all night."

I thought I would go out and find a good place to die, and was
starting, when he called out in a grieved and disappointed tone—

"Ah, you are not going, are you?"

"Yes."

"What for? Don't go—please don't."

"Are you going to keep still? Because I am not going to stay here
and see you tire yourself to death."

"Oh, it doesn't tire me in the least, I give you my word. *Do* stay."

Of course I wanted to stay, but not unless he would sit down and
act civilized, and give me a rest. For a time he could *not* seem to get
the situation through his head—for he certainly could be the dull-
est animal that ever was, at times—but at last he looked up with a
wounded expression in his big soft eyes, and said—

"August, I believe you do not *want* any more."

Of course that broke me all down and made me ashamed of
myself, and in my anxiety to heal the hurt I had given and see him
happy again I came within a hair's breadth of throwing all judgment and discretion to the winds and saying I *did* want more. But I
did not do it; the dread and terror of what would certainly follow,
tied my tongue and saved my life. I adroitly avoided a direct answer
to what he had said, by suddenly crying "ouch!" and grabbing at an

imaginary spider inside my collar, whereupon he forgot his troubles at once in his concern for me. He plunged his hand in and raked it around my neck and fetched out three spiders—real ones, whereas I had supposed there was none there but imaginary ones. It was quite unusual for any but imaginary ones to be around at that time of the year, which was February.

We had a pleasant time together, but no religious conversation, for whenever I began to frame a remark of that color he saw it in my mind and squelched it with that curious power of his whereby he barred from utterance any thought of mine it happened to suit him to bar. It was an interesting time, of course, for it was the nature of 44 to be interesting. Pretty soon I noticed that we were not in my room, but in his. The change had taken place without my knowing when it happened. It was beautiful magic, but it made me feel uneasy. Forty-Four said—

"It is because you think I am traveling toward temptation."

"I am sure you are, 44. Indeed you are already arrived there, for you are doing things of a sort which the magician has prohibited."

"Oh, that's nothing! I don't obey him except when it suits me. I mean to use his enchantments whenever I can get any entertainment out of them, and whenever I can annoy him. I know every trick he knows, and some that he doesn't know. Tricks of my own —for I bought them; bought them from a bigger expert than he is. When I play my own, he is a puzzled man, for he thinks I do it by his inspiration and command, and inasmuch as he can't remember furnishing either the order or the inspiration, he is puzzled and bothered, and thinks there is something the matter with his head. He has to father everything I do, because he has begun it and can't get out of it now, and so between working his magic and my own I mean to build him up a reputation that will leave all other second-class magicians in the shade."

"It's a curious idea. Why don't you build it up for yourself?"

"I don't want it. At home we don't care for a small vanity like that, and I shouldn't value it here."

"Where is your ho—"

It got barred before I could finish. I wished in my heart I could have that gorgeous reputation which he so despised! But he paid no attention to the thought; so I sighed, and did not pursue it. Presently I got to worrying again, and said—

"Forty-Four, I foresee that before you get far with the magician's reputation you will bring a tragedy upon yourself. And you are so unprepared. You ought to prepare, 44, you ought indeed; every moment is precious. I do wish you would become a Christian; won't you try?"

He shook his head, and said—

"I should be too lonesome."

"Lonesome? How?"

"I should be the only one."

I thought it an ill jest, and said so. But he said it was not a jest—some time he would go into the matter and prove that he had spoken the truth; at present he was busy with a thing of "importance"—and added, placidly, "I must jack-up the magician's reputation, first." Then he said in his kindest manner—

"You have a quality which I do not possess—fear. You are afraid of Katzenyammer and his pals, and it keeps you from being with me as much as you would like and as I would like. That can be remedied, in a quite simple way. I will teach you how to become invisible, whenever you please. I will give you a magic word. Utter it in your mind, for you can't do it with your tongue, though I can. Say it when you wish to disappear, and say it again when you wish to be visible again."

He uttered the word, and vanished. I was so startled and so pleased and so grateful that I did not know where I was, for a moment, nor which end of me was up; then I perceived that I was sitting by the fire in my own room, but I did not know how I got there.

Being a boy, I did what another boy would have done: as long as I could keep awake I did nothing but appear and disappear, and enjoy myself. I was very proud, and considered myself the superior of any boy in the land; and that was foolish, for I did not invent the art, it was a gift, and no merit to me that I could exercise it. Another boy with the same luck would be just as superior as I was. But these were not my thoughts, I got them later, and at second hand—where all thoughts are acquired, 44 used to say. Finally I disappeared and went to sleep happy and content, without saying one prayer for 44, and he in such danger. I never thought of it.

Chapter 16

FORTY-FOUR, by grace of his right to wear a sword, was legally a gentleman. It suited his whim, now, to come out dressed as one. He was clever, but ill balanced; and whenever he saw a particularly good chance to be a fool, pie couldn't persuade him to let it go by; he had to sample it, he couldn't seem to help it. He was as unpopular as he could be, but the hostile feeling, the intense bitterness, had been softening little by little for twenty-four hours, on account of the awful danger his life was in, so of course he must go and choose *this* time of all times, to flaunt in the faces of the comps the offensive fact that he was their social equal. And not only did he appear in the dress of a gentleman, but the quality and splendor of it surpassed even Doangivadam's best, and as for the others they were mere lilies of the valley to his Solomon. Embroidered buskins, with red heels; pink silk tights; pale blue satin trunks; cloth of gold doublet; short satin cape, of a blinding red; lace collar fit for a queen; the cunningest little blue velvet cap, with a slender long feather standing up out of a fastening of clustered diamonds; dress sword in a gold sheath, jeweled hilt. That was his outfit; and he carried himself like a princeling "doing a cake-walk," as he described it. He was as beautiful as a picture, and as satisfied with himself as if he owned the earth. He had a lace handkerchief in his hand, and now and then he would give his nose a dainty little dab or two with it, the way a duchess does. It was evident that he thought he was going to be admired, and it was pitiful to see his disappointment when the men broke out on him with insults and ridicule and called him offensive names, and asked him where he had stolen his clothes.

He defended himself the best he could, but he was so near to crying that he could hardly control his voice. He said he had come by the clothes honestly, through the generosity of his teacher the good magician, who created them instantly out of nothing just by uttering a single magic word; and said the magician was a far mightier enchanter than they supposed; that he hadn't shown the world the half of the wonders he could do, and he wished he was here now, he would not like it to have his humble servant abused so when he wasn't doing any harm; said he believed if he was here he would do Katzenyammer a hurt for calling his servant a thief and threatening to slap his face.

"He would, would he? Well, there he comes—let's *see* if he loves his poor dear servant so much," said Katzenyammer, and gave the boy a cruel slap that you could have heard a hundred yards.

The slap spun Forty-Four around, and as soon as he saw the magician he cried out eagerly and supplicatingly—

"Oh, noble master, oh greatest and sublimest of magicians, I read your command in your eyes, and I must obey if it is your will, but I pray you, I beseech you spare me the office, do it yourself with your own just hand!"

The magician stood still and looked steadily and mutely at Forty-Four as much as half a minute, we waiting and gazing and holding our breath; then at last 44 made a reverent bow, saying, "You are master, your will is law, and I obey," and turned to Katzenyammer and said—

"In not very many hours you will discover what you have brought upon yourself and the others. You will see that it is not well to offend the master."

You have seen a cloud-shadow sweep along and sober a sunlit field; just so, that darkling vague threat was a cloud-shadow to those faces there. There is nothing that is more depressing and demoralizing than the promise of an indefinite calamity when one is dealing with a powerful and malicious necromancer. It starts large, plenty large enough, but it does not stop there, the imagination goes on spreading it, till at last it covers all the space you've got, and takes away your appetite, and fills you with dreads and miseries, and you start at every noise and are afraid of your own shadow.

Old Katrina was sent by the women to beg 44 to tell what was going to happen so that they could get relieved of a part of the crushing burden of suspense, but she could not find him, nor the magician either. Neither of them was seen, the rest of the day. At supper there was but little talk, and no mention of *the* subject. In the chess-room after supper there was some private and unsociable drinking, and much deep sighing, and much getting up and walking the floor unconsciously and nervously a little while, then sitting down again unconsciously; and now and then a tortured ejaculation broke out involuntarily. At ten o'clock nobody moved to go to bed; apparently each troubled spirit found a sort of help and solace in the near presence of its kind, and dreaded to separate itself from companionship. At half past ten no one had stirred. At eleven the same. It was most melancholy to be there like this, in the dim light of unquiet and flickering candles and in a stillness that was broken by but few sounds and was all the more impressive because of the moaning of the wintry wind about the towers and battlements.

It was at half past eleven that it happened. Everybody was sitting steeped in musings, absorbed in thought, listening to that dirge the wind was chanting—Katzenyammer like the rest. A heavy step was heard, all glanced up nervously, and yonder in the door appeared a *duplicate Katzenyammer!* There was one general gasping intake of breath that nearly sucked the candles out, then the house sat paralyzed and gazing. This creature was in shop-costume, and had a "take" in its hand. It was the exact reproduction of the other Katzenyammer to the last shade and detail, a mirror couldn't have told them apart. It came marching up the room with the only gait that could be proper to it—aggressive, decided, insolent—and held out the "take" to its twin and said—

"Here! how do you want that set, leaded, or solid?"

For about a moment the original Katzenyammer was surprised out of himself; but the next moment he was all there, and jumped up shouting—

"You bastard of black magic, I'll"—he finished with his fist, delivering a blow on the twin's jaw that would have broken anybody else's, but this jaw stood it uncrushed; then the pair danced about the place hammering, banging, ramming each other like battering machines, everybody looking on with wonder and awe and admiration, and hoping neither of them would survive. They fought half an hour, then sat down panting, exhausted, and streaming with blood—they hadn't strength to go on.

The pair sat glaring at each other a while, then the original said—

"Look here, my man, who *are* you, anyway? Answer up!"

"I'm Katzenyammer, foreman of the shop. That's who I am, if you want to know."

"It's a lie. Have you been setting type in there?"

"Yes, I have."

"The hell you have! who told you you could?"

"I told myself. That's sufficient."

"Not on your life! Do you belong to the union?"

"No, I don't."

"Then you're a scab. Boys, up and at him!"

Which they did, with a will, fuming and cursing and swearing in a way which it was an education to listen to. In another minute there would not have been anything left of that Duplicate, I reckon, but he promptly set up a ringing shout of "Help, boys, help!" and in the same moment perfect Duplicates of all the *rest* of us came swarming in and plunged into the battle!

But it was another draw. It had to be, for each Duplicate fought his own mate and was his exact match, and neither could whip the other. Then they tried the issue with swords, but it was a draw once more. The parties drew apart, now, and acrimoniously discussed the situation. The Duplicates refused to join the union, neither would they throw up their job; they were stubbornly deaf to both threats and persuasion. So there it was—just a deadlock! If the Duplicates remained, the Originals were without a living—why, they couldn't even collect their waiting-time, now! Their impregnable position, which they had been so proud of and so arrogant about had turned to air and vacancy. These were very grave and serious facts, cold and clammy ones; and the deeper they sank down into the consciousness of the ousted men the colder and clammier they became.

It was a hard situation, and pitiful. A person may say that the men had only gotten what they deserved, but when that is said is all said? I think not. They were only human beings, they had been foolish, they deserved some punishment, but to take their very bread was surely a punishment beyond the measure of their fault. But there it was—the disaster was come, the calamity had fallen, and no man could see a way out of the difficulty. The more one examined it the more perplexing and baffling and irremediable it seemed. And all so unjust, so unfair; for in the talk it came out that the Duplicates did not need to eat or drink or sleep, so long as the Originals did those things—there was enough for both; but when a *Duplicate* did them, by George, his Original got no benefit out of it! Then look at that other thing: the Originals were out of work and wageless, yet they would be supporting these intruding scabs, out of *their* food and drink, and by gracious not even a thank-you for it! It came out that the scabs got no pay for their work in the shop, and didn't care for it and wouldn't ask for it. Doangivadam finally hit upon a fair and honorable compromise, as he thought, and the boys came up a little out of their droop to listen. Doangivadam's idea was, for the Duplicates to do the work, and for the Originals to take the pay, and fairly and honorably eat and sleep enough for both. It looked bright and hopeful for a moment, but then the clouds settled down again: the plan wouldn't answer; it would not be lawful for unions and scabs to have dealings together. So that idea had to be given up, and everybody was gloomier than ever. Meantime Katzenyammer had been drinking hard, to drown his exasperations, but it was not effective, he couldn't seem to hold enough, and yet he was full. He was only half drunk; the trouble was, that his Duplicate had gotten the other half of the dividend, and was just as drunk, and as insufficiently drunk, as *he* was. When he realized this he was deeply hurt, and said reproachfully to his Duplicate, who sat there blinking and suffused with a divine contentment—

"Nobody *asked* you to partake; such conduct is grossly ill-bred; no gentleman would do such a thing."

Some were sorry for the Duplicate, for he was not to blame, but several of the Originals were evidently not sorry for him, but offended at him and ashamed of him. But the Duplicate was not affected, he did not say anything, but just blinked and looked drowsy and grateful, the same as before.

The talk went on, but it arrived nowhere, of course. The situation remained despairingly incurable and desperate. Then the talk turned upon the magician and 44, and quickly became bitter and vengeful. When it was at its sharpest, the magician came mooning in; and when he saw all those Duplicates he was either thunderstruck with amazement or he played it well. The men were vexed to see him act so, and they said, indignantly—

"It's your own fiendish work and you needn't be pretending surprise."

He was frightened at their looks and their manner, and hastened to deny, with energy and apparent earnestness, that *this* was any work of his; he said he had given a quite different command, and he only wished 44 were here, he would keep his word and burn him to ashes for misusing his enchantments; he said he would go and find him; and was starting away, but they jumped in front of him and barred his way, and Katzenyammer-original was furious, and said—

"You are trying to escape, but you'll not! You don't have to stir out of your tracks to produce that limb of perdition, and you know it and we know it. Summon him—summon him and destroy him, or I give my honor I will denounce you to the Holy Office!"

That was a plenty. The poor old man got white and shaky, and put up his hand and mumbled some strange words, and in an instant, *bang!* went a thunderclap, and there stood 44 in the midst, dainty and gay in his butterfly clothes!

All sprang up with horror in their faces to protest, for at bottom no one really wanted the boy destroyed, they only *believed* they did; there was a scream, and Katrina came flying, with her gray hair streaming behind her; for one moment a blot of black darkness fell upon the place and extinguished us all; the next moment in our midst stood that slender figure transformed to a core of dazzling white fire; in the succeeding moment it crumbled to ashes and we were blotted out in the black darkness again. Out of it rose an adoring cry—broken in the middle by a pause and a sob—

"The Lord gave, the Lord hath taken away . . . . blessed be the name of the Lord!"

It was Katrina; it was the faithful Christian parting with its all, yet still adoring the smiting hand.

Chapter 17

I WENT invisible the most of the next day, for I had no heart to talk about common matters, and had rather a shrinking from talking about the matter which was uppermost in all minds. I was full of sorrow, and also of remorse, which is the way with us in the first days of a bereavement, and at such times we wish to be alone with our trouble and our bitter recallings of failings of loyalty or love toward the comrade who is gone. There were more of these sins to my charge than I could have believed; they rose up and accused me at every turn, and kept me saying with heart-wearing iteration, "Oh, if he were only back again, how true I would be, and how differently I would act." I remembered so many times when I could perhaps have led him toward the life eternal, and had let the chance go by; and now he was lost and I to blame, and where was I to find comfort?

I always came back to that, I could not long persuade myself to other and less torturing thoughts—such, for instance, as wonderings over his yielding to the temptation to overstep the bounds of the magician's prohibition when he knew so well that it could cost him his life. Over that, of a surety, I might and did wonder in vain, quite in vain; there was no understanding it. He was volatile, and lacking in prudence, I knew that; but I had not dreamed that he was *entirely* destitute of prudence, I had not dreamed that he could actually risk his life to gratify a whim. Well, and what was I trying to get out of these reasonings? This—and I had to confess it: I was trying to excuse myself for my desertion of him in his sore need; when my promised prayers, which might have saved him, were withheld, and neglected, and even forgotten. I turned here and there and yonder for solace, but in every path stood an accusing spirit and barred the way; solace for me there was none.

No one of the household was indifferent to Katrina's grief, and the most of them went to her and tried to comfort her. I was not of these, I could not have borne it if she had asked me if I had prayed as I had said I would, or if she had thanked me for my prayers, taking for granted that I had kept my word. But I sat invisible while the others offered their comforting words; and every sob that came from her broken heart was another reproach and gave me a guilty pang. But her misery could not be abated. She moaned and wept, saying over and over again that if the magician had only shown a little mercy, which could have cost him nothing, and had granted time for a priest to come and give her boy absolution, all would have been well, and now he would be happy in heaven and she in the earth—but no! he had cruelly sent the lad unassoiled to judgment and the eternal fires of hell, and so had doomed her also to the pains of hell forevermore, for in heaven she should feel them all the days of eternity, looking down upon him suffering there and she powerless to assuage his thirst with one poor drop of water!

There was another thing which wrung her heart, and she could not speak of it without new floods of tears: her boy had died unreconciled to the Church, and his ashes could not be buried in holy ground; no priest could be present, no prayer uttered above them by consecrated lips, they were as the ashes of the beasts that perish, and fit only to lie in a dishonored grave.

And now and then, with a new outburst of love and grief she would paint the graces of his form, and the beauty of his young face, and his tenderness for her, and tell this and that and the other little thing that he had done or said, so dear and fond, so prized at the time, so sacred now forevermore!

I could not endure it; and I floated from the place upon the unrevealing air, and went wandering here and there disconsolate and finding everywhere reminders of him, and a new heartbreak with each.

By reason of the strange and uncanny tragedy, all the household were in a subdued and timorous state, and full of vague and formless and depressing apprehensions and boding terrors, and they went wandering about, aimless, comfortless and forlorn; and such talking together as there was, was of the disjointed and rambling sort that indicates preoccupation. However, if the Duplicates were properly of the household, what I have just been saying does not include them. They were not affected, they did not seem interested. They stuck industriously to their work, and one met them going to it or coming from it, but they did not speak except when spoken to. They did not go to the table, nor to the chess-room; they did not seem to avoid us, they took no pains about that, they merely did not seek us. But we avoided them, which was natural. Every time I met myself unexpectedly I got a shock and caught my breath, and was as irritated for being startled as a person is when he runs up against himself in a mirror which he didn't know was there.

Of course the destruction of a youth by supernatural flames summoned unlawfully from hell was not an event that could be hidden. The news of it went quickly all about and made a great and terrifying excitement in the village and the region, and at once a summons came for the magician to appear before a commission of the Holy Office. He could not be found. Then a second summons was posted, admonishing him to appear within twenty-four hours or remain subject to the pains and penalties attaching to contumacy. It did not seem to us likely that he would accept either of these invitations, if he could get out of it.

All day long, things went as I have described—a dreary time. Next day it was the same, with the added gloom of the preparations for the burial. This took place at midnight, in accordance with the law in such cases, and was attended by all the occupants of the castle except the sick lady and the Duplicates. We buried the ashes in waste ground half a mile from the castle, without prayer or blessing, unless the tears of Katrina and our sorrow were in some sense a blessing. It was a gusty night, with flurries of snow, and a black sky with ragged cloud-rack driving across it. We came on foot, bearing flaring and unsteady torches; and when all was over, we inverted the torches and thrust them into the soft mould of the grave and so left them, sole and perishable memorial and remembrancer of him who was gone.

Home again, it was with a burdened and desolate weight at my heart that I entered my room. There sat the corpse!

Chapter 18

MY SENSES forsook me and I should have fallen, but it put up its hand and flipped its fingers toward me and this brought an influence of some kind which banished my faint and restored me; yes, more than that, for I was fresher and finer now than I had been before the fatigues of the funeral. I started away at once and with such haste as I could command, for I had never seen the day that I was not afraid of a ghost or would stay where one was if there was another place convenient. But I was stopped by a word, in a voice which I knew and which was music to my ears—

"Come back! I am alive again, it is not a ghost."

I returned, but I was not comfortable, for I could not at once realize that he was really and solidly alive again, although I knew he was, for the fact was plain enough, the cat could have recognized it. As indeed the cat did; he came loafing in, waving his tail in greeting and satisfaction, and when he saw 44 he roached his back and inflated his tail and dropped a pious word and started away on urgent business; but 44 laughed, and called him back and explained to him in the cat language, and stroked him and petted him and sent him away to the other animals with the news; and in a minute here they came, padding and pattering from all directions, and they piled themselves all over him in their joy, nearly hiding him from sight, and all talking at once, each in his own tongue, and 44 answering in the language of each; and finally he fed them liberally with all sorts of palatable things from my cupboard (where there hadn't been a thing before), and sent them away convinced and happy.

By this time my tremors were gone and I was at rest, there was nothing in my mind or heart but thankfulness to have him back again, except wonder as to how it could be, and whether he had really been dead or had only seemed to perish in a magic-show and illusion; but he answered the thought while fetching a hot supper from my empty cupboard, saying—

"It wasn't an illusion, I died;" and added indifferently, "it is nothing, I have done it many a time!"

It was a hardy statement, and I did not strain myself with trying to believe it, but of course I did not say so. His supper was beyond praise for toothsomeness, but I was not acquainted with any of the dishes. He said they were all foreign, from various corners of the globe. An amazing thing, I thought, yet it seemed to me it must be true. There was a very rare-done bird that was peculiarly heavenly; it seemed to be a kind of duck.

"Canvas-back," he said, "hot from America!"

"What is America?"

"It's a country."

"A country?"

"Yes."

"Where?"

"Oh, away off. It hasn't been discovered yet. Not quite. Next fall."

"Have you—"

"Been there? Yes; in the past, in the present, in the future. You should see it four or five centuries from now! This duck is of that period. How do you like the Duplicates?"

It was his common way, the way of a boy, and most provoking: careless, capricious, unstable, never sticking to a subject, forever flitting and sampling here and there and yonder, like a bee; always, just as he was on the point of becoming interesting, he changed the subject. I was annoyed, but concealed it as well as I could, and answered—

"Oh, well, they are well enough, but they are not popular. They won't join the union, they work for nothing, the men resent their intrusion. There you have the situation: the men dislike them, and they are bitter upon the magician for sending them."

It seemed to give 44 an evil delight. He rubbed his hands vigorously together, and said—

"They were a good idea, the Duplicates; judiciously handled, they will make a lot of trouble! Do you know, those creatures are not uninteresting, all things considered, for they are not *real* persons."

"Heavens, what are they, then!"

"I will explain. Move up to the fire."

We left the table and its savory wreckage, and took comfortable seats, each at his own customary side of the fire, which blazed up briskly now, as if in a voluntary welcome of us. Then 44 reached up and took from the mantelpiece some things which I had not noticed there before: a slender reed stem with a small red-clay cup at the end of it, and a dry and dark-colored leaf, of a breed unknown to me. Chatting along,—I watching curiously—he crushed the crisp leaf in his palm, and filled that little cup with it; then he put the stem in his mouth and touched the cup with his finger, which instantly set fire to the vegetable matter and sent up a column of smoke and I dived under the bed, thinking something might happen. But nothing did, and so upon persuasion I returned to my chair but moved it a little further, for 44 was tilting his head far back and shooting ring after ring of blue smoke toward the ceiling —delicate gauzy revolving circlets, beautiful to see; and always each new ring took enlargement and 44 fired the next one through it with a good aim and happy art, and he *did* seem to enjoy it so; but not I, for I believed his entrails were on fire, and could perhaps explode and hurt some one, and most likely the wrong person, just as happens at riots and such things.

But nothing occurred, and I grew partially reconciled to the conditions, although the odor of the smoke was nauseating and a little difficult to stand. It seemed strange that he could endure it, and stranger still that he should seem to enjoy it. I turned the mystery over in my mind and concluded it was most likely a pagan religious service, and therefore I took my cap off, not in reverence but as a matter of discretion. But he said—

"No, it is only a vice, merely a vice, but not a religious one. It originated in Mexico."

"What is Mexico?"

"It's a country."

"A country?"

"Yes."

"Where is it?"

"Away off. It hasn't been discovered yet."

"Have you ever—"

"Been there? Yes, many times. In the past, in the present, and in the future. No, the Duplicates are not real, they are fictions. I will explain about them."

I sighed, but said nothing. He was always disappointing; I wanted to hear about Mexico.

"The way of it is this," he said. "You know, of course, that you are not one person, but two. One is your Workaday-Self, and 'tends to business, the other is your Dream-Self, and has no responsibilities, and cares only for romance and excursions and adventure. It sleeps when your other self is awake; when your other self sleeps, your Dream-Self has full control, and does as it pleases. It has far more imagination than has the Workaday-Self, therefore its pains and pleasures are far more real and intense than are those of the other self, and its adventures correspondingly picturesque and extraordinary. As a rule, when a party of Dream-Selves—whether comrades or strangers—get together and flit abroad in the globe, they have a tremendous time. But you understand, they have no substance, they are only spirits. The Workaday-Self has a harder lot and a duller time; it can't get away from the flesh, and is clogged and hindered by it; and also by the low grade of its own imagination."

"But 44, these Duplicates are solid enough!"

"So they are, apparently, but it is only fictitious flesh and bone, put upon them by the magician and me. We pulled them out of the Originals and gave them this independent life."

"Why, 44, they fight and bleed, like anybody!"

"Yes, and they *feel,* too. It is not a bad job, in the solidifying line, I've never seen better flesh put together by enchantment; but no matter, it is a pretty airy fabric, and if we should remove the spell they would vanish like blowing out a candle. Ah, they are a capable lot, with their measureless imaginations! If they imagine there is a mystic clog upon them and it takes them a couple of hours to set a couple of lines, that is what happens; but on the contrary, if they imagine it takes them but half a second to set a whole galleyful of matter, *that* is what happens! A dandy lot is that handful of Duplicates, and the easy match of a thousand real printers! Handled judiciously, they'll make plenty of trouble."

"But why should you *want* them to make trouble, 44?"

"Oh, merely to build up the magician's reputation. If they once get their imaginations started . . . . . oh, the consuming intensity and effectiveness of it!" He pondered a while, then said, indolently, "Those Originals are in love with these women and are not making any headway; now then, if we arrange it so that the Duplicates . . . . . lad, it's getting late—for you; time does not exist, for me. August, that is a nice table-service—you may have it. Good-night!" and he vanished.

It was heavy silver, and ornate, and on one great piece was engraved "America Cup;" on the others were chased these words, which had no meaning for me: "New York Yacht Club, 1903."

I sighed, and said to myself, "It may be that he is not honest." After some days I obliterated the words and dates, and sold the service at a good price.

Chapter 19

D AY AFTER day went by, and Father Adolf was a busy man, for he was the head of the Commission charged with trying and punishing the magician; but he had no luck, he could come upon no trace of the necromancer. He was disappointed and exasperated, and he swore hard and drank hard, but nothing came of it, he made no progress in his hunt. So, as a vent for his wrath he turned upon the poor Duplicates, declaring them to be evil spirits, wandering devils, and condemned them to the stake on his own arbitrary authority, but 44 told me he (44,) wouldn't allow them to be hurt, they being useful in the building up of the magician's reputation. Whether 44 was really their protector or not, no matter, they certainly had protection, for every time Father Adolf chained them to the stake they vanished and left the stake empty before the fire could be applied, and straightway they would be found at work in the shop and not in any way frightened or disturbed. After several failures Father Adolf gave it up in a rage, for he was becoming ridiculous and a butt for everybody's private laughter. To cover his chagrin he pretended that he had not really tried to burn them, he only wanted to scare them; and said he was only postponing the roasting, and that it would take place presently, when he should find that the right time had come. But not many believed him, and Doangivadam, to show how little he cared for Adolf's pretensions, took out a fire insurance policy upon his Duplicate. It was an impudent thing to do, and most irreverent, and made Father Adolf very angry, but he pretended that he did not mind it.

As 44 had expected, the Duplicates fell to making love to the young women, and in such strenuous fashion that they soon cut out the Originals and left them out in the cold; which made bad blood, and constant quarrels and fights resulted. Soon the castle was no better than a lunatic asylum. It was a cat-and-dog's life all around, but there was no helping it. The master loved peace, and he tried his best to reconcile the parties and make them friendly to each other, but it was not possible, the brawling and fighting went on in spite of all he could do. Forty-Four and I went about, visible to each other but to no one else, and we witnessed these affrays, and 44 enjoyed them and was perfectly charmed with them. Well, he had his own tastes. I was not always invisible, of course, for that would have caused remark; I showed up often enough to prevent that.

Whenever I thought I saw a good opportunity I tried to interest 44 in the life eternal, but the innate frivolity of his nature contin-

ually defeated my efforts, he could not seem to care for anything
but building up the magician's reputation. He said he was interested in that, and in one other thing, *the human race*. He had
nettled me more than once by seeming to speak slightingly of the
human race. Finally, one day, being annoyed once more by some
such remark, I said, acidly—

"You don't seem to think much of the human race; it's a pity you
have to belong to it."

He looked a moment or two upon me, apparently in gentle
wonder, then answered—

"What makes you think I belong to it?"

The bland audacity of it so mixed my emotions that it was a
question which would get first expression, anger or mirth; but
mirth got precedence, and I laughed. Expecting him to laugh, too,
in response; but he did not. He looked a little hurt at my levity, and
said, as in mild reproach—

"I think the human race is well enough, in its way, all things
considered, but surely, August, I have never intimated that I belonged to it. Reflect. Now have I?"

It was difficult to know what to say; I seemed to be a little
stunned. Presently I said, wonderingly—

"It makes me dizzy; I don't quite know where I am; it is as if I
had had a knock on the head. I have had no such confusing and
bewildering and catastrophical experience as this before. It is a new
and strange and fearful idea: a person who is a person and yet *not a
human being*. I cannot grasp it, I do not know how it can be, I have
never dreamed of so tremendous a thing, so amazing a thing! Since
you are not a human being, what *are* you?"

"Ah," he said, "now we have arrived at a point where words are
useless; words cannot even convey *human* thought capably, and
they can do nothing at all with thoughts whose realm and orbit are
outside the human solar system, so to speak. I will use the language
of my country, where words are not known. During half a moment
my spirit shall speak to yours and tell you something about me. Not
much, for it is not much of me that you would be able to understand, with your limited human mentality."

While he was speaking, my head was illuminated by a single sudden flash as of lightning, and I recognised that it had conveyed to me some knowledge of him; enough to fill me with awe. Envy, too—I do not mind confessing it. He continued—

"Now then, things which have puzzled you heretofore are not a mystery to you any more, for you are now aware that there is nothing I cannot do—and lay it on the magician and increase his reputation; and you are also now aware that the difference between a human being and me is as the difference between a drop of water and the sea, a rushlight and the sun, the difference between the infinitely trivial and the infinitely sublime! I say—we'll be comrades, and have scandalous good times!" and he slapped me on the shoulder, and his face was all alight with good-fellowship.

I said I was in awe of him, and was more moved to pay him reverence than to—

"Reverence!" he mocked; "put it away; the sun doesn't care for the rushlight's reverence, put it away. Come, we'll be boys together and comrades! Is it agreed?"

I said I was too much wounded, just now, to have any heart in levities, I must wait a little and get somewhat over this hurt; that I would rather beseech and persuade him to put all light things aside for a season and seriously and thoughtfully study my unjustly disesteemed race, whereby I was sure he would presently come to estimate it at its right and true value, and worthy of the sublime rank it had always held, undisputed, as the noblest work of God.

He was evidently touched, and said he was willing, and would do according to my desire, putting light things aside and taking up this small study in all heartiness and candor.

I was deeply pleased; so pleased that I would not allow his thoughtless characterization of it as a "small" study to greatly mar my pleasure; and to this end admonishing myself to remember that he was speaking a foreign language and must not be expected to perceive nice distinctions in the values of words. He sat musing a little while, then he said in his kindest and thoughtfulest manner—

"I am sure I can say with truth that I have no prejudices against the human race or other bugs, and no aversions, no malignities. I have known the race a long time, and out of my heart I can say that I have always felt more sorry for it than ashamed of it."

He said it with the gratified look of a person who has uttered a graceful and flattering thing. By God, I think he expected thanks! He did not get them; I said not a word. That made a pause, and was a little awkward for him for the moment; then he went on—

"I have often visited this world—often. It shows that I felt an interest in this race; it is proof, proof absolute, that I felt an interest in it." He paused, then looked up with one of those inane self-approving smiles on his face that are so trying, and added, "there is nothing just like it in any other world, it is a race by itself, and in many ways amusing."

He evidently thought he had said another handsome thing; he had the satisfied look of a person who thought he was oozing compliments at every pore. I retorted, with bitter sarcasm—I couldn't help it—

"As 'amusing' as a basket of monkeys, no doubt!"

It clean failed! He didn't know it was sarcasm.

"Yes," he said, serenely, "as amusing as those—and even more so, it may be claimed; for monkeys, in their mental and moral freaks show not so great variety, and therefore are the less entertaining."

This was too much. I asked, coldly—

But he was gone.

Chapter 20

A WEEK passed.

Meantime, where was he? what was become of him? I had gone often to his room, but had always found it vacant. I was missing him sorely. Ah, he was so interesting! there was none that could approach him for that. And there could not be a more engaging mystery than he. He was always doing and saying strange and curious things, and then leaving them but half explained or not explained at all. Who was he? what was he? where was he from? I wished I knew. Could he be converted? could he be saved? Ah, if only this could happen, and I be in some humble way a helper toward it!

While I was thus cogitating about him, he appeared—gay, of course, and even more gaily clad than he was that day that the magician burnt him. He said he had been "home." I pricked up my ears hopefully, but was disappointed: with that mere touch he left the subject, just as if because it had no interest for him it couldn't have any for others. A chuckle-headed idea, certainly. He was handy about disparaging other people's reasoning powers, but it never seemed to occur to him to look nearer home. He smacked me on the thigh and said,

"Come, you need an outing, you've been shut up here quite long enough. I'll do the handsome thing by you, now—I'll show you something creditable to your race."

That pleased me, and I said so; and said it was very kind and courteous of him to find *something* to its credit, and be good enough to mention it.

"Oh, yes," he said, lightly, and paying no attention to my sarcasm, "I'll show you a really creditable thing. At the same time I'll have to show you something discreditable, too, but that's nothing —that's merely human, you know. Make yourself invisible."

I did so, and he did the like. We were presently floating away, high in the air, over the frosty fields and hills.

"We shall go to a small town fifty miles removed," he said. "Thirty years ago Father Adolf was priest there, and was thirty years old. Johann Brinker, twenty years old, resided there, with his widowed mother and his four sisters—three younger than himself, and one a couple of years older, and marriageable. He was a rising young artist. Indeed one might say that he had already risen, for he had exhibited a picture in Vienna which had brought him great praise, and made him at once a celebrity. The family had been very poor, but now his pictures were wanted, and he sold all of his little stock at fine prices, and took orders for as many more as he could paint in two or three years. It was a happy family! and was suddenly become courted, caressed and—envied, of course, for that is human. To be envied is the human being's chiefest joy.

"Then a thing happened. On a winter's morning Johann was skating, when he heard a choking cry for help, and saw that a man had broken through the ice and was struggling; he flew to the spot, and recognised Father Adolf, who was becoming exhausted by the cold and by his unwise strugglings, for he was not a swimmer. There was but one way to do, in the circumstances, and that was, to plunge in and keep the priest's head up until further help should come—which was on the way. Both men were quickly rescued by the people. Within the hour Father Adolf was as good as new, but it was not so with Johann. He had been perspiring freely, from energetic skating, and the icy water had consequences for him. Here is his small house, we will go in and see him."

We stood in the bedroom and looked about us. An elderly woman with a profoundly melancholy face sat at the fireside with her hands folded in her lap, and her head bowed, as with age-long weariness—that pathetic attitude which says so much! Without audible words the spirit of 44 explained to me—

"The marriageable sister. There was no marriage."

On a bed, half reclining and propped with pillows and swathed in wraps was a grizzled man of apparently great age, with hollow cheeks, and with features drawn by immemorial pains; and now and then he stirred a little, and softly moaned—whereat a faint spasm flitted across the sister's face, and it was as if that moan had carried a pain to her heart. The spirit of 44 breathed upon me again:

"Since that day it has been like this—thirty years!—"

"My God!"

"It is true. Thirty years. He has his wits—the worse for him—the cruelty of it! He cannot speak, he cannot hear, he cannot see, he is wholly helpless, the half of him is paralysed, the other half is but a house of entertainment for bodily miseries. At risk of his life he saved a fellow-being. It has cost him ten thousand deaths!"

Another sad-faced woman entered. She brought a bowl of gruel with her, and she fed it to the man with a spoon, the other woman helping.

"August, the four sisters have stood watches over this bed day and night for thirty years, ministering to this poor wreck. Marriage, and homes and families of their own was not for them; they gave up all their hopeful young dreams and suffered the ruin of their lives, in order to ameliorate as well as they might the miseries of their brother. They laid him upon this bed in the bright morning of his youth and in the golden glory of his new-born fame—and look at him now! His mother's heart broke, and she went mad. Add up the sum: one broken heart, five blighted and blasted young lives. All this it costs to save a priest for a life-long career of vice and all forms of shameless rascality! Come, come, let us go, before these enticing rewards for well-doing unbalance my judgment and persuade me to become a human being myself!"

In our flight homeward I was depressed and silent, there was a heavy weight upon my spirit; then presently came a slight uplift and a glimmer of cheer, and I said—

"Those poor people will be richly requited for all they have sacrificed and suffered."

"Oh, perhaps," he said, indifferently.

"It is my belief," I retorted. "And certainly a large mercy has been shown the poor mother, in granting her a blessed mental oblivion and thus emancipating her from miseries which the others, being younger, were better able to bear."

"The madness was a mercy, you think?"

"With the broken heart, yes; for without doubt death resulted quickly and she was at rest from her troubles."

A faint spiritual cackle fell upon my ear. After a moment 44 said—

"At dawn in the morning I will show you something."

Chapter 21

I spent a wearying and troubled night, for in my dreams I was a member of that ruined family and suffering with it through a dragging long stretch of years; and the infamous priest whose life had been saved at cost of these pains and sorrows seemed always present and drunk and mocking. At last I woke. In the dimmest of cold gray dawns I made out a figure sitting by my bed—an old and white-headed man in the coarse dress of a peasant.

"Ah," I said, "who are you, good man?"

It was 44. He said, in a wheezy old voice, that he was merely showing himself to me so that I would recognize him when I saw him later. Then he disappeared, and I did the same, by his order. Soon we were sailing over the village in the frosty air, and presently we came to earth in an open space behind the monastery. It was a solitude, except that a thinly and rustily clad old woman was there, sitting on the frozen ground and fastened to a post by a chain around her waist. She could hardly hold her head up for drowsiness and the chill in her bones. A pitiful spectacle she was, in the vague dawn and the stillness, with the faint winds whispering around her and the powdery snow-whorls frisking and playing and chasing each other over the black ground. Forty-Four made himself visible, and stood by, looking down upon her. She raised her old head wearily, and when she saw that it was a kindly face that was before her she said appealingly—

"Have pity on me—I am *so* tired and so cold, and the night has been so long, so long! light the fire and put me out of my misery!"

"Ah, poor soul, I am not the executioner, but tell me if I can serve you, and I will."

She pointed to a pile of fagots, and said,

"They are for me, a few can be spared to warm me, they will not be missed, there will be enough left to burn me with, oh, much more than enough, for this old body is sapless and dry. Be good to me!"

"You shall have your wish," said 44, and placed a fagot before her and lit it with a touch of his finger.

The flame flashed crackling up, and the woman stretched her lean hands over it, and out of her eyes she looked the gratitude that was too deep for words. It was weird and pathetic to see her getting comfort and happiness out of that fuel that had been provided to inflict upon her an awful death! Presently she looked up wistfully and said—

"You are good to me, you are very good to me, and I have no friends. I am not bad—you must not think I am bad, I am only poor and old, and smitten in my wits these many many years. They think I am a witch; it is the priest, Adolf, that caught me, and it is he that has condemned me. But I am not that—no, God forbid! You do not believe I am a witch?—say you do not believe that of me."

"Indeed I do not."

"Thank you for that kind word! . . . . . How long it is that I have wandered homeless—oh, many years, many! . . . . Once I had a home—I do not know where it was; and four sweet girls and a son—how dear they were! The name . . . . . the name . . . . . but I have forgotten the name. All dead, now, poor things, these many years . . . . . . If you could have seen my son! ah, so good he was, and a painter . . . . oh, such pictures he painted! . . . . Once he saved a man's life . . . . . or it could have been a woman's . . . . . . a person drowning in the ice—"

She lost her way in a tangle of vague memories, and fell to nodding her head and mumbling and muttering to herself, and I whispered anxiously in the ear of 44—

"You will save her? You will get the word to the priest, and when he knows who she is he will set her free and we will restore her to her family, God be praised!"

"No," answered 44.

"No? Why?"

"She was appointed from the beginning of time to die at the stake this day."

"How do *you* know?"

He made no reply. I waited a moment, in growing distress, then said—

"At least *I* will speak! I will tell her story. I will make myself visible, and I—"

"It is not so written," he said; "that which is not foreordained will not happen."

He was bringing a fresh fagot. A burly man suddenly appeared, from the monastery, and ran toward him and struck the fagot from his hand, saying roughly—

"You meddling old fool, mind what you are about! Pick it up and carry it back."

"And if I don't—what then?"

In his fury at being so addressed by so mean and humble a person the man struck a blow at 44's jaw with his formidable fist, but 44 caught the fist in his hand and crushed it; it was sickening to hear the bones crunch. The man staggered away, groaning and cursing, and 44 picked up the fagot and renewed the old woman's fire with it. I whispered—

"Quick—disappear, and let us get away from here; that man will soon—"

"Yes, I know," said 44, "he is summoning his underlings; they will arrest me."

"Then come—come along!"

"What good would it do? It is written. What is written must happen. But it is of no consequence, nothing will come of it."

They came running—half a dozen—and seized him and dragged him away, cuffing him with fists and beating him with sticks till he was red with his own blood. I followed, of course, but I was merely a substanceless spirit, and there was nothing that I could do in his defence. They chained him in a dim chamber under the monastery and locked the doors and departed, promising him further attentions when they should be through with burning the witch. I was troubled beyond measure, but he was not. He said he would use this opportunity to increase the magician's reputation: he would spread the report that the aged hand-crusher was the magician in disguise.

"They will find nothing here but the prisoner's clothes when they come," he said, "then they will believe."

He vanished out of the clothes, and they slumped down in a pile. He could certainly do some wonderful things, feather-headed and frivolous as he was! There was no way of accounting for 44. We soared out through the thick walls as if they had been made of air, and followed a procession of chanting monks to the place of the burning. People were gathering, and soon they came flocking in crowds, men, women, youths, maidens; and there were even children in arms.

There was a half hour of preparation: a rope ring was widely drawn around the stake to keep the crowd at a distance; within this a platform was placed for the use of the preacher—Adolf. When all was ready he came, imposingly attended, and was escorted with proper solemnity and ceremony to this pulpit. He began his sermon at once and with business-like energy. He was very bitter upon witches, "familiars of the Fiend, enemies of God, abandoned of the angels, foredoomed to hell;" and in closing he denounced this present one unsparingly, and forbade any to pity her.

It was all lost upon the prisoner; she was warm, she was comfortable, she was worn out with fatigue and sorrow and privation, her gray head was bowed upon her breast, she was asleep. The executioners moved forward and raised her upon her feet and drew her chains tight, around her breast. She looked drowsily around upon the people while the fagots were being piled, then her head drooped again, and again she slept.

The fire was applied and the executioners stepped aside, their mission accomplished. A hush spread everywhere: there was no movement, there was not a sound, the massed people gazed, with lips apart and hardly breathing, their faces petrified in a common expression, partly of pity, mainly of horror. During more than a minute that strange and impressive absence of motion and movement continued, then it was broken in a way to make any being with a heart in his breast shudder—a man lifted his little child and sat her upon his shoulder, that she might see the better!

The blue smoke curled up about the slumberer and trailed away upon the chilly air; a red glow began to show at the base of the fagots; this increased in size and intensity and a sharp crackling sound broke upon the stillness; suddenly a sheet of flame burst upward and swept the face of the sleeper, setting her hair on fire, she uttered an agonizing shriek which was answered by a horrified groan from the crowd, then she cried out "Thou art merciful and good to Thy sinful servant, blessed be Thy holy Name—sweet Jesus receive my spirit!"

Then the flames swallowed her up and hid her from sight. Adolf stood sternly gazing upon his work. There was now a sudden movement upon the outskirts of the crowd, and a monk came plowing his way through and delivered a message to the priest—evidently a pleasant one to the receiver of it, if signs go for anything. Adolf cried out—

"Remain, everybody! It is reported to me that that arch malignant the magician, that son of Satan, is caught, and lies a chained prisoner under the monastery, disguised as an aged peasant. He is already condemned to the flames, no preliminaries are needed, his time is come. Cast the witch's ashes to the winds, clear the stake! Go—you, and you, and you—bring the sorcerer!"

The crowd woke up! this was a show to their taste. Five minutes passed—ten. What might the matter be? Adolf was growing fiercely impatient. Then the messengers returned, crestfallen. They said the magician was gone—gone, through the bolted doors and the massive walls; nothing was left of him but his peasant clothes! And they held them up for all to see.

The crowd stood amazed, wondering, speechless—and disappointed. Adolf began to storm and curse. Forty-Four whispered—

"The opportunity is come. I will personate the magician and make some more reputation for him. Oh, just watch me raise the limit!"

So the next moment there was a commotion in the midst of the crowd, which fell apart in terror exposing to view the supposed magician in his glittering oriental robes; and his face was white with fright, and he was trying to escape. But there was no escape for him, for there was one there whose boast it was that he feared neither Satan nor his servants—this being Adolf the admired. Others fell back cowed, but not he; he plunged after the sorcerer, he chased him, gained upon him, shouted, "Yield—in His Name I command!"

An awful summons! Under the blasting might of it the spurious magician reeled and fell as if he had been smitten by a bolt from the sky. I grieved for him with all my heart and in the deepest sincerity, and yet I rejoiced for that at last he had learned the power of that Name at which he had so often and so recklessly scoffed. And all too late, too late, forever and ever too late—ah, why had he not listened to me!

There were no cowards there, now! Everybody was brave, everybody was eager to help drag the victim to the stake, they swarmed about him like raging wolves; they jerked him this way and that, they beat him and reviled him, they cuffed him and kicked him, he wailing, sobbing, begging for pity, the conquering priest exulting, scoffing, boasting, laughing. Briskly they bound him to the stake and piled the fagots around him and applied the fire; and there the forlorn creature stood weeping and sniffling and pleading in his fantastic robes, a sorry contrast to that poor humble Christian who but a little while before had faced death there so bravely. Adolf lifted his hand and pronounced with impressive solemnity the words—

"Depart, damned soul, to the regions of eternal woe!"

Whereat the weeping magician laughed sardonically in his face and vanished away, leaving his robes empty and hanging collapsed in the chains! There was a whisper at my ear—

"Come, August, let us to breakfast and leave these animals to gape and stare while Adolf explains to them the unexplainable—a job just in his line. By the time I have finished with the sorcerer he will have a dandy reputation—don't you think?"

So all his pretence of being struck down by the Name was a blasphemous jest. And I had taken it so seriously, so confidingly, innocently, exultantly. I was ashamed. Ashamed of him, ashamed of myself. Oh, manifestly nothing was serious to him, levity was the blood and marrow of him, death was a joke; his ghastly fright, his moving tears, his frenzied supplications—by God, it was all just coarse and vulgar horse-play! The only thing he was capable of being interested in, was his damned magician's reputation! I was too disgusted to talk, I answered him nothing, but left him to chatter over his degraded performance unobstructed, and rehearse it and chuckle over it and glorify it up to his taste.

Chapter 22

I T W A S in my room. He brought it—the breakfast—dish after dish, smoking hot, from my empty cupboard, and briskly set the table, talking all the while—ah, yes, and pleasantly, fascinatingly, winningly; and not about that so-recent episode, but about these fragrant refreshments and the far countries he had summoned them from—Cathay, India, and everywhere; and as I was famishing, this talk was pleasing, indeed captivating, and under its influence my sour mood presently passed from me. Yes, and it was healing to my bruised spirit to look upon the rich and costly table-service—quaint of shape and pattern, delicate, ornate, exquisite, beautiful!—and presently quite likely to be mine, you see.

"Hot corn-pone from Arkansas—split it, butter it, close your eyes and enjoy! Fried spring chicken—milk-and-flour gravy—from Alabama. Try it, and grieve for the angels, for they have it not! Cream-smothered strawberries, with the prairie-dew still on them —let them melt in your mouth, and don't try to say what you feel! Coffee from Vienna—fluffed cream—two pellets of saccharin— drink, and have compassion for the Olympian gods that know only nectar!"

I ate, I drank, I reveled in these alien wonders; truly I was in Paradise!

"It is intoxication," I said, "it is delirium!"

"It's a jag!" he responded.

I inquired about some of the refreshments that had outlandish names. Again that weird detail: they were non-existent as yet, they were products of the unborn *future!* Understand it? How could I? Nobody could. The mere *trying* muddled the head. And yet it was a pleasure to turn those curious names over on the tongue and taste them: Corn-pone! Arkansas! Alabama! Prairie! Coffee! Saccharin! Forty-Four answered my thought with a stingy word of explanation—

"Corn-pone is made from maize. Maize is known only in America. America is not discovered yet. Arkansas and Alabama will be States, and will get their names two or three centuries hence. Prairie—a future French-American term for a meadow like an ocean. Coffee: they have it in the Orient, they will have it here in Austria two centuries from now. Saccharin—concentrated sugar, 500 to 1; as it were, the sweetness of five hundred pretty maids concentrated in a young fellow's sweetheart. Saccharin is not due yet for nearly four hundred years; I am furnishing you several advance-privileges, you see."

"Tell me a little, *little* more, 44—please! You starve me so! and I am so hungry to know how you find out these strange marvels, these impossible things."

He reflected a while, then he said he was in a mood to enlighten me, and would like to do it, but did not know how to go about it, because of my mental limitations and the general meanness and poverty of my construction and qualities. He said this in a most casual and taken-for-granted way, just as an archbishop might say it to a cat, never suspecting that the cat could have any feelings about it or take a different view of the matter. My face flushed, and I said with dignity and a touch of heat—

"I must remind you that I am made in the image of God."

"Yes," he said carelessly, but did not seem greatly impressed by it, certainly not crushed, not overpowered. I was more indignant than ever, but remained mute, coldly rebuking him by my silence. But it was wasted on him; he did not see it, he was thinking. Presently he said—

"It is difficult. Perhaps impossible, unless I should make you over again." He glanced up with a yearningly explanatory and apologetic look in his eyes, and added, "For you are an animal, you see—you understand that?"

I could have slapped him for it, but I austerely held my peace, and answered with cutting indifference—

"Quite so. It happens to happen that all of us are that."

Of course I was including him, but it was only another waste— he didn't perceive the inclusion. He said, as one might whose way has been cleared of an embarrassing obstruction—

"Yes, that is just the trouble! It makes it ever so difficult. With my race it is different; we have no limits of any kind, we comprehend all things. You see, for your race there is such a thing as *time* —you cut it up and measure it; to your race there is a past, a present and a future—out of one and the same thing you make *three;* and to your race there is also such a thing as *distance*—and hang it, you measure *that,* too! . . . . . Let me see: if I could only . . . . if I . . . . oh, no, it is of no use—there is no such thing as enlightening that kind of a mind!" He turned upon me despairingly, pathetically, adding, "If it only had *some* capacity, some depth, or breadth, or—or—but you see it doesn't *hold* anything; one cannot pour the starred and shoreless expanses of the universe into a jug!"

I made no reply; I sat in frozen and insulted silence; I would not have said a word to save his life. But again he was not aware of what was happening—he was thinking. Presently he said—

"Well, it is *so* difficult! If I only had a starting-point, a basis to proceed from—but I can't find any. If—look here: *can't* you extinguish time? *can't* you comprehend eternity? can't you conceive of a thing like that—a thing with *no* beginning—a thing that *always* was? Try it!"

"Don't! I've tried it a hundred times," I said, "It makes my brain whirl just to think of it!"

He was in despair again.

"Dear me—to think that there can be an ostensible Mind that cannot conceive of so simple a trifle as that! . . . . Look here, August: there are really no divisions of time—none at all. The past is always present when I want it—the *real* past, not an image of it; I can summon it, and there it *is*. The same with the future: I can summon it out of the unborn ages, and there it is, before my eyes, alive and real, not a fancy, an image, a creation of the imagination. Ah, these troublesome limitations of yours!—they hamper me. Your race cannot even conceive of something being made out of nothing —I am aware of it, your learned men and philosophers are always confessing it. They say there had to be *something* to start with— meaning a solid, a substance—to build the world out of. Man, it is perfectly simple—it was built out of *thought*. Can't you comprehend that?"

"No, I can't! *Thought!* There is no substance to thought; then how is a material thing going to be constructed out of it?"

"But August, I don't mean *your* kind of thought, I mean my kind, and the kind that the gods exercise."

"Come, what is the difference? Isn't thought just *thought*, and all said?"

"No. A man *originates* nothing in his head, he merely observes exterior things, and *combines* them in his head—puts several observed things together and draws a conclusion. His mind is merely a machine, that is all—an *automatic* one, and he has no control over it; it cannot conceive of a *new* thing, an original thing, it can only gather material from the outside and combine it into new *forms* and patterns. But it always has to have the *materials* from the *outside*, for it can't make them itself. That is to say, a man's mind cannot *create*—a god's can, and my race can. That is the difference. *We* need no contributed materials, we *create* them—out of thought. All things that exist were made out of thought—and out of nothing else."

It seemed to me charitable, also polite, to take him at his word and not require proof, and I said so. He was not offended. He only said—

"Your automatic mind has performed its function—its sole function—and without help from you. That is to say, it has listened, it has observed, it has put this and that together, and drawn a conclusion—the conclusion that my statement was a doubtful one. It is now privately beginning to wish for a test. Is that true?"

"Well, yes," I said, "I won't deny it, though for courtesy's sake I would have concealed it if I could have had my way."

"Your mind is automatically suggesting that I offer a specific proof—that I create a dozen gold coins out of nothing; that is to say, out of *thought*. Open your hand—they are there."

And so they were! I wondered; and yet I was not very greatly astonished, for in my private heart I judged—and not for the first time—that he was using magic learned from the magician, and that he had no gifts in this line that did not come from that source. But was this so? I dearly wanted to ask this question, and I started to do it. But the words refused to leave my tongue, and I realized that he had applied that mysterious check which had so often shut off a question which I wanted to ask. He seemed to be musing. Presently he ejaculated—

"That poor old soul!"

It gave me a pang, and brought back the stake, the flames and the death-cry; and I said—

"It was a shame and a pity that she wasn't rescued."

"Why a pity?"

"*Why?* How can you ask, 44?"

"What would she have gained?"

"An extension of life, for instance; is that nothing?"

"Oh, there spoke the human! He is always pretending that the eternal bliss of heaven is such a priceless boon! Yes, and always keeping out of heaven just as long as he can! At bottom, you see, he is far from being certain about heaven."

I was annoyed at my carelessness in giving him that chance. But I allowed it to stand at that, and said nothing; it could not help the matter to go into it further. Then, to get away from it I observed that there was at least one gain that the woman could have had if she had been saved: she might have entered heaven by a less cruel death.

"She isn't going there," said 44, placidly.

It gave me a shock, and also it angered me, and I said with some heat—

"You seem to know a good deal about it—*how* do you know?"

He was not affected by my warmth, neither did he trouble to answer my question; he only said—

"The woman could have gained nothing worth considering—certainly nothing worth measuring by your curious methods. What are ten years, subtracted from ten billion years? It is the ten-thousandth part of a second—that is to say, it is nothing at all. Very well, she is in hell now, she will remain there forever. Ten years subtracted from it wouldn't count. Her bodily pain at the stake lasted six minutes—to save her from *that* would not have been worthwhile. That poor creature is in hell; see for yourself!"

Before I could beg him to spare me, the red billows were sweeping by, and she was there among the lost.

The next moment the crimson sea was gone, with its evoker, and I was alone.

Chapter 23

Young as I was—I was barely seventeen—my days were now sodden with depressions, there was little or no rebound. My interest in the affairs of the castle and of its occupants faded out and disappeared; I kept to myself and took little or no note of the daily happenings; my Duplicate performed all my duties, and I had nothing to do but wander aimlessly about and be unhappy.

Thus the days wore heavily by, and meantime I was missing something; missing something, and growing more and more conscious of it. I hardly had the daring to acknowledge to myself what it was. It was the master's niece—Marget! I was a secret worshipper; I had been that a long time; I had worshipped her face and her form with my eyes, but to go further would have been quite beyond my courage. It was not for me to aspire so high; not yet, certainly; not in my timid and callow youth. Every time she had blessed me with a passing remark, the thrill of it, the bliss of it had tingled through me and swept along every nerve and fibre of me with a sort of celestial ecstasy and given me a wakeful night which was better than sleep. These casual and unconsidered remarks, unvalued by her were treasures to me, and I hoarded them in my memory, and knew when it was that she had uttered each of them, and the occasion and the circumstance that had produced each one, and the tone of her voice and the look of her face and the light in her eye; and there was not a night that I did not pass them through my mind caressingly, and turn them over and pet them and play with them, just as a poor girl possessed of half a dozen cheap seed-pearls might do with her small hoard. But that Marget should ever give me an actual thought—any word or notice above what she might give the cat—ah, I never dreamed of it! As a rule she had never been conscious of my presence at all; as a rule she gave me merely a glance of recognition and nothing more when she passed me by in hall or corridor.

As I was saying, I had been missing her, a number of days. It was because her mother's malady was grown a trifle worse and Marget was spending all her time in the sick room. I recognized, now, that I was famishing to see her, and be near that gracious presence once more. Suddenly, not twenty steps away, she rose upon my sight—a fairy vision! That sweet young face, that dainty figure, that subtle exquisite something that makes seventeen the perfect year and its bloom the perfect bloom—oh, there it all was, and I stood transfixed and adoring! She was coming toward me, walking slowly, musing, dreaming, heeding nothing, absorbed, unconscious. As she drew near I stepped directly in her way; and as she passed through me the contact invaded my blood as with a delicious fire! She stopped, with a startled look, the rich blood rose in her face, her breath came quick and short through her parted lips, and she gazed wonderingly about her, saying twice, in a voice hardly above a whisper—

"What could it have been?"

I stood devouring her with my eyes, she remained as she was, without moving, as much as a minute, perhaps more; then she said in that same low soliloquising voice, "I was surely asleep—it was a dream—it must have been that—why did I wake?" and saying this, she moved slowly away, down the great corridor.

Nothing can describe my joy. I believed she loved me, and had been keeping her secret, as maidens will; but now I would persuade it out of her; I would be bold, brave, and speak! I made myself visible, and in a minute had overtaken her and was at her side. Excited, happy, confident, I touched her arm, and the warm words began to leap from my mouth—

"Dear Marget! oh, my own, my dar—"

She turned upon me a look of gentle but most chilly and dignified rebuke, allowed it a proper time to freeze where it struck, then moved on, without a word, and left me there. I did not feel inspired to follow.

No, I could not follow, I was petrified with astonishment. Why should she act like that? Why should she be glad to dream of me and not glad to meet me awake? It was a mystery; there was something very strange about this; I could make nothing out of it. I went on puzzling and puzzling over the enigma for a little while, still gazing after her and half crying for shame that I had been so fresh and had gotten such a blistering lesson for it, when I saw her stop. Dear me, she might turn back! I was invisible in half an instant—I wouldn't have faced her again for a province.

Sure enough, she did turn back. I stepped to the wall, and gave her the road. I wanted to fly, but I had no power to do that, the sight of her was a spell that I could not resist; I had to stay, and gaze, and worship. She came slowly along in that same absorbed and dreamy way, again; and just as she was passing by me she stopped, and stood quite still a moment—two or three moments, in fact—then moving on, she said, with a sigh, "I was mistaken, but I thought I faintly felt it again."

Was she sorry it was a mistake? It certainly sounded like that. It put me in a sort of ecstasy of hope, it filled me with a burning desire to test the hope, and I could hardly refrain from stepping out and barring her way again, to see what would happen; but that rebuff was too recent, its smart was still too fresh, and I hadn't the pluck to do it.

But I could feast my eyes upon her loveliness, at any rate, and in safety, and I would not deny myself that delight. I followed her at a distance, I followed all her wanderings; and when at last she entered her apartment and closed the door, I went to my own place and to my solitude, desolate. But the fever born of that marvelous first contact came back upon me and there was no rest for me. Hour after hour I fought it, but still it prevailed. Night came, and dragged along, there was no abatement. At ten the castle was asleep and still, but I could not sleep. I left my room and went wandering here and there, and presently I was floating through the great corridor again. In the vague light I saw a figure standing motionless in that memorable spot. I recognized it—even less light would have answered for that. I could not help approaching it, it drew me like a magnet. I came eagerly on; but when I was within two or three steps of it I remembered, with a chill, who I was, and stopped. No matter: To be so near to Marget was happiness enough, riches enough! With a quick movement she lifted her head and poised it in the attitude of one who listens—listens with a tense and wistful and breathless interest; it was a happy and longing face that I saw in the dim light; and out of it, as through a veil, looked darkling and humid the eyes I loved so well. I caught a whisper: "I cannot hear anything—no, there is no sound—but it is near, I know it is near, and the dream is come again!" My passion rose and overpowered me and I floated to her like a breath and put my arms about her and drew her to my breast and put my lips to hers, unrebuked, and drew intoxication from them! She closed her eyes, and with a sigh which seemed born of measureless content, she said dreamily, "I love you so—and have so longed for you!"

Her body trembled with each kiss received and repaid, and by the power and volume of the emotions that surged through me I realized that the sensations I knew in my fleshly estate were cold and weak by contrast with those which a spirit feels.

I was invisible, impalpable, substanceless, I was as transparent as the air, and yet I seemed to support the girl's weight and bear it up. No, it was more than seeming, it was an actuality. This was new; I had not been aware that my spirit possessed this force. I must exploit this valuable power, I must examine it, test it, make experiments. I said—

"When I press your hand, dear, do you feel it?"

"Why, of course."

"And when I kiss you?"

"Indeed yes!" and she laughed.

"And do you *feel* my arms about you when I clasp you in them?"

"Why, certainly. What strange questions!"

"Oh, well, it's only to make talk, so that I can hear your voice. It is such music to me, Marget, that I—"

"Marget? Marget? Why do you call me that?"

"Oh, you little stickler for the conventions and proprieties! Have I got to call you Miss Regen? Dear me, I thought we were further along than that!"

She seemed puzzled, and said—

"But why should you call me *that*?"

It was my turn to be puzzled.

"Why should I? I don't know any really good reason, except that it's your name, dear."

"My name, indeed!" and she gave her comely head a toss. "I've never heard it before!"

I took her face between my hands and looked into her eyes to see if she were jesting, but there was nothing there but sweet sincerity. I did not quite know what to say, so at a venture I said—

"Any name that will be satisfactory to you will be lovely to me, you unspeakably adorable creature! Mention it! What shall I call you?"

"Oh, what a time you do have, to make talk, as you call it! What shall you *call* me? Why, call me by my own name—my *first* name —and don't put any Miss to it!"

I was still in the fog, but that was no matter—the longer it might take to work out of it the pleasanter and the better. So I made a start:

"Your first name . . . . your first name . . . . . how annoying, I've forgotten it! What is it, dear?"

The music of her laugh broke out rich and clear, like a bird-song, and she gave me a light box on the ear, and said—

"Forgotten it?—oh, no, that won't do! You are playing some kind of a game—I don't know what it is, but you are not going to catch me. You want me to say it, and then—then—why then you are going to spring a trap or a joke or something and make me feel foolish. Is that it? What *is* it you are going to do if I say it, dearheart?"

"*I'll* tell you," I said, sternly, "I am going to bend your head back and cradle your neck in the hollow of my left arm,—so—and squeeze you close—so—and the moment you say it I am going to kiss you on the mouth."

She gazed up from the cradling arm with the proper play-acting humility and resignation, and whispered—

"Lisabet!" and took her punishment without a protest.

"You have been a very good girl," I said, and patted her cheek approvingly. "There wasn't any trap, Lisabet—at least none but this: I pretended that forgetfulness because when the sweetest of all names comes from the sweetest of all lips it is sweeter then than ever, and I wanted to hear you say it."

"Oh, you dear thing! I'll say the rest of it at the same price!"

"Done!"

"Elisabeth von Arnim!"

"One—two—three: a kiss for each component!"

I was out of the fog, I had the name. It was a triumph of diplomacy, and I was proud of it. I repeated the name several times, partly for the pleasure of hearing it and partly to nail it in my memory, then I said I wished we had some more things to trade between us on the same delicious basis. She caught at that, and said—

"We can do *your* name, Martin."

Martin! It made me jump. Whence had she gathered this batch of thitherto unheard-of names? What was the secret of this mystery, the how of it, the why of it, the explanation of it? It was too deep for me, much too deep. However, this was no time to be puzzling over it, I ought to be resuming trade and finding out the rest of my name; so I said—

"Martin is a poor name, except when you say it. Say it again, sweetheart."

"Martin. Pay me!"

Which I did.

"Go on, Betty dear; more music—say the rest of it."

"Martin von Giesbach. I wish there was more of it. Pay!"

I did, and added interest.

Boom-m-m-m! from the solemn great bell in the main tower.

"Half-past eleven—oh, what will mother say! I did not dream it was so late, did you Martin?"

"No, it seemed only fifteen minutes."

"Come, let us hurry," she said, and we hurried—at least after a sort of fashion—with my left arm around her waist and the hollow of her right hand cupped upon my left shoulder by way of having a support. Several times she murmured dreamily, "How happy I am, how happy, happy, happy!" and seemed to lose herself in that thought and be conscious of nothing else. By and by I had a rare start—my Duplicate stepped suddenly out from a bunch of shadows, just as we were passing by! He said, reproachfully—

"Ah, Marget, I waited so long by your door, and you broke your promise! Is this kind of you? is it affectionate?"

Oh, jealousy—I felt the pang of it for the first time.

To my surprise—and joy—the girl took no more notice of him than if he had not been there. She walked right on, she did not seem to see him nor hear him. He was astonished, and stopped still and turned, following her with his eyes. He muttered something, then in a more definite voice he said—

"What a queer attitude—to be holding her hand up in the air like that! . . . . . Why, she's walking in her sleep!"

He began to follow, a few steps behind us. Arrived at Marget's door, I took her—no, Lisbet's!—peachy face between my hands and kissed the eyes and the lips, her delicate hands resting upon my shoulders the while; then she said "Good-night—good-night and blessed dreams," and passed within. I turned toward my Duplicate. He was standing near by, staring at the vacancy where the girl had been. For a time he did only that. Then he spoke up and said joyfully—

"I've been a jealous fool! That was a kiss—and it was for me! She was dreaming of me. I understand it all, now. And that loving good-night—it was for me, too. Ah, it makes all the difference!" He went to the door and knelt down and kissed the place where she had stood.

I could not endure it. I flew at him and with all my spirit-strength I fetched him an open-handed slat on the jaw that sent him lumbering and spinning and floundering over and over along the stone floor till the wall stopped him. He was greatly surprised. He got up rubbing his bruises and looking admiringly about him for a minute or two, then went limping away, saying—

"I wonder what in hell *that* was!"

Chapter 24

I FLOATED off to my room through the unresisting air, and stirred up my fire and sat down to enjoy my happiness and study over the enigma of those names. By ferreting out of my memory certain scraps and shreds of information garnered from 44's talks I presently untangled the matter, and arrived at an explanation— which was this: the presence of my flesh-and-blood personality was not a circumstance of any interest to Marget Regen, but my presence as a spirit acted upon her hypnotically—as 44 termed it—and plunged her into the somnambulic sleep. This removed her Day-Self from command and from consciousness, and gave the command to her Dream-Self for the time being. Her Dream-Self was a quite definite and independent personality, and for reasons of its own it had chosen to name itself Elisabeth von Arnim. It was entirely unacquainted with Marget Regen, did not even know she existed, and had no knowledge of her affairs, her feelings, her opinions, her religion, her history, nor of any other matter concerning her. On the other hand, Marget was entirely unacquainted with Elisabeth and wholly ignorant of her existence and of all other matters concerning her, including her name.

Marget knew me as August Feldner, her Dream-Self knew me as Martin von Giesbach—*why*, was a matter beyond guessing. Awake, the girl cared nothing for me; steeped in the hypnotic sleep, I was the idol of her heart.

There was another thing which I had learned from 44, and that was this: each human being contains not merely two independent entities, but three—the Waking-Self, the Dream-Self, and the Soul. This last is immortal, the others are functioned by the brain and the nerves, and are physical and mortal; they are not functionable when the brain and nerves are paralysed by a temporary hurt or stupefied by narcotics; and when the man dies *they* die, since their life, their energy and their existence depend solely upon physical sustenance, and they cannot get that from dead nerves and a dead brain. When I was invisible the whole of my physical make-up was gone, nothing connected with it or depending upon it was left. My soul—my immortal spirit—alone remained. Freed from the encumbering flesh, it was able to exhibit forces, passions and emotions of a quite tremendously effective character.

It seemed to me that I had now ciphered the matter out correctly, and unpuzzled the puzzle. I was right, as I found out afterward.

And now a sorrowful thought came to me: all three of my Selves were in love with the one girl, and how could we all be happy? It made me miserable to think of it, the situation was so involved in difficulties, perplexities and unavoidable heart-burnings and resentments.

Always before, I had been tranquilly unconcerned about my Duplicate. To me he was merely a stranger, no more no less; to him I was a stranger; in all our lives we had never chanced to meet until 44 had put flesh upon him; we could not have met if we had wanted to, because whenever one of us was awake and in command of our common brain and nerves the other was of necessity asleep and unconscious. All our lives we had been what 44 called Box and Cox lodgers in the one chamber: aware of each other's existence but not interested in each other's affairs, and never encountering each other save for a dim and hazy and sleepy half-moment on the threshold, when one was coming in and the other going out, and never in any case halting to make a bow or pass a greeting.

And so it was not until my Dream-Self's fleshing that he and I met and spoke. There was no heartiness; we began as mere acquaintances, and so remained. Although we had been born together, at the same moment and of the same womb, there was no spiritual kinship between us; spiritually we were a couple of distinctly independent and unrelated individuals, with equal rights in a common fleshly property, and we cared no more for each other than we cared for any other stranger. My fleshed Duplicate did not even bear my name, but called himself Emil Schwarz.

I was always courteous to my Duplicate, but I avoided him. This was natural, perhaps, for he was my superior. My imagination, compared with his splendid dream-equipment, was as a lightning bug to the lightning; in matters of our trade he could do more with his hands in five minutes than I could do in a day; he did all my work in the shop, and found it but a trifle; in the arts and graces of beguilement and persuasion I was a pauper and he a Croesus; in passion, feeling, emotion, sensation—whether of pain or pleasure—I was phosphorus, he was fire. In a word he had all the intensities one suffers or enjoys in a dream!

This was the creature that had chosen to make love to Marget! In my coarse dull human form, what chance was there for me? Oh, none in the world, none! I knew it, I realized it, and the heartbreak of it was unbearable.

But my Soul, stripped of its vulgar flesh—what was my Duplicate in competition with *that?* Nothing, and less than nothing. The conditions were reversed, as regarded passions, emotions, sensations, and the arts and graces of persuasion. Lisbet was mine, and I could hold her against the world—but only when she was Lisbet, only when her Dream-Self was in command of her person! when she was Marget she was her Waking-Self, and the slave of that reptile! Ah, there could be no help for this, no way out of this fiendish complication. I could have only half of her; the other half, no less dear to me, must remain the possession of another. She was mine, she was his, turn-about.

These desolating thoughts kept racing and chasing and scorching and blistering through my brain without rest or halt, and I could find no peace, no comfort, no healing for the tortures they brought. Lisbet's love, so limitlessly dear and precious to me, was almost lost sight of because I couldn't have Marget's too. By this sign I perceived that I was still a human being; that is to say, a person who wants the earth, and cannot be satisfied unless he can have the whole of it. Well, we are made so; even the humblest of us has the voracity of an emperor.

At early mass the next morning my happiness came back to me, for Marget was there, and the sight of her cured all my sorrows. For a time! She took no notice of me, and I was not expecting she would, therefore I was not troubled about that, and was content to look at her, and breathe the same air with her, and note and admire everything she did and everything she didn't do, and bless myself in these privileges; but when I found she had over-many occasions to glance casually and fleetingly around to her left I was moved to glance around, myself, and see if there was anything particular there. Sure enough there was. It was Emil Schwarz. He was already become a revolting object to me, and I now so detested him that I could hardly look at anything else during the rest of the service; except, of course, Marget.

When the service was over, I lingered outside, and made myself invisible, purposing to follow Marget and resume the wooing. But she did not come. Everybody came out but two,—*those* two. After a little, Marget put her head out and looked around to see if any one was in sight, then she glanced back, with a slight nod, and moved swiftly away. That saddened me, for I interpreted it to mean that the other wooing was to have first place. Next came Schwarz, and him I followed—upward, always upward, by dim and narrow stairways seldom used; and so, to a lofty apartment in the south tower, the luxurious quarters of the departed magician. He entered, and closed the door, but I followed straight through the heavy panels, without waiting, and halted just on the inside. There was a great fire of logs at the other end of the room, and Marget was there! She came briskly to meet this odious Dream-stuff, and flung herself into his arms, and kissed him—and he her, and she him again, and he her again, and so on, and so on, and so on, till it was most unpleasant to look at. But I bore it, for I wanted to know all my misfortune, the full magnitude of it and the particulars. Next, they went arm-in-arm and sat down and cuddled up together on a sofa, and did that all over again—over and over and over and over—the most offensive spectacle I had ever seen, as it seemed to me. Then Schwarz tilted up that beautiful face, using his profane forefinger as a fulcrum under the chin that should have been sacred to me, and looked down into the luminous eyes which should have been wholly mine by rights, and said, archly—

"Little traitor!"

"Traitor? I? How, Emil?"

"You didn't keep your tryst last night."

"Why, Emil, I did!"

"Oh, not you! Come—what did we do? where did we go? For a ducat you can't tell!"

Marget looked surprised—then nonplussed—then a little frightened.

"It is very strange," she said, "very strange . . . . . unaccountable. I seem to have forgotten everything. But I know I was out; I was out till near midnight; I know it because my mother chided me, and tried her best to make me confess what had kept me out so late; and she was very uneasy, and I was cruelly afraid she would suspect the truth. I remember nothing at all of what happened before. Isn't it strange!"

Then the devil Schwarz laughed gaily and said that for a kiss he would unriddle the riddle. So he told her how he had encountered her, and how she was walking in her sleep, and how she was dreaming of him, and how happy it made him to see her kiss the air, imagining she was kissing him. And then they both laughed at the odd incident, and dropped the trifle out of their minds, and fell to trading caresses and endearments again, and thought no more about it.

They talked of the "happy day!"—a phrase that scorched me like a coal. They would win over the mother and the uncle presently—yes, they were quite sure of it. Then they built their future—built it out of sunshine and rainbows and rapture; and went on adding and adding to its golden ecstasies until they were so intoxicated with the prospect that words were no longer adequate to express what they were foreseeing and pre-enjoying, and so died upon their lips and gave place to love's true and richer language, wordless soul-communion: the heaving breast, the deep sigh, the unrelaxing embrace, the shoulder-pillowed head, the bliss-dimmed eyes, the lingering kiss . . . .

By God, my reason was leaving me! I swept forward and enveloped them as with a viewless cloud! In an instant Marget was Lisbet again; and as she sprang to her feet divinely aflame with passion for me I stepped back, and back, and back, she following, then I stopped and she fell panting in my arms, murmuring—

"Oh, my own, my idol, how wearily the time has dragged—do not leave me again!"

That Dream-mush rose astonished, and stared stupidly, his mouth working, but fetching out no words. Then he thought he understood, and started toward us, saying—

"Walking in her sleep again—how suddenly it takes her! . . . . . I wonder how she can lean over like that without falling?"

He arrived and put his arms through me and around her to support her, saying tenderly—

"Wake, dearheart, shake it off, I cannot bear to see you so!"

Lisbet freed herself from his arms and bent a stare of astonishment and wounded dignity upon him, accompanied by words to match—

"Mr. Schwarz, you forget yourself!"

It knocked the reptile stupid for a moment; then he got his bearings and said—

"Oh, please come to yourself, dear, it is so hard to see you like this. But if you can't wake, do come to the divan and sleep it off, and I will so lovingly watch over you, my darling, and protect you from intrusion and discovery. Come, Marget—do!"

"*Marget!*" Lisbet's eyes kindled, as at a new affront. "*What* Marget, please? Whom do you take me for? And why do you venture these familiarities?" She softened a little then, seeing how dazed and how pitiably distressed he looked, and added, "I have always treated you with courtesy, Mr. Schwarz, and it is very unkind of you to insult me in this wanton way."

In his miserable confusion he did not know what to say, and so he said the wrong thing—

"Oh, my poor afflicted child, shake it off, be your sweet self again, and let us steep our souls once more in dreams of our happy marriage day and—"

It was too much. She would not let him finish, but broke wrathfully into the midst of his sentence.

"Go away!" she said; "your mind is disordered, you have been drinking. Go—go at once! I cannot bear the sight of you!"

He crept humbly away and out at the door, mopping his eyes with his handkerchief and muttering "Poor afflicted thing, it breaks my heart to see her so!"

Dear Lisbet, she was just a girl—alternate sunshine and shower, peremptory soldier one minute, crying the next. Sobbing, she took refuge on my breast, saying—

"Love me, oh my precious one, give me peace, heal my hurts, charm away the memory of the shame this odious creature has put upon me!"

During half an hour we re-enacted that sofa-scene where it had so lately been played before, detail by detail, kiss for kiss, dream for dream, and the bliss of it was beyond words. But with an important difference: in Marget's case there was a mamma to be pacified and persuaded, but Lisbet von Arnim had no such incumbrances; if she had a relative in the world she was not aware of it; she was free and independent, she could marry whom she pleased and when she pleased. And so, with the dearest and sweetest naivety she suggested that to-day and now was as good a time as any! The suddenness of it, the unexpectedness of it, would have taken my breath if I had had any. As it was, it swept through me like a delicious wind and set my whole fabric waving and fluttering. For a moment I was gravely embarrassed. Would it be right, would it be honorable, would it not be treason to let this confiding young creature marry herself to a viewless detail of the atmosphere? I knew how to accomplish it, and was burning to do it, would it be fair? Ought I not to at least tell her my condition, and let her decide for herself? Ah . . . . . She might decide the wrong way!

No, I couldn't bring myself to it, I couldn't run the risk. I must think—think—think. I must hunt out a good and righteous reason for the marriage without the revelation. That is the way we are made; when we badly want a thing, we go to hunting for good and righteous reasons for it; we give it that fine name to comfort our consciences, whereas we privately know we are only hunting for plausible ones.

I seemed to find what I was seeking, and I urgently pretended to myself that it hadn't a defect in it. Forty-Four was my friend; no doubt I could persuade him to return my Dream-Self into my body and lock it up there for good. Schwarz being thus put out of the way, wouldn't my wife's Waking-Self presently lose interest in him and cease from loving him? That looked plausible. Next, by throwing *my* Waking-Self in the way of *her* Waking-Self a good deal and using tact and art, would not a time come when . . . . . oh, it was all as clear as a bell! Certainly. It wouldn't be long, it couldn't be long, before I could retire my Soul into my body, then both Lisbet and Marget being widows and longing for solace and tender companionship, would yield to the faithful beseechings and supplications of my poor inferior Waking-Self and marry *him*. Oh, the scheme was perfect, it was flawless, and my enthusiasm over it was without measure or limit. Lisbet caught that enthusiasm from my face and cried out—

"I know what it is! It is going to be *now!*"

I began to volley the necessary "suggestions" into her head as fast as I could load and fire—for by "suggestion," as 44 had told me, you make the hypnotised subject see and do and feel whatever you please: see people and things that are not there, hear words that are not spoken, eat salt for sugar, drink vinegar for wine, find the rose's sweetness in a stench, carry out all suggested acts—and forget the whole of it when he wakes, and remember the whole of it again whenever the hypnotic sleep returns!

In obedience to suggestion, Lisbet clothed herself as a bride; by suggestion she made obeisance to imaginary altar and priest, and smiled upon imaginary wedding-guests; made the solemn responses; received the ring, bent her dear little head to the benediction, put up her lips for the marriage kiss, and blushed as a new-made wife should before people!

Then, by suggestion altar and priest and friends passed away and we were alone—alone, immeasurably content, the happiest pair in the Duchy of Austria!

Ah . . . . . footsteps! some one coming! I fled to the middle of the room, to emancipate Lisbet from the embarrassment of the hypnotic sleep and be Marget again and ready for emergencies. She began to gaze around and about, surprised, wondering, also a little frightened, I thought.

"Why, where is Emil?" she said. "How strange; I did not see him go. How could he go and I not see him? . . . . Emil! . . . . No answer! Surely this magician's den is bewitched. But we've been here many times, and nothing happened."

At that moment Emil slipped in, closed the door, and said, apologetically and in a tone and manner charged with the most respectful formality—

"Forgive me, Miss Regen, but I was afraid for you and have stood guard—it would not do for you to be found in this place, and asleep. Your mother is fretting about your absence—her nurse is looking for you everywhere—I have misdirected her . . . . . pardon, what is the matter?"

Marget was gazing at him in a sort of stupefaction, with the tears beginning to trickle down her face. She began to sob in her hands, and said—

"If I have been asleep it was cruel of you to leave me. Oh, Emil, how could you desert me at such a time, if you love me?"

The astonished and happy bullfrog had her in his arms in a minute and was blistering her with kisses, which she paid back as fast as she could register them, and she not cold yet from her marriage-oath! A man—and such a man as that—hugging my wife before my eyes, and she getting a gross and voracious satisfaction out of it!—I could not endure the shameful sight. I rose and winged my way thence, intending to kick a couple of his teeth out as I passed over, but his mouth was employed and I could not get at it.

Chapter 25

THAT NIGHT I had a terrible misfortune. The way it came about was this. I was so unutterably happy and so unspeakably unhappy that my life was become an enchanted ecstasy and a crushing burden. I did not know what to do, and took to drink. Merely for that evening. It was by Doangivadam's suggestion that I did this. He did not know what the matter was, and I did not tell him; but he could see that something *was* the matter and wanted regulating, and in his judgment it would be well to try drink, for it might do good and couldn't do harm. He was ready to do any kindness for me, because I had been 44's friend; and he loved to have me talk about 44, and mourn with him over his burning. I couldn't tell him 44 was alive again, for the mysterious check fell upon my tongue whenever I tried to. Very well; we were drinking and mourning together, and I took a shade too much and it biased my judgment. I was not what one could call at all far gone, but I had reached the heedless stage, the unwatchful stage, when we parted, and I forgot to make myself invisible! And so, eager and unafraid, I entered the boudoir of my bride confident of the glad welcome which would of course have been mine if I had come as Martin von Giesbach, whom she loved, instead of as August Feldner, whom she cared nothing about. The boudoir was dark, but the bedroom door was standing open, and through it I saw an enchanting picture and stopped to contemplate it and enjoy it. It was Marget. She was sitting before a pier glass, snowily arrayed in her dainty nightie, with her left side toward me; and upon her delicate profile and her shining cataract of dark red hair streaming unvexed to the floor a strong light was falling. Her maid was busily grooming her with brush and comb, and gossiping, and now and then Marget smiled up at her and she smiled back, and I smiled at both in sympathy and good-fellowship out of the dusk, and altogether it was a gracious and contenting condition of things, and my heart sang with happiness. But the picture was not quite complete, not wholly perfect—there was a pair of lovely blue eyes that persistently failed to turn my way. I thought I would go nearer and correct that defect. Supposing that I was invisible I tranquilly stepped just within the room and stood there; at the same moment Marget's mother appeared in the further door; and also at the same moment the three indignant women discovered me and began to shriek and scream in the one breath!

I fled the place. I went to my quarters, resumed my flesh, and sat mournfully down to wait for trouble. It was not long coming. I expected the master to call, and was not disappointed. He came in anger—which was natural,—but to my relief and surprise I soon found that his denunciations were not for me! What an uplift it was! No, they were all for my Duplicate—all that the master wanted from me was a denial that I was the person who had profaned the sanctity of his niece's bedchamber. When he said *that* . . . . well, it took the most of the buoyancy out of the uplift. If he had stopped there and challenged me to testify, I—but he didn't. He went right on recounting and re-recounting the details of the exasperating episode, never suspecting that they were not news to me, and all the while he freely lashed the Duplicate and took quite for granted that he was the criminal and that my character placed me above suspicion. This was all so pleasant to my ear that I was glad to let him continue: indeed the more he abused Schwarz the better I liked it, and soon I was feeling grateful that he had neglected to ask for my testimony. He was very bitter, and when I perceived that he was minded to handle my detestable rival with severity I rejoiced exceedingly in my secret heart. Also I became evilly eager to keep him in that mind, and hoped for chances to that end.

It appeared that both the mother and the maid were positive that the Duplicate was the offender. The master kept dwelling upon that, and never referring to Marget as a witness, a thing that seemed so strange to me that at last I ventured to call his attention to the omission.

"Oh, her unsupported opinion is of no consequence!" he said, indifferently. "She says it was you—which is nonsense, in the face of the other evidence and your denial. She is only a child—how can *she* know one of you from the other? To satisfy her I said I would bring your denial; as for Emil Schwarz's testimony I don't want it and shouldn't value it. These Duplicates are ready to say anything that comes into their dreamy heads. This one is a good enough fellow, there's no deliberate harm in him, but—oh, as a witness he is not to be considered. He has made a blunder—in another person it would have been a crime—and by consequence my niece is compromised, for sure, for the maid can't keep the secret; poor thing, she's like all her kind—a secret, in a lady's-maid, is water in a basket. Oh, yes, it's true that this Duplicate has merely committed a blunder, but all the same my mind is made up as to one thing . . . . . the bell is tolling midnight, it marks a change for him . . . . . when I am through with him to-day, let him blunder as much as he likes he'll not compromise my niece again!"

I suppose it was wicked to feel such joy as I felt, but I couldn't help it. To have that hated rival put summarily out of my way and my road left free—the thought was intoxicating! The master asked me—as a formality—to deny that I was the person who had invaded Marget's chamber.

I promptly furnished the denial. It had always cost me shame to tell an injurious lie before, but I told this one without a pang, so eager was I to ruin the creature that stood between me and my worshipped little wife. The master took his leave, then, saying—

"It is sufficient. It is all I wanted. He shall marry the girl before the sun sets!"

Good heavens! in trying to ruin the Duplicate, I had only ruined myself.

Chapter 26

I was so miserable! A whole endless hour dragged along. Oh, why didn't he come, *why* didn't he come! wouldn't he *ever* come, and I so in need of his help and comfort!

It was awfully still and solemn and midnighty, and this made me feel creepy and shivery and afraid of ghosts; and that was natural, for the place was foggy with them, as Ernest Wasserman said, who was the most unexact person in his language in the whole castle, foggy being a noun of multitude and not applicable to ghosts, for they seldom appear in large companies, but mostly by ones and twos, and then—oh, then, when they go flitting by in the gloom like forms made of delicate smoke, and you see the furniture through them—

My, what is that! . . . . I heard it again! . . . . I was quaking like a jelly, and my heart was so cold and scared! Such a dry, bony noise, such a kl—lackety klackclack, kl—lackety klackclack!—dull, muffled, far away down the distant caverns and corridors—but approaching! oh, dear, approaching! It shriveled me up like a spider in a candle-flame, and I sat scrunched together and quivering, the way the spider does in his death-agony, and I said to myself, "skeletons a-coming, oh, what *shall* I do!"

Do? Shut my door, of course! if I had the strength to get to it—which I wouldn't have, on my legs, I knew it well; but I collapsed to the floor and crawled to the door, and panted there and listened, to see if the noise was certainly coming my way—which it was!—and I took a look; and away down the murky hall a long square of moonlight lay across the floor, and a tall figure was capering across it, with both hands held aloft and violently agitated and clacking out that clatter—and next moment the figure was across and blotted out in the darkness, but not the racket, which was getting loud and sharp, now—then I pushed the door to, and crept back a piece and lay exhausted and gasping.

It came, and came,—that dreadful noise—straight to my door, then that figure capered in and slammed the door to, and went on capering gaily all around me and everywhere about the room; and it was not a skeleton; no, it was a tall man, clothed in the loudest and most clownish and outlandish costume, with a vast white collar that stood above its ears, and a battered hat like a bucket, tipped gallusly to one side, and betwixt the fingers of the violent hands were curved fragments of dry bone which smote together and made that terrible clacking; and the man's mouth reached clear across his face and was unnaturally red, and had extraordinarily thick lips, and the teeth showed intensely white between them, and the face was as black as midnight. It was a terrible and ferocious spectre, and would bound as high as the ceiling, and crack its heels together, and yah-yah-yah! like a fiend, and keep the bones going, and soon it broke into a song in a sort of bastard English,

> "Buffalo gals can't you come out to-night,
> Can't you come out to-night,

> Can't you come out to-night,
> O, Buffalo gals can't you come out to-night—
> A-n-d *dance* by de light er de moon!"

And then it burst out with a tremendous clatter of laughter, and flung itself furiously over and over in the air like the wings of a windmill in a gale, and landed with a whack! on its feet alongside of me and looked down at me and shouted most cheerfully—

"*Now* den, Misto' Johnsing, how does yo' corporsosity seem to segashuate!"

I gasped out—

"Oh, dread being, have pity, oh—if—if—"

"Bress yo' soul, honey, *I* ain' no dread being, I's Cunnel Bludso's nigger fum Souf C'yarlina, en I's heah th'ee hund'd en fifty year ahead o' time, caze you's down in de mouf en I got to 'muse you wid de banjo en make you feel all right en comfy agin. So you jist lay whah you is, boss, en listen to de music; I gwineter sing to you, honey, de way de po' slave-niggers sings when dey's sol' away fum dey home en is homesick en down in de mouf."

Then out of nowhere he got that thing that he called a banjo, and sat down and propped his left ancle on his right knee, and canted his bucket-hat a little further and more gallusly over his ear, and rested the banjo in his lap, and set the grip of his left fingers on the neck of it high up, and fetched a brisk and most thrilling rake across the strings low down, giving his head a toss of satisfaction, as much as to say "I reckon *that* gets in to where you live, oh I guess not!" Then he canted his head affectionately toward the strings, and twisted the pegs at the top and tuned the thing up with a musical plunkety-plunk or so; then he re-settled himself in his chair and lifted up his black face toward the ceiling, grave, far-away, kind of pathetic, and began to strum soft and low—and then! Why then his voice began to tremble out and float away toward heaven —such a sweet voice, such a divine voice, and so touching—

> "Way down upon de Swanee river,
> Far, far away,
> Dah's whah my heart is turnin' ever,
> Dah's whah de ole folks stay."

And so on, verse after verse, sketching his humble lost home, and the joys of his childhood, and the black faces that had been dear to him, and which he would look upon no more—and there he sat lost in it, with his face lifted up that way, and there was never anything so beautiful, never anything so heart-breaking, oh, never any music like it below the skies! and by the magic of it that uncouth figure lost its uncouthness and became lovely like the song, because it so fitted the song, so belonged to it, and was such a part *of* it, so helped to body forth the feeling of it and make it visible, as it were, whereas a silken dress and a white face and white graces would have profaned it, and cheapened its noble pathos.

I closed my eyes, to try if I could picture to myself that lost home; and when the last notes were dying away, and apparently receding into the distance, I opened them again: the singer was gone, my room was gone, but afar off the home was there, a cabin of logs nestling under spreading trees, a soft vision steeped in a mellow summer twilight—and steeped in that music, too, which was dying, dying, fading, fading; and with it faded the vision, like a dream, and passed away; and as it faded and passed, my room and my furniture began to dimly reappear—spectrally, with the perishing home showing vaguely, through it, as through a veil; and when the transformation was accomplished my room was its old self again, my lights were burning, and in the black man's place sat Forty-Four beaming a self-complimenting smile. He said—

"Your eyes are wet; it's the right applause. But it's nothing, I could fetch that effect if they were glass. Glass? I could do it if they were knot-holes. Get up, and let's feed."

I *was* so glad to see him again! The very sight of him was enough to drive away my terrors and despairs and make me forget my deplorable situation. And then there was that mysterious soul-refreshment, too, that always charged the atmosphere as with wine and set one's spirits a-buzzing whenever he came about, and made you perceive that he was come, whether he was visible or not.

***When we had finished feeding, he lit his smoke-factory and we drew up to the fire to discuss my unfortunate situation and see what could be done about it. We examined it all around, and I said it seemed to me that the first and most urgent thing to be done was to stop the lady's-maid's gossiping mouth and keep her from compromising Marget; I said the master hadn't a doubt that she would spread the fact of the unpleasant incident of an hour or two ago. Next, I thought we ought to stop that marriage, if possible. I concluded with—

"Now, 44, the case is full of intolerable difficulties, as you see, but do try and think of some way out of them, won't you?"

To my grief I soon saw that he was settling down into one of his leather-headed moods. Ah, how often they came upon him when there was a crisis and his very brightest intelligence was needed!

He said he saw no particular difficulties in the situation if I was right about it: the first and main necessity was to silence the maid and stop Schwarz from proceeding with his marriage—and then blandly proposed that we *kill* both of them!

It almost made me jump out of my clothes. I said it was a perfectly insane idea, and if he was actually in earnest—

He stopped me there, and the argument-lust rose in his dull eye. It always made me feel depressed to see that look, because he loved to get a chance to show off how he could argue, and it was so dreary to listen to him—dreary and irritating, for when he was in one of his muddy-minded moods he couldn't argue any more than a clam. He said, big-eyed and asinine—

"What makes you think it insane, August?"

What a hopeless question! what could a person answer to such a foolishness as that?

"Oh, dear, me," I said, "can't you *see* that it's insane?"

He looked surprised, puzzled, pathetically mystified for a little while, then said—

"Why, *I* don't see how you make it out, August. We don't need those people, you know. No one needs them, so far as I can see. There's a plenty of them around, you can get as many as you want. Why, August, you don't seem to have any practical ideas—business ideas. You stay shut up here, and you don't know about these things. There's dozens and dozens of those people. I can turn out and in a couple of hours I can fetch a whole swarm of—"

"Oh, wait, 44! Dear me, is supplying their places the whole thing? is it the important thing? Don't you suppose *they* would like to have something to say about it?"

That simple aspect of it did seem to work its way into his head—after boring and tugging a moment or two—and he said, as one who had received light—

"Oh, I didn't think of that. Yes—yes, I see now." Then he brightened, and said, "but you know, they've got to die anyway, and so the *when* isn't any matter. Human beings aren't of any particular consequence; there's plenty more, plenty. Now then, after we've got them killed—"

"Damnation, we are not *going* to kill them!—now don't say another word about it; it's a perfectly atrocious idea; I should think you would be ashamed of it; and ashamed to hang to it and stick to it the way you do, and be so reluctant to give it up. Why, you act as if it was a child, and the first one you ever had."

He was crushed, and looked it. It hurt me to see him look cowed, that way; it made me feel mean, and as if I had struck a dumb animal that had been doing the best it knew how, and not meaning any harm; and at bottom I was vexed at myself for being so rough with him at such a time; for *I* know at a glance when he has a leather-headed mood on, and that he is not responsible when his brains have gone mushy; but I just *couldn't* pull myself together right off and say the gentle word and pet away the hurt I had given. I had to take time to it and work down to it gradually. But I managed it, and by and by his smiles came back, and his cheer, and then he was all right again, and as grateful as a child to see me friends with him once more.

Then he went zealously to work on the problem again, and soon evolved another scheme. The idea this time was to turn the maid into a cat, and make some *more* Schwarzes, then Marget would not be able to tell t'other from which, and couldn't choose the right one, and it wouldn't be lawful for her to marry the whole harem. That would postpone the wedding, he thought.

It certainly had the look of it! Any blind person could see that. So I gave praise, and was glad of the chance to do it and make up for bygones. He was as pleased as could be. In about ten minutes or so we heard a plaintive sound of meyow-yowing wandering around and about, away off somewhere, and 44 rubbed his hands joyfully and said—

"There she is, now!"

"Who?"

"The lady's-maid."

"No! Have you already transmuted her?"

"Yes. She was sitting up waiting for her room-mate to come, so she could tell her. Waiting for her mate to come from larking with the porter's new yunker. In a minute or two it would have been too late. Set the door ajar; she'll come when she sees the light, and we'll see what she has to say about the matter. She mustn't recognize me; I'll change to the magician. It will give him some more reputation. Would you like me to make you able to understand what she says?"

"Oh, *do*, 44, do, please!"

"All right. Here she is."

It was the magician's voice, exactly counterfeited; and there he stood, the magician's duplicate, official robes and all. I went invisible; I did not want to be seen in the condemned enchanter's company, even by a cat.

She came sauntering sadly in, a very pretty cat. But when she saw the necromancer her tail spread and her back went up and she let fly a spit or two and would have scurried away, but I flew over her head and shut the door in time. She backed into the corner and fixed her glassy eyes on 44, and said—

"It was you who did this, and it was mean of you. I never did you any harm."

"No matter, you brought it on yourself."

"How did I bring it on myself?"

"You were going to tell about Schwarz; you would have compromised your young mistress."

"It's not so; I wish I may never die if—"

"Nonsense! Don't talk so. You were waiting up to tell. I know all about it."

The cat looked convicted. She concluded not to argue the case.

After thinking a moment or two she said, with a kind of sigh—

"Will they treat me well, do you think?"

"Yes."

"Do you know they will?"

"Yes, I know it."

After a pause and another sigh—

"I would rather be a cat than a servant—a slave, that has to smile, and look cheerful, and pretend to be happy, when you are scolded for every little thing, the way Frau Stein and her daughter do, and be sneered at and insulted, and they haven't any right to, *they* didn't pay my wage, I wasn't *their* slave—a hateful life, an odious life! I'd rather be a cat. Yes, I would. Will everybody treat me well?"

"Yes, everybody."

"Frau Stein, too, and the daughter?"

"Yes."

"Will *you* see that they do?"

"I will. It's a promise."

"Then I thank you. They are all afraid of you, and the most of them hate you. And it was the same with me—but not now. You seem different to me now. You have the same voice and the same clothes, but you seem different. You seem kind; I don't know why, but you do; you seem kind and good, and I trust you; I think you will protect me."

"I will keep my promise."

"I believe it. And keep me as I am. It was a bitter life. You would think those Steins would not have been harsh with me, seeing I was a poor girl, with not a friend, nor anybody that was mine, and I never did them any harm. I *was* going to tell. Yes, I was. To get revenge. Because the family said I was bribed to let Schwarz in there—and it was a lie! Even Miss Marget believed that lie—I could see it, and she—well, she tried to defend me, but she let them convince her. Yes, I was going to tell. I was hot to tell. I was angry. But I am glad I didn't get the chance, for I am not angry any more; cats do not carry anger, I see. Don't change me back, leave me as I am. Christians go—I know where they go; some to the one place some to the other; but I think cats—where do *you* think cats go?"

"Nowhere. After they die."

"Leave me as I am, then; don't change me back. Could I have these leavings?"

"And welcome—yes."

"Our supper was there, in our room, but the other maid was frightened of me because I was a strange cat, and drove me out, and I didn't get any. This is wonderful food, I wonder how it got to this room? there's never been anything like it in this castle before. Is it enchanted food?"

"Yes."

"I just guessed it was. Safe?"

"Perfectly."

"Do you have it here a good deal?"

"Always—day and night."

"How gaudy! But this isn't your room?"

"No, but I'm here a great deal, and the food is here all the time. Would you like to do your feeding here?"

"Too good to be true!"

"Well, you can. Come whenever you like, and speak at the door."

"How dear and lovely! I've had a narrow escape—I can see it now."

"From what?"

"From not getting to be a cat. It was just an accident that that idiot came blundering in there drunk; if I hadn't been there—but I *was*, and never shall I get done being thankful. This is amazing good food; there's never been anything like it in this castle before —not in my time, I can tell you. I am thankful I may come here when I'm hungry."

"Come whenever you like."

"I'll do what I can for pay. I've never caught a mouse, but I feel it in me that I could do it, and I will keep a lookout here. I'm not so sad, now; no, things look very different; but I was pretty sad when I came. Could I room here, do you think? Would you mind?"

"Not at all. Make yourself quite at home. There'll be a special bed for you. I'll see to it."

"What larks! I never knew what nuts it was to be a cat before."

"It has its advantages."

"Oh, I should smile! I'll step out, now, and browse around a little, and see if there's anything doing in my line. Au revoir, and many many thanks for all you have done for me. I'll be back before long."

And so she went out, waving her tail, which meant satisfaction.

"There, now," said 44, "that part of the plan has come out all right, and no harm done."

"No, indeed," I said, resuming my visible form, "we've done her a favor. And in her place I should feel about it just as she does. Forty-Four, it was beautiful to hear that strange language and understand it—I understood every word. Could I learn to speak it, do you think?"

"You won't have to learn it, I'll put it *into* you."

"Good. When?"

"Now. You've already got it. Try! Speak out—do The Boy Stood on the Burning Deck—in catapult, or cataplasm, or whatever one might call that tongue."

"The Boy—what was it you said?"

"It's a poem. It hasn't been written yet, but it's very pretty and stirring. It's English. But I'll empty it into you, where you stand, in cataplasm. Now you've got it. Go ahead—recite."

I did it, and never missed a wail. It was certainly beautiful in that tongue, and quaint and touching; 44 said if it was done on a back fence, by moonlight, it would make people cry—especially a quartette would. I was proud; he was not always so complimentary. I said I was glad to have the cat, particularly now that I could talk to her; and she would be happy with me, didn't he think? Yes, he said, she would. I said—

"It's a good night's work we've done for that poor little blonde-haired lady's-maid, and I believe, as you do, that quite soon she is going to be contented and happy."

"As soon as she has kittens," he said, "and it won't be long."

Then we began to think out a name for her, but he said—

"Leave that, for the present, you'd better have a nap."

He gave a wave of his hand, and that was sufficient; before the wave was completed I was asleep.

Chapter 27

I woke up fresh and fine and vigorous, and found I had been asleep a little more than six minutes. The sleeps which he furnished had no dependence upon time, no connection with it, no relation to it; sometimes they did their work in one interval, sometimes in another, sometimes in half a second, sometimes in half a day, according to whether there was an interruption or wasn't; but let the interval be long or short, the result was the same: that is to say, the reinvigoration was perfect, the physical and mental refreshment complete.

There had been an interruption, a voice had spoken. I glanced up, and saw myself standing there, within the half-open door. That is to say, I saw Emil Schwarz, my Duplicate. My conscience gave me a little prod, for his face was sad. Had he found out what had been happening at midnight, and had he come at three in the morning to reproach me?

Reproach me? What for? For getting him falsely saddled with a vulgar indiscretion? What of it? Who was the loser by it? Plainly, I, myself—I had lost the girl. And who was the gainer? He himself, and none other—he had acquired her. Ah, very well, then—let him reproach me; if he was dissatisfied, let him trade places: he wouldn't find me objecting. Having reached solid ground by these logical reasonings, I advised my conscience to go take a tonic, and leave me to deal with this situation as a healthy person should.

Meantime, during these few seconds, I was looking at myself, standing there—and for once, I was admiring. Just because I had been doing a very handsome thing by this Duplicate, I was softening toward him, my prejudices were losing strength. I hadn't intended to do the handsome thing, but no matter, it had happened, and it was natural for me to take the credit of it and feel a little proud of it, for I was human. Being human accounts for a good many insanities, according to 44—upwards of a thousand a day was his estimate.

It is actually the truth that I had never looked this Duplicate over before. I never could bear the sight of him. I wouldn't look at him when I could help it; and until this moment I *couldn't* look at him dispassionately and with fairness. But now I could, for I had done him a great and creditable kindness, and it quite changed his aspects.

In those days there were several things which I didn't know. For instance I didn't know that my voice was not the same voice to me that it was to others; but when 44 made me talk into the thing which he brought in, one day, when he had arrived home from one of his plundering-raids among the unborn centuries, and then reversed the machine and allowed me to listen to my voice as other people were used to hearing it, I recognized that it had so little resemblance to the voice *I* was accustomed to hearing that I should have said it was not my voice at all if the proof had not been present that it was.

Also, I had been used to supposing that the person I saw in the mirror was the person others saw when they looked at me—whereas that was not the case. For once, when 44 had come back from robbing the future he brought a camera and made some photographs of me—those were the names which he gave the things, names which he invented out of his head for the occasion, no doubt, for that was his habit, on account of his not having any principles—and *always* the pictures which were like me as I saw myself in the glass he pronounced poor, and those which I thought exceedingly bad, he pronounced almost supernaturally good.

And here it was again. In the figure standing by the door I was now seeing myself as others saw me, but the resemblance to the self which I was familiar with in the glass was *merely* a resemblance, nothing more; not approaching the common resemblance of brother to brother, but reaching only as far as the resemblance which a person usually bears to his brother-in-law. Often one does not notice that, at all, until it is pointed out; and sometimes, even then, the resemblance owes as much to imagination as to fact. It's like a cloud which resembles a horse after some one has pointed out the resemblance. You perceive it, then, though I have often seen a cloud that didn't. Clouds often have nothing more than a brother-in-law resemblance. I wouldn't say this to everybody, but I believe it to be true, nevertheless. For I myself have seen clouds which looked like a brother-in-law, whereas I knew very well they didn't. Nearly all such are hallucinations, in my opinion.

Well, there he stood, with the strong white electric light flooding him, (more plunder,) and he hardly even reached the brother-in-law standard. I realized that I had never really seen this youth before. Of course I could recognize the general pattern, I don't deny it, but that was only because I knew who the creature was; but if I had met him in another country, the most that could have happened would have been this: that I would turn and look after him and say "I wonder if I have seen him somewhere before?" and then I would drop the matter out of my mind, as being only a fancy.

Well, there he was; that is to say, there *I* was. And I was interested; interested at last. He was distinctly handsome, distinctly trim and shapely, and his attitude was easy, and well-bred and graceful. Complexion—what it should be at seventeen, with a blonde ancestry: peachy, bloomy, fresh, wholesome. Clothes—precisely like mine, to a button—or the lack of it.

I was well satisfied with this front view. I had never seen my back; I was curious to see it. I said, very courteously—

"Would you please turn around for a moment?—only a moment? . . . Thank you."

Well, well, how little we know what our backs are like! This one was all right, I hadn't a fault to find with it, but it was all new to me, it was the back of a stranger—hair-aspects and all. If I had seen it walking up the street in front of me it would not have occurred to me that I could be in any personal way interested in it.

"Turn again, please, if you will be so good . . . . Thank you kindly."

I was to inspect the final detail, now—mentality. I had put it last,

for I was reluctant, afraid, doubtful. Of course one glance was
enough—I was expecting that. It saddened me: he was of a loftier
world than I, he moved in regions where I could not tread, with my
earth-shod feet. I wished I had left that detail alone.

"Come and sit down," I said, "and tell me what it is. You wish to
speak with me about something?"

"Yes," he said, seating himself, "if you will kindly listen."

I gave a moment's thought to my defence, as regards the impend-
ing reproach, and was ready. He began, in a voice and manner
which were in accord with the sadness which sat upon his young
face—

"The master has been to me and has charged me with profaning
the sanctity of his niece's chamber."

It was a strange place to stop, but there he stopped, and looked
wistfully at me, just as a person might stop in a dream, and wait for
another person to take up the matter there, without any definite
text to talk to. I had to say something, and so for lack of anything
better to offer, I said—

"I am truly sorry, and I hope you will be able to convince him
that he is mistaken. You can, can't you?"

"Convince him?" he answered, looking at me quite vacantly,
"Why should I wish to convince him?"

I felt pretty vacant myself, now. It was a most unlooked-for
question. If I had guessed a week I should not have hit upon that
one. I said—and it was the only thing a body would ever think of
saying—

"But you do, don't you?"

The look he gave me was a look of compassion, if I know the
signs. It seemed to say, gently, kindly, but clearly, "alas, this poor
creature doesn't know anything." Then he uttered his answer—

"Wh-y, no, I do not see that I have that wish. It—why, you see,
it isn't any matter."

"Good heavens! It isn't any matter whether you stand disgraced
or not?"

He shook his head, and said quite simply—

"No, it isn't any matter, it is of no consequence."

It was difficult to believe my ears. I said—

"Well, then, if disgrace is nothing to you, consider *this* point. If the report gets around, it can mean disgrace for the young *lady*."

It had no effect that I could see! He said—

"Can it?" just as an idiot child might have said it.

"*Can* it? Why of course it can! You wouldn't want *that* to happen, would you?"

"We-ll," (reflectively), "I don't know. I don't see the bearing of it."

"Oh, great guns, this infantile stu—this—this—why, it's perfectly disheartening! You love her, and yet you don't care whether her good name is ruined or not?"

"Love her?" and he had the discouraged aspect of a person who is trying to look through a fog and is not succeeding, "why, I don't love her; what makes you think I do?"

"Well, I must say! Well, certainly this is too many for *me*. Why, hang it, *I* know you've been courting her."

"Yes—oh, yes, that is true."

"Oh, it is, is it! Very well, then, how is it that you were courting her and yet didn't love her?"

"No, it isn't that way. No, I loved her."

"Oh—go on, I'll take a breath or two—I don't know where I am, I'm all at sea."

He said, placidly—

"Yes, I remember about that. I loved her. It had escaped me. No —it hadn't escaped me; it was not important, and I was thinking of something else."

"Tell me," I said, "is *anything* important to you?"

"Oh, yes!" he responded, with animation and a brightening face; then the animation and the brightness passed, and he added, wearily, "but not these things."

Somehow, it touched me; it was like the moan of an exile. We were silent a while, thinking, ruminating, then I said—

"Schwarz, I'm not able to make it out. It is a sweet young girl, you certainly did love her, and—"

"Yes," he said, tranquilly, "it is quite true. I believe it was yesterday . . . . yes, I think it was yesterday."

"Oh, you *think* it was! But of course it's not important. Dear me, why should it be?—a little thing like that. Now then, something has changed it. What was it? What has happened?"

"Happened? Nothing, I think. Nothing that I know of."

"Well, then, why the devil . . . . oh, great Scott, I'll never get my wits back again! Why, look here, Schwarz, you wanted to *marry* her!"

"Yes. Quite true. I think . . . . yesterday? Yes, I think it was yesterday. I am to marry her to-day. I think it's to-day; anyway, it is pretty soon. The master requires it. He has told me so."

"Well . . . . upon my word!"

"What is the matter?"

"Why, you are as indifferent about this as you are about everything else. You show no feeling whatever, you don't even show interest. Come! surely you've got a heart hidden away somewhere; open it up; give it air; show at least some little corner of it. Land, I wish I were in your place! Don't you *care* whether you marry her or not?"

"Care? Why, *no,* of course I don't. You do ask the *strangest* questions! I wander, wander, wander! I try to make you out, I try to understand you, but it's all fog, fog, fog—you're just a riddle, nobody *can* understand you!"

Oh, the idea! the impudence of it! this to *me!*—from this frantic chaos of unimaginable incomprehensibilities, who couldn't by any chance utter so much as half a sentence that Satan himself could make head or tail of!

"Oh, I like *that!*" I cried, flying out at him. "*You* can't understand *me!* Oh, but that *is* good! It's immortal! Why, look here, when you came, I thought I knew what you came for—I thought I knew all about it—I would have said you were coming to reproach me for—for—"

I found it difficult to get it out, and so I left it in, and after a pause, added—

"Why, Schwarz, you certainly had something on your mind when you came—I could see it in your face—but if ever you've got to it I've not discovered it—oh, not even a sign of it! You *haven't* got to it, *have* you?"

"*Oh*, no!" he answered, with an outburst of very real energy. "These things were of no sort of consequence. *May* I tell it now? Oh, *will* you be good and hear me? I shall be so grateful, if you will!"

"Why, certainly, and glad to! Come, *now* you're waking up, at last! You've got a heart in you, sure enough, and plenty of feeling —why, it burns in your eye like a star! Go ahead—I'm all interest, all sympathy."

Oh, well, he was a different creature, now. All the fogs and puzzlings and perplexities were gone from his face, and had left it clear and full of life. He said—

"It was no idle errand that brought me. No, far from it! I came with my heart in my mouth, I came to beg, to plead, to pray—to beseech you, to implore you, to have mercy upon me!"

"Mercy—upon *you?*"

"Yes, mercy. Have mercy, oh, be merciful, and set me free!"

"Why, I—I—Schwarz, I don't understand. You say, yourself, that if they want you to marry, you are quite indif—"

"Oh, not *that!* I care nothing for that—it is these bonds"— stretching his arms aloft—"oh, free me from *them; these bonds of flesh*—this decaying vile matter, this foul weight, and clog, and burden, this loathsome sack of corruption in which my spirit is imprisoned, her white wings bruised and soiled—oh, be merciful and set her free! Plead for me with that malicious magic-monger— he has been here—I saw him issue from this door—he will come again—say you will be my friend, as well as brother! for brothers indeed we are; the same womb was mother to us both, I live by you, I perish when you die—brother, be my friend! plead with him to take away this rotting flesh and set my spirit free! Oh, this human life, this earthy life, this weary life! It is so groveling, and so mean; its ambitions are so paltry, its prides so trivial, its vanities so childish; and the glories that it values and applauds—lord, how empty! Oh, here I am a servant!—I who never served before; here I am a slave—slave among little mean kings and emperors made of clothes, the kings and emperors slaves themselves, to mud-built carrion that are *their* slaves!

"To think you should think I came here concerned about those other things—those inconsequentials! Why should they concern me, a spirit of air, habitant of the august Empire of Dreams? *We* have no morals; the angels have none; morals are for the impure; we have no principles, those chains are for men. We love the lovely whom we meet in dreams, we forget them the next day, and meet and love their like. They are dream-creatures—no others are real. Disgrace? We care nothing for disgrace, we do not know what it is. Crime? we commit it every night, while you sleep; it is nothing to us. We have no character, no *one* character, we have *all* characters; we are honest in one dream, dishonest in the next; we fight in one battle and flee from the next. We wear no chains, we cannot abide them; we have no home, no prison, the universe is our province; we do not know time, we do not know space—we live, and love, and labor, and enjoy, fifty years in an hour, while you are sleeping, snoring, repairing your crazy tissues; we circumnavigate your little globe while you wink; we are not tied within horizons, like a dog with cattle to mind, an emperor with human sheep to watch—we visit hell, we roam in heaven, our playgrounds are the constellations and the Milky Way. Oh, help, help! be my friend and brother in my need—beseech the magician, beg him, plead with him; he will listen, he will be moved, he will release me from this odious flesh!"

I was powerfully stirred—so moved, indeed, that in my pity for him I brushed aside unheeded or but half-heeded the scoffs and slurs which he had flung at my despised race, and jumped up and seized him by both hands and wrung them passionately, declaring that with all my heart and soul I would plead for him with the magician, and would not rest from these labors until my prayers should succeed or their continuance be peremptorily forbidden.

Chapter 28

H E   C O U L D not speak, for emotion; for the same cause my voice forsook me; and so, in silence we grasped hands again; and that grip, strong and warm, said for us what our tongues could not utter. At that moment the cat entered, and stood looking at us. Under her grave gaze a shame-faced discomfort, a sense of embarrassment, began to steal over me, just as would have been the case if she had been a human being who had caught me in that gushy and sentimental situation, and I felt myself blushing. Was it because I was aware that she had lately been that kind of a being? It annoyed me to see that my brother was not similarly affected. And yet, why mind it? didn't I already know that no human intelligence could guess what occurrence would affect *him* and what event would leave him cold? With an uncomfortable feeling of being critically watched by the cat, I pressed him with clumsy courtesy into his seat again, and slumped into my own.

The cat sat down. Still looking at us in that disconcerting way, she tilted her head first to one side and then the other, inquiringly and cogitatively, the way a cat does when she has struck the unexpected and can't quite make out what she had better do about it. Next she washed one side of her face, making such an awkward and unscientific job of it that almost anybody would have seen that she was either out of practice or didn't know how. She stopped with the one side, and looked bored, and as if she had only been doing it to put in the time, and wished she could think of something else to do to put in some more time. She sat a while, blinking drowsily, then she hit an idea, and looked as if she wondered she hadn't thought of it earlier. She got up and went visiting around among the furniture and belongings, sniffing at each and every article, and elaborately examining it. If it was a chair, she examined it all around, then jumped up in it and sniffed all over its seat and its back; if it was any other thing she could examine all around, she examined it all around; if it was a chest and there was room for her between it and the wall, she crowded herself in behind there and gave it a thorough overhauling; if it was a tall thing, like a washstand, she would stand on her hind toes and stretch up as high as she could, and reach across and paw at the toilet things and try to rake them to where she could smell them; if it was the cupboard, she stood on her toes and reached up and pawed the knob; if it was the table she would squat, and measure the distance, and make a leap, and land in the wrong place, owing to newness to the business; and, part of her going too far and sliding over the edge, she would scramble, and claw at things desperately, and save herself and make good; then she would smell everything on the table, and archly and daintily paw everything around that was movable, and finally paw something off, and skip cheerfully down and paw it some more, throwing herself into the prettiest attitudes, rising on her hind feet and curving her front paws and flirting her head this way and that and glancing down cunningly at the object, then pouncing on it and spatting it half the length of the room, and chasing it up and spatting it again, and again, and racing after it and fetching it another smack—and so on and so on; and suddenly she would tire of it and try to find some way to get to the top of the cupboard or the wardrobe, and if she couldn't she would look troubled and disappointed; and toward the last, when you could see she was getting her bearings well lodged in her head and was satisfied with the place and the arrangements, she relaxed her intensities, and got to purring a little to herself, and praisefully waving her tail between inspections—and at last she was done— done, and everything satisfactory and to her taste.

Being fond of cats, and acquainted with their ways, if I had been a stranger and a person had told me that this cat had spent half an hour in that room before, but hadn't happened to think to examine it until now, I should have been able to say with conviction, "Keep an eye on her, that's no orthodox cat, she's an imitation, there's a flaw in her make-up, you'll find she's born out of wedlock or some other arrested-development accident has happened, she's no true Christian cat, if *I* know the signs."

She couldn't think of anything further to do, now, so she thought she would wash the other side of her face, but she couldn't remember which one it was, so she gave it up, and sat down and went to nodding and blinking; and between nods she would jerk herself together and make remarks. I heard her say—

"One of them's the Duplicate, the other's the Original, but I can't tell t'other from which, and I don't suppose *they* can. I am sure I couldn't if I were them. The missuses said it was the Duplicate that broke in there last night, and I voted with the majority for policy's sake, which is a servant's only protection from

trouble, but I would like to know how *they* knew. *I* don't believe
they could tell them apart if they were stripped. Now my idea is—"
   I interrupted, and intoned musingly, as if to myself,—

> "The boy stood on the burning deck,
>   Whence all but him had fled—"

and stopped there, and seemed to sink into a reverie.
   It gave her a start! She muttered—
   "*That's* the Duplicate. Duplicates know languages—everything,
sometimes, and then again they don't know anything at all. That is
what Fischer says, though of course it could have been his Duplicate that said it, there's never any telling, in this bewitched place,
whether you are talking to a person himself, or only to his heathen
image. And Fischer says they haven't any morals nor any principles
—though of course it could have been his Duplicate that said
it—one never knows. Half the time when you say to a person *he*
said so-and-so, he says he didn't—so then you recognize it was the
other one. As between living in such a place as this and being crazy,
you don't know *which* it is, the most of the time. I would rather be
a cat and not have any Duplicate, then I always know which one I
am. Otherwise, not. If they haven't any principles, it was this
Duplicate that broke in there, though of course, being drunk he
wouldn't know which one he was, and so it could be the other
without him suspecting it, which leaves the matter where it was
before—not certain enough to be certain, and just uncertain
enough to be *un*certain. So I don't see that anything's decided. In
fact I know it isn't. Still, I think this one that wailed is the
Duplicate, because sometimes they know all languages a minute,
and next minute they don't know their own, if they've got one,
whereas a *man* doesn't. Doesn't, and can't even *learn* it—can't learn
cat-language, anyway. It's what Fischer says—Fischer or his Duplicate. So this is the one—*that's* decided. He couldn't talk cataract,
nor ever learn it, either, if it was the Christian one . . . . . I'm
awful tired!"
   I didn't let on, but pretended to be dozing; my brother was a

little further along than that—he was softly snoring. I wanted to wait and see, if I could, what was troubling the cat, for it seemed plain to me that she had something on her mind, she certainly was not at her ease. By and by she cleared her throat, and I stirred up and looked at her, as much as to say, "well, I'm listening—proceed." Then she said, with studied politeness—

"It is very late. I am sorry to disturb you gentlemen, but I am very tired, and would like to go to bed."

"Oh, dear me," I said, "don't wait up on our account I beg of you. Turn right in!"

She looked astonished.

"With you present?" she said.

So then I was astonished myself, but did not reveal it.

"Do you mind it?" I asked.

"Do I *mind* it! You will grant, I make no doubt, that so extraordinary a question is hardly entitled to the courtesy of an answer from one of my sex. You are offensive, sir; I beg that you will relieve me of your company at once, and take your friend with you."

"Remove him? I could not do that. He is my guest, and it is his place to make the first move. This is my room."

I said it with a submerged chuckle, as knowing quite well, that soft-spoken as it was, it would knock some of the starch out of her. As indeed it did.

"*Your* room! Oh, I beg a thousand pardons, I am ashamed of my rude conduct, and will go at once. I assure you sir, I was the innocent victim of a mistake: I thought it was my room."

"And so it is. There has been no mistake. Don't you see?—there is your bed."

She looked whither I was pointing, and said with surprise—

"How strange that is! it wasn't there five seconds ago. Oh, *isn't* it a love!"

She made a spring for it—cat-like, forgetting the old interest in the new one; and feminine-like, eager to feast her native appetite for pretty things upon its elegancies and daintinesses. And really it *was* a daisy! It was a canopied four-poster, of rare wood, richly carved, with bed twenty inches wide and thirty long, sumptuously bepillowed and belaced and beruffled and besatined and all that; and when she had petted it and patted it and searched it and sniffed it all over, she cried out in an agony of delight and longing—

"Oh, I would just *love* to stretch out on that!"

The enthusiasm of it melted me, and I said heartily—

"Turn right in, Mary Florence Fortescue Baker G. Nightingale, and make yourself at home—that is the magician's own present to you, and it shows you he's no imitation-friend, but the true thing!"

"Oh, what a pretty name!" she cried; "is it mine for sure enough, and may I keep it? Where *did* you get it?"

"I don't know—the magician hooked it from somewhere, he is always at that, and it just happened to come into my mind at the psychological moment, and I'm glad it did, for your sake, for it's a dandy! Turn in, now, Baker G., and make yourself entirely at home."

"You are *so* good, dear Duplicate, and I am just as grateful as I can be, but—but—well, you see how it is. I have never roomed with any person not of my own sex, and—"

"You will be perfectly safe here, Mary, I assure you, and—"

"I should be an ingrate to doubt it, and I do not doubt it, be sure of that; but at this particular time—at this time of all others—er—well, you know, for a smaller matter than this, Miss Marget is already compromised beyond repair, I fear, and if I—"

"Say no more, Mary Florence, you are perfectly right, perfectly. My dressing-room is large and comfortable, I can get along quite well without it, and I will carry your bed in there. Come along . . . Now then, there you are! Snug and nice and all right, isn't it? Contemplate that! Satisfactory?—yes?"

She cordially confessed that it was. So I sat down and chatted along while she went around and examined *that* place all over, and pawed everything and sampled the smell of each separate detail, like an old hand, for she was getting the hang of her trade by now; then she made a final and special examination of the button on our communicating-door, and stretched herself up on her hind-toes and fingered it till she got the trick of buttoning-out inquisitives and undesirables down fine and ship-shape, then she thanked me hand-

somely for fetching the bed and taking so much trouble; and gave
me good-night, and when I asked if it would disturb her if I talked
a while with my guest, she said no, talk as much as we pleased, she
was tired enough to sleep through thunderstorms and earthquakes.
So I said, right cordially—

"Good-night, Mary G., und schlafen Sie wohl!" and passed out
and left her to her slumbers. As delicate-minded a cat as ever I've
struck, and I've known a many of them.

Chapter 29

I stirred my brother up, and we talked the time away while
waiting for the magician to come. I said his coming was a most
uncertain thing, for he was irregular, and not at all likely to come
when wanted, but Schwarz was anxious to stay and take the
chances; so we did as I have said—talked and waited. He told me a
great deal about his life and ways as a dream-sprite, and did it in a
skipping and disconnected fashion proper to his species. He would
side-track a subject right in the middle of a sentence if another
subject attracted him, and he did this without apology or explanation—well, just as a dream would, you know. His talk was scatter-
ingly seasoned with strange words and phrases, picked up in a
thousand worlds, for he had been everywhere. Sometimes he could
tell me their meaning and where he got them, but not always; in
fact not very often, the dream-memory being pretty capricious, he
said—sometimes good, oftener bad, and always flighty. "Side-track,"
for instance. He was not able to remember where he had picked
that up, but thought it was in a star in the belt of Orion where he
had spent a summer one night with some excursionists from Sirius
whom he had met in space. That was as far as he could remember
with anything like certainty; as to *when* it was, that was a blank
with him; perhaps it was in the past, maybe it was in the future, he
couldn't tell which it was, and probably didn't know, at the time it

happened. *Couldn't* know, in fact, for Past and Future were human terms and not comprehendable by him, past and future being all one thing to a dream-sprite, and not distinguishable the one from the other. "And not important, anyway." How natural that sounded, coming from him! His notions of the important were just simply elementary, as you may say.

He often dropped phrases which had clear meanings to him, but which he labored in vain to make comprehensible by me. It was because they came from countries where none of the conditions resembled the conditions I had been used to; some from comets where nothing was solid, and nobody had legs; some from our sun, where nobody was comfortable except when white-hot, and where you needn't talk to people about cold and darkness, for you would not be able to explain the words so that they could understand what you were talking about; some from invisible black planets swimming in eternal midnight and thick-armored in perpetual ice, where the people have no eyes, nor any use for them, and where you might wear yourself out trying to make them understand what you meant by such words as warmth and light, you wouldn't ever succeed; and some from *general space*—that sea of ether which has no shores, and stretches on, and on, and arrives nowhere; which is a waste of black gloom and thick darkness through which you may rush forever at thought-speed, encountering at weary long intervals spirit-cheering archipelagoes of suns which rise sparkling far in front of you, and swiftly grow and swell, and burst into blinding glories of light, apparently measureless in extent, but you plunge through and in a moment they are far behind, a twinkling archipelago again, and in another moment they are blotted out in darkness; constellations, these? yes; and the earliest of them the property of your own solar system; the rest of that unending flight is through solar systems not known to men.

And he said that in that flight one came across *such* interesting dream-sprites! coming from a billion worlds, bound for a billion others; always friendly, always glad to meet up with you, always full of where they'd been and what they'd seen, and dying to tell

you about it; doing it in a million foreign languages, which sometimes you understood and sometimes you didn't, and the tongue
you understood to-day you forgot to-morrow, there being *nothing*
permanent about a dream-sprite's character, constitution, beliefs,
opinions, intentions, likes, dislikes, or anything else; all he cares for
is to travel, and talk, and see wonderful things and have a good
time. Schwarz said dream-sprites are well-disposed toward their
fleshly brothers, and did what they could to make them partakers of
the wonders of their travels, but it couldn't be managed except on a
poor and not-worth-while scale, because they had to communicate
through the flesh-brothers' Waking-Self imagination, and *that* medi-
um—oh, well, it was like "emptying rainbows down a rat-hole."

His tone was not offensive. I think his tone was never that, and
was never meant to be that; *it* was all right enough, but his
phrasing was often hurtful, on account of the ideal frankness of it.
He said he was once out on an excursion to Jupiter with some
fellows about a million years ago, when—

I stopped him there, and said—

"I am only seventeen, and you said you were born with me."

"Yes," he said, "I've been with you only about two million years,
I believe—counting as you count; *we* don't measure time at all.
Many a time I've been abroad five or ten or twenty thousand years
in a single night; I'm always abroad when you are asleep; I always
leave, the moment you fall asleep, and I never return until you
wake up. You are dreaming all the time I am gone, but you get
little or nothing of what I see—never more than some cheap odds
and ends, such as your groping Mortal Mind is competent to
perceive—and sometimes there's nothing for you at all, in a whole
night's adventures, covering many centuries; it's all above your dull
Mortal Mind's reach."

Then he dropped into his "chances." That is to say, he went to
discussing my health—as coldly as if I had been a piece of mere
property that he was commercially interested in, and which ought
to be thoughtfully and prudently taken care of for *his* sake. And he
even went into particulars, by gracious! advising me to be very
careful about my diet, and to take a good deal of exercise, and keep

regular hours, and avoid dissipation and religion, and not get married, because a family brought love, and distributed it among many objects, and intensified it, and this engendered wearing cares and anxieties, and when the objects suffered or died the miseries and anxieties multiplied and broke the heart and shortened life; whereas if I took good care of myself and avoided these indiscretions, there was no reason why he should not live ten million years and be hap—

I broke in and changed the subject, so as to keep from getting inhospitable and saying language; for really I was a good deal tried. I started him on the heavens, for he had been to a good many of them and liked ours the best, on account of there not being any Sunday there. They kept Saturday, and it was very pleasant: plenty of rest for the tired, and plenty of innocent good times for the others. But no Sunday, he said; the Sunday-Sabbath was a commercial invention and quite local, having been devised by Constantine to equalize prosperities in this world between the Jews and the Christians. The government statistics of that period showed that a Jew could make as much money in five days as a Christian could in six; and so Constantine saw that at this rate the Jews would by and by have all the wealth and the Christians all the poverty. There was nothing fair nor right about this, a righteous government should have equal laws for all, and take just as much care of the incompetent as of the competent—more, if anything. So he added the Sunday-Sabbath, and it worked just right, because it equalized the prosperities. After that, the Jew had to lie idle 104 days in the year, the Christian only 52, and this enabled the Christian to catch up. But my brother said there was now talk among Constantine and other early Christians up there, of some more equalizing; because, in looking forward a few centuries they could notice that along in the twentieth century somewhere it was going to be necessary to furnish the Jews another Sabbath to keep, so as to save what might be left of Christian property at that time. Schwarz said he had been down into the first quarter of the twentieth century lately, and it looked so to him.

Then he "side-tracked" in his abrupt way, and looked avidly at

my head and said he did wish he was back in my skull, he would
sail out the first time I fell asleep and have a scandalous good time!
—wasn't that magician *ever* coming back?

"And oh," he said, "what wouldn't I see! wonders, spectacles,
splendors which your fleshly eyes couldn't endure; and what
wouldn't I hear! the music of the spheres—no mortal could live
through five minutes of *that* ecstasy! If he would only come! If he
. . . ." He stopped, with his lips parted and his eyes fixed, like one
rapt. After a moment he whispered, *"do you feel that?"*

I recognized it; it was that life-giving, refreshing, mysterious
something which invaded the air when 44 was around. But I
dissembled, and said—

"What is it?"

"It's the magician; he's coming. He doesn't always let that influence go out from him, and so we dream-sprites took him for an
ordinary necromancer for a while; but when he burnt 44 we were
all there and close by, and he let it out then, and in an instant we
knew what he was! We knew he was a . . . we knew he was a
. . . . a . . . a . . . how curious!—my tongue won't *say* it!"

Yes, you see, 44 wouldn't let him say it—and I so near to getting
that secret at last! It was a sorrowful disappointment.

Forty-Four entered, still in the disguise of the magician, and
Schwarz flung himself on his knees and began to beg passionately
for release, and I put in my voice and helped. Schwarz said—

"Oh, mighty one, you imprisoned me, you can set me free, and no
other can. You have the power; you possess *all* the powers, all the
forces that defy Nature, nothing is impossible to you, for you are a
. . . a . . ."

So there it was again—he couldn't say it. I was that close to it a
second time, you see; 44 wouldn't let him say that word, and I
would have given anything in the world to hear it. It's the way we
are made, you know: if we can get a thing, we don't want it, but if
we can't get it, why—well, it changes the whole aspect of it, you
see.

Forty-Four was very good about it. He said he would let this one
go—Schwarz was hugging him around the knees and lifting up the

hem of his robe and kissing it and kissing it before he could get any further with his remark—yes, he would let this one go, and make some fresh ones for the wedding, the family could get along very well that way. So he told Schwarz to stand up and melt. Schwarz did it, and it was very pretty. First, his clothes thinned out so you could see him through them, then they floated off like shreds of vapor, leaving him naked, then the cat looked in, but scrambled out again; next, the flesh fell to thinning, and you could see the skeleton through it, very neat and trim, a good skeleton; next the bones disappeared and nothing was left but the empty form—just a statue, perfect and beautiful, made out of the delicatest soap-bubble stuff, with rainbow-hues dreaming around over it and the furniture showing through it the same as it would through a bubble; then—poof! and it was gone!

Chapter 30

THE CAT walked in, waving her tail, then gathered it up in her right arm, as she might a train, and minced her way to the middle of the room, where she faced the magician and rose up and bent low and spread her hands wide apart, as if it was a gown she was spreading, then sank her body grandly rearward—certainly the neatest thing you ever saw, considering the limitedness of the materials. I think a curtsy is the very prettiest thing a woman ever does, and I think a lady's-maid's curtsy is prettier than any one else's; which is because they get more practice than the others, on account of being at it all the time when there's nobody looking. When she had finished her work of art she smiled quite Cheshirely (my dream-brother's word, he knew it was foreign and thought it was future, he couldn't be sure), and said, very engagingly—

"Do you think I could have a bite now, without waiting for the second table, there'll be *such* goings-on this morning, and I would just give a whole basket of rats to be in it! and if I—"

At that moment the wee-wee'est little bright-eyed mousie you ever saw went scrabbling across the floor, and Baker G. gave a skip and let out a scream and landed in the highest chair in the room and gathered up her imaginary skirts and stood there trembling. Also at that moment her breakfast came floating out of the cupboard on a silver tray, and she asked that it come to the chair, which it did, and she took a hurried bite or two to stay her stomach, then rushed away to get her share of the excitements, saying she would like the rest of her breakfast to be kept for her till she got back.

"Now then, draw up to the table," said 44. "We'll have Vienna coffee of two centuries hence—it is the best in the world—buckwheat cakes from Missouri, vintage of 1845, French eggs of last century, and deviled breakfast-whale of the post-pliocene, when he was whitebait size, and just *too* delicious!"

By now I was used to these alien meals, raked up from countries I had never heard of and out of seasons a million years apart, and was getting indifferent about their age and nationalities, seeing that they always turned out to be fresh and good. At first I couldn't stand eggs a hundred years old and canned manna of Moses's time, but that effect came from habit and prejudiced imagination, and I soon got by it, and enjoyed what came, asking few or no questions. At first I would not have touched whale, the very thought of it would have turned my stomach, but now I ate a hundred and sixty of them and never turned a hair. As we chatted along during breakfast, 44 talked reminiscently of dream-sprites, and said they used to be important in the carrying of messages where secrecy and dispatch were a desideratum. He said they took a pride in doing their work well, in old times; that they conveyed messages with perfect verbal accuracy, and that in the matter of celerity they were up to the telephone and away beyond the telegraph. He instanced the Joseph-dreams, and gave it as his opinion that if they had gone per Western Union the lean kine would all have starved to death before the telegrams arrived. He said the business went to pot in Roman times, but that was the fault of the interpreters, not of the dream-sprites, and remarked—

"You can easily see that accurate interpreting was as necessary as accurate wording. For instance, suppose the Founder sends a telegram in the Christian Silence dialect, what are you going to do? Why, there's nothing to do but *guess* the best you can, and take the chances, because there isn't anybody in heaven or earth that can understand *both* ends of it, and so, there you are, you see! Up a stump."

"Up a which?"

"Stump. American phrase. Not discovered yet. It means defeated. You are bound to misinterpret the end you do not understand, and so the matter which was to have been accomplished by the message miscarries, fails, and vast damage is done. Take a specific example, then you will get my meaning. Here is a telegram from the Founder to her disciples. Date, June 27, four hundred and thirteen years hence; it's in the paper—Boston paper—I fetched it this morning."

"What is a Boston paper?"

"It can't be described in just a mouthful of words—pictures, scare-heads and all. You wait, I'll tell you all about it another time; I want to read the telegram, now."

"Hear, O Israel, the Lord God is one Lord.

"I now request that the members of my Church cease special prayer for the peace of nations, and cease in full faith that God does not hear our prayers only because of oft speaking; but that He will bless all the inhabitants of the earth, and 'none can stay His hand nor say unto Him what doest thou.' Out of His allness He must bless all with His own truth and love.

"MARY BAKER G. EDDY."

"Pleasant View, Concord, N.H., June 27, 1905."

"You see? Down to the word 'nations' anybody can understand it. There's been a prodigious war going on for about seventeen months, with destruction of whole fleets and armies, and in seventeen words she indicates certain things, to-wit: I believed we could squelch the war with prayer, therefore I ordered it; it was an error of Mortal Mind, whereas I had supposed it was an inspiration; I now order you to cease from praying for peace and take hold of something nearer our size, such as strikes and insurrections. The rest seems to mean—seems to mean . . . . Let me study it a minute. It seems to mean that He does not listen to our prayers any more because we pester Him too much. This carries us to the phrase 'oft-speaking.' At that point the fog shuts down, black and impenetrable, it solidifies into uninterpretable irrelevancies. Now then, you add up, and get these results: the praying must be stopped—which is clear and definite; the reason for the stoppage is—well, uncertain. Don't you know that the incomprehensible and uninterpretable remaining half of the message may be of *actual* importance? we may be even sure of it, I think, because the first half wasn't; then what are we confronted with? what is the world confronted with? Why, possible disaster—isn't it so? Possible disaster, absolutely impossible to avoid; and all because one cannot get at the meaning of the words intended to describe it and tell how to prevent it. You now understand how important is the interpreter's share in these matters. If you put part of the message in school-girl and the rest in Choctaw, the interpreter is going to be defeated, and colossal harm can come of it."

"I am sure it is true. What is His allness?"

"I pass."

"You which?"

"Pass. Theological expression. It probably means that she entered the game because she thought only His halfness was in it and would need help; then perceiving that His allness was there and playing on the other side, she considered it best to cash-in and draw out. I think that that must be it; it looks reasonable, you see, because in seventeen months she hadn't put up a single chip and got it back again, and so in the circumstances it would be natural for her to want to go out and see a friend. In Roman times the business went to pot through bad interpreting, as I told you before. Here in Suetonius is an instance. He is speaking of Atia, the mother of Augustus Caesar:

" 'Before her delivery she dreamed that her bowels stretched to the stars, and expanded through the whole circuit of heaven and earth.'

"Now how would you interpret that, August?"

"Who—me? I do not think I could interpret it at all, but I do wish I could have seen it, it must have been magnificent."

"Oh, yes, like enough; but doesn't it suggest anything to you?"

"Why, n-no, I can't see that it does. What would *you* think— that there had been an accident?"

"Of course not! It wasn't real, it was only a dream. It was sent to inform her that she was going to be delivered of something remarkable. What should you think it was?"

"I—why, I don't know."

"Guess."

"Do you think—well, would it be a slaughter-house?"

"Sho, you've no talent for interpretation. But that is a striking instance of what the interpreter had to deal with, in that day. The dream-messages had become loose and rickety and indefinite, like the Founder's telegram, and soon the natural thing happened: the interpreters became loose and careless and discouraged, and got to guessing instead of interpreting, and the business went to ruin. Rome had to give up dream-messages, and the Romans 'took to entrails for prophetic information."

"Why, then, these ones must have come good, 44, don't you think?"

"I mean *bird* entrails—entrails of chickens."

"I would stake my money on the others; what does a chicken know about the future?"

"Sho, you don't get the idea, August. It isn't what the chicken knows; a chicken doesn't know anything, but by examining the condition of its entrails when it was slaughtered, the augurs could find out a good deal about what was going to happen to emperors, that being the way the Roman gods had invented to communicate with them when dream-transportation went out and Western Union hadn't come in yet. It was a good idea, too, because often a chicken's entrails knew more than a Roman god did, if he was drunk, and he generally was."

"Forty-Four, aren't you afraid to speak like that about a god?"

"No. Why?"

"Because it's irreverent."

"No, it isn't."

"Why isn't it? What do you *call* irreverence?"

"Irreverence is *another person's* disrespect to *your* god; there isn't any word that tells what your disrespect to *his* god is."

I studied it over and saw that it was the truth, but I hadn't ever happened to look at it in that way before.

"Now then, August, to come back to Atia's dream. It beat every soothsayer. None of them got it right. The real meaning of it was—"

The cat dashed in, excited, and said, "I heard Katzenyammer say there's hell to pay down below!" and out she dashed again. I jumped up, but 44 said—

"Sit down. Keep your head. There's no hurry. Things are working; I think we can have a good time. I have shut down the prophecy-works and prepared for it."

"The prophecy-works?"

"Yes. Where I come from, we—"

"*Where* do you co—"

It was as far as I could get. My jaw caught, there, and he gave me a look and went on as if nothing had happened:

"Where I come from we have a gift which we get tired of, now and then. We foresee everything that is going to happen, and so when it happens there's nothing *to* it, don't you see? we don't get any surprises. We can't shut down the prophecy-works there, but we can here. That is one of the main reasons that I come here so much. I do love surprises! I'm only a youth, and it's natural. I love shows and spectacles, and stunning dramatics, and I love to astonish people, and show off, and be and do all the gaudy things a boy loves to be and do; and whenever I'm here and have got matters worked up to where there is a good prospect to the fore, I shut down the works and have a time! I've shut them down now, two hours ago, and I don't know a thing that's ahead, any more than you do. That's all—now we'll go. I wanted to tell you that. I had plans, but I've thrown them aside. I haven't any now. I will let things go their own way, and act as circumstances suggest. Then there will be surprises.

They may be small ones, and nothing to you, because you are used to them; but even the littlest ones are grand to me!"

The cat came racing in, greatly excited, and said—

"Oh, I'm so glad I'm in time! Shut the door—there's people everywhere—don't let them see in. Dear magician, get a disguise, you are in greater danger now than ever before. You have been seen, and everybody knows it, everybody is watching for you, it was most imprudent in you to show yourself. Do put on a disguise and come with me, I know a place in the castle where they'll never find you. Oh, please, please hurry! don't you hear the distant noises? they're hunting for you—do *please* hurry!"

Forty-Four was that gratified, you can't think! He said—

"There it is, you see! I hadn't any idea of it, any more than you! And there'll be more—I just feel it."

"Oh, please don't stop to talk, but get the disguise! you don't know what may happen any moment. Everybody is searching for me, and for you, too, Duplicate, and for your Original; they've been at it some time, and are coming to think all three of us is murdered—"

"*Now* I know what I'll do!" cried 44; "oh but we'll have the gayest time! go on with your news!"

"—and Katrina is wild to get a chance at you because you burnt up 44, which was the idol of her heart, and she's got a carving knife three times as long as my tail, and is ambushed behind a marble column in the great hall, and it's awful to see how savagely she rakes it and whets it up and down that column and makes the sparks fly, and darts her head out, with her eyes glaring, to see if she can see you—oh, *do* get the disguise and come with me, quick! and laws bless me, there's a conspiracy, and—"

"Oh, it's grand, August, it's just grand! and I didn't know a thing about it, any more than you. *What* conspiracy are you talking about, pussy?"

"It's the strikers, going to kill the Duplicates—I sat in Fischer's lap and heard them talk the whole thing in whispers; and they've got signs and grips and passwords and all that, so't they can tell which is themselves and which is other people, though I hope to goodness if I can, not if I had a thousand such; *do* get the disguise and come, I'm just ready to cry!"

"Oh, bother the disguise, I'm going just so, and if they offer to do anything to me I will give them a piece of my mind."

And so he opened the door and started away, Mary following him, with the tears running down, and saying—

"Oh, *they* won't care for your piece of mind—why *will* you be so imprudent and throw your life away, and you *know* they'll abuse me and bang me when you are gone!"

I became invisible and joined them.

Chapter 31

I T W A S a dark, sour, gloomy morning, and bleak and cold, with a slanting veil of powdery snow driving along, and a clamorous hollow wind bellowing down the chimneys and rumbling around the battlements and towers—just the right weather for the occasion, 44 said, nothing could improve it but an eclipse. That gave him an idea, and he said he would do an eclipse; not a real one, but an artificial one that nobody but Simon Newcomb could tell from the original Jacobs—so he started it at once, and it certainly did make those yawning old stone tunnels pretty dim and sepulchral, and also of course it furnished an additional uncanniness and muffledness to way-off footfalls, taking the harshness out of them and the edge off their echoes, because when you walk on that kind of eclipsy gloominess on a stone floor it squshes under the foot and makes that dull effect which is so shuddery and uncomfortable in these crumbly old castles where there has been such ages of cruelty and captivity and murder and mystery. And to-night would be Ghost-Night besides, and 44 did not forget to remember that, and said he wished eclipses weren't so much trouble after sundown, hanged if he wouldn't run this one all night, because it could be a great help, and a lot of ghastly effects could be gotten out of it, because all the castle ghosts turn out then, on account of its coming only every ten years, which makes it kind of select and distinguished, and still more so every Hundredth Year—which this one was—because the best ghosts from many other castles come by invitation, then, and take a hand at the great ball and banquet at midnight, a good spectacle and full of interest, insomuch that 44 had come more than once on the Hundredth Night to see it, he said, and it was very pathetic and interesting to meet up with shadowy friends that way that you haven't seen for one or two centuries and hear them tell the same mouldy things over again that they've told you several times before; because they don't have anything fresh, the way they are situated, poor things. And besides, he was going to make this the swellest Hundredth Night that had been celebrated in this castle in twelve centuries, and said he was inviting A 1 ghosts from everywhere in the world and from all the ages, past and future, and each could bring a friend if he liked—any friend, character no object, just so he is dead—and if I wanted to invite some I could, he hoped to accumulate a thousand or two, and make this *the* Hundredth Night of Hundredth Nights, and discourage competition for a thousand years.

We didn't see a soul, all the murky way from my door to the central grand staircase and half way down it—then we began to see plenty of people, our own and men from the village—and they were armed, and stood in two ranks, waiting, a double fence across the spacious hall—for the magician to pass between, if it might please him to try it; and Katrina was there, between the fences, grim and towering and soldierly, and she was watching and waiting, with her knife. I glanced back, by chance, and there was also a living fence *behind!* dim forms, men who had been keeping watch in ambush, and had silently closed in upon the magician's tracks as he passed along. Mary G. had apparently had enough of this grisly journey—she was gone.

When the people below saw that their plans had succeeded, and that their quarry was in the trap they had set, they set up a loud cheer of exultation, but it didn't seem to me to ring true; there was a doubtful note in it, and I thought likely those folks were not as

glad they had caught their bird as they were letting on to be; and
they kept crossing themselves industriously; I took that for a sign,
too.

Forty-Four moved steadily down. When he was on the last step
there was turmoil down the hall, and a volley of shoutings, with
cries of "make way—Father Adolf is come!" then he burst panting
through one of the ranks and threw himself in the way, just as
Katrina was plunging for the disguised 44, and stormed out—

"Stop her, everybody! Donkeys, would you let her butcher him,
and cheat the Church's fires!"

They jumped for Katrina, and in a moment she was struggling in
the jumble of swaying forms, with nothing visible above it but her
head and her long arm with the knife in it; and her strong voice
was pouring out her feelings with energy, and easily making itself
heard above the general din and the priest's commands:

"Let me at him—he burnt my child, my darling!" . . . . "*Keep
her off, men, keep her off!*" . . . . "He is *not* the Church's, his
blood is *mine* by rights—out of my way! I *will* have it!" . . . .
"*Back! woman, back, I tell you—force her back, men, have you no
strength? are you nothing but boys?*" . . . . "A hundred of you
shan't stay me, woman though I be!"

And sure enough, with one massy surge she wrenched herself
free, and flourished her knife, and bent her head and body forward
like a foot-racer and came charging down the living lane through
the gathering darkness—

Then suddenly there was a great light! she lifted her head and
caught it full in her swarthy face, which it transfigured with its
white glory, as it did also all that place, and its marble pillars, and
the frightened people, and Katrina dropped her knife and fell to
her knees, with her hands clasped, everybody doing the same; and
so there they were, all kneeling, like that, with hands thrust forward
or clasped, and they and the stately columns all awash in that
unearthly splendor; and there where the magician had stood, stood
44 now, in his supernal beauty and his gracious youth; and it was
from him that that flooding light came, for all his form was clothed
in that immortal fire, and flashing like the sun; and Katrina crept

on her knees to him, and bent down her old head and kissed his feet, and he bent down and patted her softly on the shoulder and touched his lips to the gray hair—*and was gone!*—and for two or three minutes you were so blinded you couldn't see your next neighbor in that submerging black darkness. Then after that it was better, and you could make out the murky forms, some still kneeling, some lying prone in a swoon, some staggering about, here and there, with their hands pressed over their eyes, as if that light had hurt them and they were in pain. Katrina was wandering off, on unsteady feet, and her knife was lying there in the midst.

It was good he thought of the eclipse, it helped out ever so much; the effects would have been fine and great in any case, but the eclipse made them grand and stunning—just letter-perfect, as it seemed to me; and he said himself it beat Barnum and Bailey hands down, and was by as much as several shades too good for the provinces—which was all Sanscrit to me, and hadn't any meaning even in Sanscrit I reckon, but was invented for the occasion, because it had a learned sound, and he liked sound better than sense as a rule. There's been others like that, but he was the worst.

I judged it would take those people several hours to get over that, and accumulate their wits again and get their bearings, for it had knocked the whole bunch dizzy; meantime there wouldn't be anything doing. I must put in the time some way until they should be in a condition to resume business at the old stand. I went to my room and put on my flesh and stretched myself out on a lounge before the fire with a book, first setting the door ajar, so that the cat could fetch news if she got hold of any, which I wished she might; but in a little while I was asleep. I did not stir again until ten at night. I woke then, and found the cat finishing her supper, and my own ready on the table and hot; and very welcome, for I hadn't eaten anything since breakfast. Mary came and occupied a chair at my board, and washed herself and delivered her news while I ate. She had witnessed the great transformation scene, and had been so astonished by it and so interested in it that she did not wait to see the end, but went up a chimney and stayed there half an hour freezing, until somebody started a fire under her, and then she was

"It's a thing he calls a paper—Boston paper."

"That's right, that's what he said. And he said it is future English and you know present English and can read it. Did he say right?"

"The *fact* is right, but he didn't say it, because he's dead."

"You wait—that's all. He said look at the date."

"Very well. He didn't say it, because he's dead, and of course wouldn't think of it; but here it is, all the same—June 28, 1905."

"That's right, it's what he said. Then he said ask you what was the Founder's message to her disciples, that was in the other Boston paper. What was it?"

"Well, he told me there was an immense war going on, and she got tired having her people pray for peace and never take a trick for seventeen months, so she ordered them to quit, and put their battery out of commission. And he said nobody could understand the rest of the message, and like enough that very ignorance would bring on an immense disaster."

"Aha! well, it *did!* He says the very minute she was stopping the praying, the two fleets were meeting, and the uncivilized one utterly annihilated the civilized one, and it wouldn't have happened if she had let the praying go on. Now then, you didn't know *that*, did you!"

"No, and I don't know it yet."

"Well, you soon will. The message was June 27, wasn't it?"

"Yes."

"Well, the disaster was *that very day*—right after the praying was stopped—and you'll find the news of it in the very next day's paper, which you've got in your hand—date, *June 28*."

I took a glance at the big headings, and said—

"M-y word! why it's absolutely *so!* Baker G., don't you know this is the most astounding thing that ever happened? It proves he *is* alive—nobody else could bring this paper. He certainly is alive, and back with us, after that tremendous abolishment and extinction which we witnessed; yes, he's alive, Mary, alive, and glad am I, oh, grateful beyond words!"

"Oh!" she cried, in a rapture, "it's just splendid, oh, just too lovely! I knew I could prove it; I knew it just as well! I thought he was gone, when he blazed up and went out, that way, and I *was* so scared and grieved—and isn't he a wonder! Duplicate, there isn't another necromancer in the business that can begin with him, now *is* there?"

"You can stake your tale and your ears on it, Mary, and don't you forget it—as he used to say. In my opinion he can give the whole trade ninety-nine in the hundred and go out every time, cross-eyed and left-handed."

"But he isn't, Duplicate."

"Isn't what?"

"Cross-eyed and left-handed."

"Who said he was, you little fool?"

"Why, you did."

"I never said anything of the kind; I said he could if he *was*. That isn't *saying* he was; it was a supposititious case, and literary; it was a figure, a metaphor, and its function was to augment the force of the—"

"Well, he *isn't*, anyway; because I've noticed, and—"

"Oh, shut up! don't I tell you it was only a *figure,* and I never meant—"

"I don't care, you'll never make *me* believe he's cross-eyed and left-handed, because the time he—"

"Baker G., if you open your mouth again I'll jam the boot-jack down it! you're as random and irrelevant and incoherent and mentally impenetrable as the afflicted Founder herself."

But she was under the bed by that time; and reflecting, probably, if she had the machinery for it.

Chapter 32

FORTY-FOUR, still playing Balthasar Hoffman the magician, entered briskly now, and threw himself in a chair. The cat emerged with confidence, spread herself, purring, in his lap, and said—

"This Duplicate wouldn't believe me when I told him, and when

I proved it he tried to cram a boot-jack down my throat, thinking to scare me, which he didn't, *didn't* you, Duplicate?"

"Didn't I *what*?"

"Why, what I just *said*."

"I don't know what you just said; it was Christian Silence and untranslatable; but I'll say yes to the whole of it if that will quiet you. Now then, keep still, and let the master tell what is on his mind."

"Well, this is on my mind, August. Some of the most distinguished people can't come. Flora McFlimsey—nothing to wear; Eve, ditto; Adam, previous engagement, and so on and so on; Nero and ever so many others find the notice too short, and are urgent to have more time. Very well, we've got to accommodate them."

"But how can we do it? The show is due to begin in an hour. Listen!"

Boom-m-m—boom-m-m—boom-m-m!—

It was the great bell of the castle tolling the hour. Our American clock on the wall struck in, and simultaneously the clock of the village—faint and far, and half of the notes overtaken in their flight and strangled by the gusty wind. We sat silent and counted, to the end.

"You see?" said I.

"Yes, I see. Eleven. Now there are two ways to manage. One is, to have time stand still—which has been done before, a lot of times; and the other one is, to turn time backward for a day or two, which is comparatively new, and offers the best effects, besides.

" 'Backward, turn backward, O Time, in thy flight—
Make me a child again, just for to-night!'—

"—'Beautiful Snow,' you see; it hasn't been written yet. *I* vote to reverse—and that is what we will do, presently. We will make the hands of the clocks travel around in the other direction."

"But will they?"

"Sure. It will attract attention—make yourself easy, as to that. But the stunning effect is going to be the sun."

"How?"

"Well, when they see him come rising up out of the west, about half a dozen hours from now, it will secure the interest of the entire world."

"I should think as much."

"Oh, yes, depend upon it. There is going to be more early rising than the human race has seen before. In my opinion it'll be a record."

"I believe you are right about it. I mean to get up and see it myself. Or stay up."

"I think it will be a good idea to have it rise in the south-west, instead of the west. More striking, you see; and hasn't been done before."

"Master, it will be wonderful! It will be the very greatest marvel the world has ever seen. It will be talked about and written about as long as the human race endures. And there'll not be any disputing over it, because every human being that's alive will get up to look at it, and there won't be one single person to say it's a lie."

"It's so. It will be the only perfectly authenticated event in all human history. All the other happenings, big and little, have got to depend on minority-testimony, and very little of that—but not so, this time, dontcherknow. And this one's patented. There aren't going to be any encores."

"How long shall we go backwards, Balthasar?"

"Two or three days or a week; long enough to accommodate Robert Bruce, and Henry I and such, who have hearts and things scattered around here and there and yonder, and have to get a basket and go around and collect; so we will let the sun and the clocks go backwards a while, then start them ahead in time to fetch up all right at midnight to-night—then the shades will begin to arrive according to schedule."

"It grows on me! It's going to be the most prodigious thing that ever happened, and—"

"Yes," he burst out, in a rapture of eloquence, "and will round out and perfect the reputation I've been building for Balthasar Hoffman, and make him the most glorious magician that ever lived, and get him burnt, to a dead moral certainty. You know I've taken a lot of pains with that reputation; I've taken more interest in it than anything I've planned out in centuries; I've spared neither labor nor thought, and I feel a pride in it and a sense of satisfaction such as I have hardly ever felt in a mere labor of love before; and when I get it completed, now, in this magnificent way, and get him burnt, or pulverized, or something showy and picturesque, like that, I shan't mind the trouble I've had, in the least; not in the least, I give you my word."

Boom-m-m—boom-m-m—boom-m-m—

"There she goes! striking eleven again."

"Is it really?"

"Count—you'll see."

It woke the cat, and she stretched herself out about a yard and a half, and asked if time was starting back—which showed that she had heard the first part of the talk. And understood it of course, because it was in German. She was informed that time was about to start back; so she arranged herself for another nap, and said that when we got back to ten she would turn out and catch that rat again.

I was counting the clock-strokes—counting aloud—

"*Eight . . . . nine . . . . ten . . . . eleven—*"

Forty-Four shouted—

"Backward! turn backward! O Time in thy flight! Look at the clock-hands! Listen!"

Instantly I found myself counting the strokes again, aloud—

"Eleven . . . ten . . . . nine . . . eight . . . . seven . . . six . . . . five . . . . four . . . two . . . one!"

At once the cat woke and repeated her remark about re-catching the rat—saying it backwards!

Then Forty-Four said—

"see you'll—Count."

Whereupon I said—

"really? it Is"

And he remarked—the booming of the great castle clock mixing with his words—

"again. eleven striking goes! she There word (here his voice began to become impressive, then to nobly rise, and swell, and grow in eloquent feeling and majestic expression), my you give I least, the in not least; the in had, I've trouble the mind shan't I that, like picturesque, and showy something or pulverized, or burnt, him get and way, magnificent this in now, completed, it get I when and before; love of labor mere a in felt ever hardly have I as such satisfaction of sense a and it in pride (here his voice was near to breaking, so deeply were his feelings stirred) a feel I and thought, nor labor neither spared I've centuries; in out planned I've anything than it in interest more taken I've reputation; that with pains of lot a taken I've know You (here his winged eloquence reached its loftiest flight, and in his deep organ-tones he thundered forth his sublime words) certainty. moral dead a to burnt, him get and lived, ever that magician glorious most the him make and Hoffman, Balthasar for building been I've reputation the perfect and out round will and Yes,"—

My brain was spinning, it was audibly whizzing, I rose reeling, and was falling lifeless to the floor, when 44 caught me. His touch restored me, and he said—

"I see it is too much for you, you cannot endure it, you would go mad. Therefore I relieve you of your share in this grand event. You shall look on and enjoy, taking no personal part in the backward flight of time, nor in its return, until it reaches the present hour again and resumes its normal march forward. Go and come as you please, amuse yourself as you choose."

Those were blessed words! I could not tell him how thankful I was.

A considerable blank followed—a silent one, for it represented the unrepeated conversation which he and I had had about the turning back of time and the sun.

Then another silent blank followed; it represented the interval occupied by my dispute with the cat as to whether the magician was come alive again or not.

I filled in these intervals not wearily nor drearily—oh, no indeed, just the reverse; for my gaze was glued to that American clock—

watching its hands creeping backward around its face, an uncanny spectacle!

Then I fell asleep, and when I woke again the clock had gone back seven hours, and it was mid-afternoon. Being privileged to go and come as I pleased, I threw off my flesh and went down to see the grand transformation-spectacle repeated backwards.

It was as impressive and as magnificent as ever. In the darkness some of the people lay prone, some were kneeling, some were wandering and tottering about with their hands over their eyes, Katrina was walking backwards on unsteady feet; she backed further and further, then knelt and bowed her head—then that white glory burst upon the darkness and 44 stood clothed as with the sun; and he bent and kissed the old head—and so on and so on, the scene repeated itself backwards, detail by detail, clear to the beginning; then the magician, the cat and I walked backward up the stairs and through the gathering eclipse to my room.

After that, as time drifted rearward, I skipped some things and took in others, according to my humor. I watched my Duplicate turn from nothing into a lovely soap-bubble statue with delicate rainbow-hues playing over it; watched its skeleton gather form and solidity; watched it put on flesh and clothes, and all that; but I skipped the interviews with the cat; I also skipped the interview with the master; and when the clock had gone back twenty-three hours and I was due to appear drunk in Marget's chamber, I took the pledge and stayed away.

Then, for amusement and to note effects, 44 and I—invisible—appeared in China, where it was noonday. The sun was just ready to turn downward on his new north-eastern track, and millions of yellow people were gazing at him, dazed and stupid, while other millions lay stretched upon the ground everywhere, exhausted with the terrors and confusions they had been through, and now blessedly unconscious. We loafed along behind the sun around the globe, tarrying in all the great cities on the route, and observing and admiring the effects. Everywhere weary people were re-chattering previous conversations backwards and not understanding each other, and oh, they did look so tuckered out and tired of it all! and always there were groups gazing miserably at the town-clocks; in every city funerals were being held again that had already been held once, and the hearses and the processions were marching solemnly backwards; where there was war, yesterday's battles were being refought, wrong-end-first; the previously killed were getting killed again, the previously wounded were getting hit again in the same place and complaining about it; there were blood-stirring and tremendous charges of masses of steel-clad knights across the field —backwards; and on the oceans the ships, with full-bellied sails were speeding backwards over the same water they had traversed the day before, and some of each crew were scared and praying, some were gazing in mute anguish at the crazy sun, and the rest were doing profanity beyond imagination.

At Rouen we saw Henry I gathering together his split skull and his other things.

Chapter 33

S URELY Forty-Four was the flightiest creature that ever was! Nothing interested him long at a time. He would contrive the most elaborate projects, and put his whole mind and heart into them, then he would suddenly drop them, in the midst of their fulfilment, and start something fresh. It was just so with his Assembly of the Dead. He summoned those forlorn wrecks from all the world and from all the epochs and ages, and then, when everything was ready for the exhibition, he wanted to flit back to Moses's time and see the Egyptians floundering around in the Dead Sea, and take me along with him. He said he had seen it twice, and it was one of the handsomest and most exciting incidents a body ever saw. It was all I could do to persuade him to wait a while.

To me the Procession was very good indeed, and most impressive. First, there was an awful darkness. All visible things gloomed down gradually, losing their outlines little by little, then disappeared utterly. The thickest and solidest and blackest darkness followed, and a silence which was so still it was as if the world was holding its breath. That deep stillness continued, and continued, minute after minute, and got to be so oppressive that presently I was holding *my* breath—that is, only half-breathing. Then a wave of cold air came drifting along, damp, searching, and smelling of the grave, and was shivery and dreadful. After about ten minutes I heard a faint clicking sound coming as from a great distance. It came slowly nearer and nearer, and a little louder and a little louder, and increasing steadily in mass and volume, till all the place was filled with a dry sharp clacking and was right abreast of us and passing by! Then a vague twilight suffused the place and through it and drowned in it we made out the spidery dim forms of thousands of skeletons marching! It made me catch my breath. It was that grewsome and grisly and horrible, you can't think.

Soon the light paled to a half dawn, and we could distinguish details fairly well. Forty-Four had enlarged the great hall of the castle, so as to get effects. It was a vast and lofty corridor, now, and stretched away for miles and miles, and the Procession drifted solemnly down it sorrowfully clacking, losing definiteness gradually, and finally fading out in the far distances, and melting from sight.

Forty-Four named no end of those poor skeletons, as they passed by, and he said the most of them had been distinguished, in their day and had cut a figure in the world. Some of the names were familiar to me, but the most of them were not. Which was natural, for they belonged to nations that perished from the earth ten, and twenty, and fifty, and a hundred, and three hundred, and six hundred thousand years ago, and so of course I had never heard of them.

By force of 44's magic each skeleton had a tab on him giving his name and date, and telling all about him, in brief. It was a good idea, and saved asking questions. Pharaoh was there, and David and Goliath and several other of the sacred characters; and Adam and Eve, and some of the Caesars, and Cleopatra, and Charlemagne, and Dagobert, and kings, and kings and kings till you couldn't count them—the most of them from away back thousands and thousands of centuries before Adam's time. Some of them fetched their crowns along, and had a rotten velvet rag or two dangling about their bones, a kind of pathetic spectacle.

And there were skeletons whom I had known, myself, and been at their funerals, only three or four years before—men and women, boys and girls; and they put out their poor bony hands and shook with me, and looked so sad. Some of the skeletons dragged the rotting ruins of their coffins after them by a string, and seemed pitifully anxious that that poor property shouldn't come to harm.

But to think how long the pathos of a thing can last, and still carry its touching effect, the same as if it was new and happened yesterday! There was a slim skeleton of a young woman, and it went by with its head bowed and its bony hands to its eyes, crying, apparently. Well, it was a young mother whose little child disappeared one day and was never heard of again, and so her heart was broken, and she cried her life away. It brought the tears to my eyes and made my heart ache to see that poor thing's sorrow. When I looked at her tab I saw it had happened five hundred thousand years ago! It seemed strange that it should still affect me, but I suppose such things never grow old, but remain always new.

King Arthur came along, by and by, with all his knights. That interested me, because we had just been printing his history, copying it from Caxton. They rode upon bony crates that had once been horses, and they looked very stately in their ancient armor, though it was rusty and lacked a piece here and there, and through those gaps you could see the bones inside. They talked together, skeletons as they were, and you could see their jawbones go up and down through the slits in their helmets. By grace of Forty-Four's magic I could understand them. They talked about Arthur's last battle, and seemed to think it happened yesterday, which shows that a thousand years in the grave is merely a night's sleep, to the dead, and counts for nothing.

It was the same with Noah and his sons and their wives. Evidently they had forgotten that they had ever left the Ark, and could not understand how they came to be wandering around on land.

They talked about the weather; they did not seem to be interested in anything else.

The skeletons of Adam's predecessors outnumbered the later representatives of our race by myriads, and they rode upon un-dreamt-of monsters of the most extraordinary bulk and aspect. They marched ten thousand abreast, our walls receding and melt-ing away and disappearing, to give them room, and the earth was packed with them as far as the eye could reach. Among them was the Missing Link. That is what 44 called him. He was an under-sized skeleton, and he was perched on the back of a long-tailed and long-necked creature ninety feet long and thirty-three feet high; a creature that had been dead eight million years, 44 said.

For hours and hours the dead passed by in continental masses, and the bone-clacking was so deafening you could hardly hear yourself think. Then, all of a sudden 44 waved his hand and we stood in an empty and soundless world.

Chapter 34

"AND YOU are going away, and will not come back any more."

"Yes," he said. "We have comraded long together, and it has been pleasant—pleasant for both; but I must go now, and we shall not see each other any more."

"In this life, 44, but in another? We shall meet in another, surely, 44?"

Then all tranquilly and soberly he made the strange answer—

"There is no other."

A subtle influence blew upon my spirit from his, bringing with it a vague, dim, but blessed and hopeful feeling that the incredible words might be true—even *must* be true.

"Have you never suspected this, August?"

"No—how could I? But if it can only be true—"

"It is true."

A gush of thankfulness rose in my breast, but a doubt checked it before it could issue in words, and I said—

"But—but—we have *seen* that future life—seen it in its actuality, and so—"

"It was a vision—it had no existence."

I could hardly breathe for the great hope that was struggling in me—

"A vision?—a vi—"

"Life itself is only a vision, a dream."

It was electrical. By God I had had that very thought a thousand times in my musings!

"*Nothing* exists; all is a dream. God—man—the world,—the sun, the moon, the wilderness of stars: a dream, all a dream, they have no existence. *Nothing exists save empty space—and you!*"

"I!"

"And you are not you—you have no body, no blood, no bones, you are but a *thought*. I myself have no existence, I am but a dream —your dream, creature of your imagination. In a moment you will have realized this, then you will banish me from your visions and I shall dissolve into the nothingness out of which you made me . . . . .

"I am perishing already—I am failing, I am passing away. In a little while you will be alone in shoreless space, to wander its limitless solitudes without friend or comrade forever—for you will remain a *Thought*, the only existent Thought, and by your nature inextinguishable, indestructible. But I your poor servant have revealed you to yourself and set you free. Dream other dreams, and better! . . . .

"Strange! that you should not have suspected, years ago, centuries, ages, æons ago! for you have existed, companionless, through all the eternities. Strange, indeed, that you should not have suspected that your universe and its contents were only dreams, visions, fictions! Strange, because they are so frankly and hysterically insane—like all dreams: a God who could make good children as easily as bad, yet preferred to make bad ones; who could have made every one of them happy, yet never made a single happy one; who made them prize their bitter life, yet stingily cut it short; who gave his angels eternal happiness unearned, yet required his other children to earn it; who gave his angels painless lives, yet cursed his other children with biting miseries and maladies of mind and body; who mouths justice, and invented hell—mouths mercy, and invented hell—mouths Golden Rules, and foregiveness multiplied by seventy times seven, and invented hell; who mouths morals to other people, and has none himself; who frowns upon crimes, yet commits them all; who created man without invitation, then tries to shuffle the responsibility for man's acts upon man, instead of honorably placing it where it belongs, upon himself; and finally, with altogether divine obtuseness, invites this poor abused slave to worship him! . . . .

"You perceive, *now,* that these things are all impossible, except in a dream. You perceive that they are pure and puerile insanities, the silly creations of an imagination that is not conscious of its freaks—in a word, that they are a dream, and you the maker of it. The dream-marks are all present—you should have recognized them earlier . . . . .

"It is true, that which I have revealed to you: there is no God, no universe, no human race, no earthly life, no heaven, no hell. It is all a Dream, a grotesque and foolish dream. Nothing exists but You. And You are but a *Thought*—a vagrant Thought, a useless Thought, a homeless Thought, wandering forlorn among the empty eternities!"

He vanished, and left me appalled; for I knew, and realized, that all he had said was true.

THE END

Explanatory Notes

Notes are keyed to page and line: 5.3–18 means page 5, lines 3–18. Chapter titles are not included when counting lines.

title.5–6   BEING AN ANCIENT TALE FOUND IN A JUG, AND FREELY TRANSLATED FROM THE JUG] The author was not consistent in maintaining his role as translator, but the significance of his subtitle is made clear in chapter 22. There his supernatural character, 44, who is having difficulty enlightening August, laments that the human mind "doesn't *hold* anything; one cannot pour the starred and shoreless expanses of the universe into a jug!" (114.2–4).

3.9–4.3   Yes, Austria . . . shade-trees.] In sketching Eseldorf, Mark Twain used his notes made in July 1897 about the Swiss village of Weggis. Like his home town, Hannibal (Missouri), Weggis was a small village backed by forested heights and fronting on an expanse of water. It also had the air of repose and lethargy that he associated with Hannibal, described in *Life on the Mississippi* (1883) as a "town drowsing in the sunshine" (chapter 4). Impressions of the recently observed European village are blended here with those of the well-remembered American one. For further dis-

189

cussion of the setting, see Henry Nash Smith, "Mark Twain's Images of Hannibal: From St. Petersburg to Eseldorf," *Texas Studies in English* 37 (1958): 3–23; and John S. Tuckey, "Hannibal, Weggis, and Mark Twain's Eseldorf," *American Literature* 42 (May 1970): 235–240.

5.3–18   He was . . . saying is.] Mark Twain based his characterization of Father Adolf on his unfavorable impressions of Dr. Karl Lueger, leader of the anti-Jewish Christian Socialist Party and Burgomeister of Vienna. Lueger had been prominent in events leading to an outbreak of rioting on the floor of the Austrian parliament in the fall of 1897, which Mark Twain witnessed. The manuscript for this chapter, which Mark Twain salvaged from an earlier version of his novel called "The Chronicle of Young Satan," shows that he first called the bad priest "Lueger," but changed the name to "Adolf" before reaching the end of the chapter.

11.10–16.6   stretched . . . myself.] Sometime after Mark Twain decided to call his novel "The Mysterious Stranger" in 1902 or 1903, he wrote a note to himself on the manuscript: "Put in (Description of the region from the 'Young Satan.')." This long passage was in fact salvaged from the earlier manuscript, "The Chronicle of Young Satan," which he abandoned about 1900.

11.20–22   In some . . . sadder still.] Mark Twain's own "castle," the great house in Hartford, had been standing empty and neglected since the death of his daughter Susy there in 1896. He and his wife could not bear to live in the house after that event, and he sold it in the spring of 1903.

13.27   *pi*] Pi is jumbled or mixed type, requiring resorting. Here and in subsequent passages, Mark Twain uses the jargon of the printshop that he had known since 1847 when he worked as a printer's devil and jack-of-all-trades in the office of the Hannibal *Gazette*. He did not abandon the printer's trade until 1857, when he turned to piloting. For a glossary of the printing terms used in the novel, see William M. Gibson, ed.,

> *Mark Twain's Mysterious Stranger Manuscripts* (Berkeley and Los Angeles: University of California Press, 1969), pp. 475–480.

20.25   "Number 44, New Series 864,962."] Mark Twain's rationale for this arresting number-name is not certainly known, but there are several interesting speculations. Henry Nash Smith has suggested that the name may derive from Mark Twain's early acquaintance with the two Levin boys in Hannibal. They were the first Jews he had ever seen and they seemed to him "clothed invisibly in the damp and cobwebby mould of antiquity." The youths of Hannibal jokingly nicknamed them "Twenty-two," that is, "twice Levin" ("Mark Twain's Images of Hannibal," p. 20). William M. Gibson has noted a joke that appeared in "A Mystery," a newspaper sketch about Mark Twain's "Double" which he published in the Cleveland *Herald* on 16 November 1868. Complaining that his "Double" was going about the countryside misbehaving and giving the author a bad reputation, Mark Twain said: "I am fading, still fading. Shortly, if my distress of mind continues, there may be only four of us left. [That is a joke, and it naturally takes the melancholy tint of my own feelings. I will explain it: I am Twain, which is two; my Double is Double-Twain, which is four more; four and two are six; two from six leave four. It is very sad.]" Gibson observes that "in a punning non-mathematical sense, 44 might be Twain twice doubled" (*Mark Twain's Mysterious Stranger Manuscripts*, p. 473).

For many psychologists, four or a multiple of four symbolizes psychic wholeness. The number forty-four would intensify this significance. See, for example, C. G. Jung, *Man and His Symbols* (Garden City, N.Y.: Doubleday, 1969), p. 200. Mark Twain's work of course antedates Jung's; however, Jung did not claim to have invented the signification of fourness, but only to have elucidated it as an abiding symbol of the whole personality, the greater Self that includes both the conscious and the unconscious mind. The number forty-four would, in this respect, express a high degree of psychic wholeness. See the note to 187.27.

37.21–30   Moses was setting type . . . double-leaded at that.]
                Mark Twain here displays his print-shop expertise.
                The incompetent Moses Haas needs a guide to keep his
                place in the copy he is following, and he spaces his
                lines of type very unevenly. He sets only 600 ems of
                type an hour on a fat take (copy having much open
                space, as for example poetry) that is double-leaded
                (has lines widely spaced).

45.31   *B.-A.*"] The letters signify "Bottle-Assed" (from the
                shape of a tapered kind of type) and apparently refer
                in this context to August's "girl-boy" figure.

55.20   "In the year 1453] Mark Twain here pinned to his
                manuscript clippings from a religious pamphlet issued
                in 1902. On a manuscript page inserted at the end of
                the preceding chapter he wrote: "NOTE: It is curious
                and interesting to find that the miracles recounted by
                Father Peter in the next chapter are still kept on tap,
                in Father Peter's identical words, in the pious publica-
                tions of the convent of the Perpetual Adoration at
                Clyde, Missouri, an institution devoted to good and
                charitable works and rest from intellectual activity.—
                TRANSLATOR." He later deleted the note. The clip-
                pings, in which Mark Twain made minor changes,
                provide the text for Father Peter's sermon at 55.20–
                56.8, 56.14–25, 56.28–31, 57.6–13, and 57.24–58.6.

122.6   "Elisabeth von Arnim!"] Elisabeth (Bettina) von
                Arnim was a young friend of Goethe's, whose wife
                found her devotion excessive. After Goethe's death
                Elisabeth wrote about their friendship and published
                some of his letters to her.

124.26–27   Waking-Self, the Dream-Self, and the Soul] Mark
                Twain had explored these psychological concepts in
                his notebook, seven or eight years before writing this
                passage. In an extended entry dated 7 January 1897,
                he distinguished three selves: the waking self; "that
                other person [who] is in command during the somnam-
                bulic sleep"; and a *"spiritualized self* which can *detach
                itself* & go wandering off upon affairs of its own—for
                recreation, perhaps" (*Mark Twain's Notebooks*, ed.
                Albert Bigelow Paine [New York and London: Har-

per & Brothers, 1935], p. 349; corrected against the manuscript).

125.20–21   Box and Cox lodgers] Box was the name of the journeyman printer in a farce by John Maddison Morton, *Box and Cox* (1847).

135.18–19   I had only ruined myself.] Mark Twain carried his novel this far at Florence in the spring of 1904. He resumed composition at the end of June 1905 and then wrote, at the bottom of the last manuscript page of chapter 25, "June 30/05[.] Burned the rest (30,000 words) of this book this morning. Too diffusive." That he did in fact destroy a substantial amount of what he had already written is confirmed by his letter to his daughter Clara on the preceding day: "I have spent the day reading the book I wrote in Florence. I destroyed 125 pages of it, & expect to go over it again tomorrow & destroy 25 more. Then I think I will take hold of it and finish it" (29 June 1905, typescript, Mark Twain Papers). Mark Twain's wife had died in Florence on 5 June 1904; it is likely that the "too diffusive" portion of the manuscript he destroyed had been written in the extremity of his grief. Chapter 26 begins the part he wrote in 1905.

136.21–138.11 that figure capered in . . . noble pathos.] Forty-four cheers up August by putting on a one-man minstrel show, playing the parts of both end men. Mark Twain was a long-time fan of the authentic (as opposed to the black-face) minstrel show. In 1873, writing in praise of the Jubilee Singers from Nashville, he said: "I think these gentlemen and ladies make eloquent music—and what is as much to the point, they reproduce the true melody of the plantations. . . . I was reared in the South, and my father owned slaves, and I do not know when anything has so moved me as did the plaintive melodies of the Jubilee Singers. It was the first time for twenty-five or thirty years that I had heard such songs, or heard them sung in the genuine old way—and it is a way, I think, that white people cannot imitate—and never can, for that matter, for one must have been a slave himself in order to feel what that life was and so convey the pathos of it in the music" (Samuel Clemens to Tom Hood, et al., 10 March 1873, *Mark Twain's Collected Letters, Volume 3*, ed. Michael B. Frank, Berkeley and Los Angeles: University of California Press, 1983).

137.25–26   "I reckon *that* gets in to where you live, oh I guess not!"] Mark Twain wrote in 1865: "When you want *genuine music*—music that will come right home to you like a bad quarter, suffuse your system like strychnine whisky, go right through you like Brandreth's pills, ramify your whole constitution like the measles, and break out on your hide like the pin-feather pimples on a picked goose,—when you want all this, just smash your piano, and invoke the glory-beaming banjo!" ("Enthusiastic Eloquence," San Francisco *Dramatic Chronicle*, 23 June 1865, reprinted in *Early Tales & Sketches, Volume 2*, ed. Edgar Marquess Branch and Robert H. Hirst, with the assistance of Harriet Elinor Smith [Berkeley and Los Angeles: University of California Press, 1981], p. 235).

151.29   set my spirit free!] This plea from August's Dream-Self foreshadows the concluding chapter, where 44 tells August, "But I your poor servant have revealed you to yourself and set you free" (186.27–28).

160.27–30   groping Mortal Mind . . . dull Mortal Mind's reach."] The "Mortal Mind" is a basic concept in the doctrines of Christian Science.

165.19–27   "Hear, O Israel . . . June 27, 1905."] A clipping from the Boston *Herald*, which Mark Twain pinned to his manuscript, is the source for this quotation.

175.17–18   the very minute . . . two fleets were meeting] Here Mark Twain rearranged history for dramatic effect and for a joke on Mary Baker Eddy, the founder of Christian Science and a favorite satirical target. The battle of Tsushima, which resulted in the destruction of the Russian fleet and led to the end of the Russo-Japanese War, occurred on 27 May 1905—one month before the date assigned it in the novel.

177.10   Flora McFlimsey—nothing to wear] A popular poem by William Allen Butler, first published in *Harper's*

Weekly on 7 February 1857, concerned a Miss Flora M'Flimsey who had "Nothing to Wear."

177.27–29   " 'Backward, turn backward . . . hasn't been written yet.] Mark Twain quotes the first two lines of Elizabeth Akers Allen's poem "Rock Me to Sleep," first published in the *Saturday Evening Post* on 9 January 1860. Mark Twain probably expected his readers to recall the widely publicized controversy in 1867 and 1868 about who had, in fact, written the poem.

182.16   his other things.] The part of the manuscript written in 1905 ends here. The next chapter, comprising eight manuscript pages, was written in 1908.

185.17–187.29   AND YOU are going away . . . THE END] Mark Twain wrote this chapter in Florence in 1904; he headed it "Conclusion of the Book." That he intended it as the ending for *No. 44, The Mysterious Stranger*, and not for any earlier version of the story, is established by the names "44" and "August," which appear together only in this version. The manuscript shows that Albert Bigelow Paine altered these names when he edited the chapter for his 1916 edition of the novel.

187.27   He vanished] This conclusion suggests the psychic wholeness implied by 44's name. In psychological terms, if a full assimilation of the unconscious to the conscious were to be achieved, 44 and August would in effect merge. There would no longer be a projection on the part of August by which the unconscious component of the total psyche would be seen as a strange and mysterious otherness. The illusion of separateness would dissolve, even as at the last moment 44 vanishes in the act of completing August's enlightenment.

Note on the Text

The text of Mark Twain's novel published here is a photographic reproduction of the typesetting first published in 1969 by the University of California Press in *Mark Twain's Mysterious Stranger Manuscripts*, edited by William M. Gibson (pp. 201–405). That text was carefully established from the manuscript, and the typesetting meticulously checked, by Professor Gibson and the staff of the Mark Twain Project in accord with the standards of the Center for Editions of American Authors (CEAA) and with generous financial support from the Editing Program of the National Endowment for the Humanities (NEH), an independent federal agency. The 1969 edition brought into print, for the first time, three quite different versions of Mark Twain's story about a superhuman character, which the author left in manuscript at the time of his death in 1910: "The Chronicle of Young Satan," some 55,000 words written in several stints during the years from 1897 to 1900, and left incomplete; "Schoolhouse Hill," some 15,000 words written in 1898 and also left incomplete; and "No. 44, The Mysterious Stranger," some 65,000 words written mostly between 1902 and 1905, and last worked on in 1908. All three manuscripts are in the Mark Twain Papers in The Bancroft Library at the University of California, Berkeley.

These materials were available to Albert Bigelow Paine, Mark Twain's literary executor, and Frederick A. Duneka, an editor at Harper and Brothers, when they prepared a posthumous publication of the story which appeared in 1916, bearing the title *The Mysterious Stranger*. For their edition they used the earliest rather than the latest of the manuscripts ("Chronicle" instead of "No. 44"), and they took extraordinary liberties with what Mark Twain had written. They deleted fully one-fourth of the author's words; they wrote into the story the character of an astrologer, who did not even appear in the manuscript, letting him assume most of the villainies Mark Twain had assigned to the bad priest, Father Adolf. And, since the "Chronicle" version was incomplete, they appropriated the concluding chapter Mark Twain had written for his latest and longest version, "No. 44, The Mysterious Stranger," altering the names of the characters in order to make the ending consistent with "Chronicle." The editors said nothing about their alterations, and the facts were not known even to scholars familiar with the manuscripts until John S. Tuckey published *Mark Twain and Little Satan* in 1963. These events may suffice to show why the version of his novel that Mark Twain wrote last, and the only one that he completed, has so long remained unknown and unread.

The present text differs from the original 1969 typesetting in only one feature: it adopts the full title and subtitle preserved in Mark Twain's manuscript.

Further information about Mark Twain's composition of this novel and about related matters will be found in the original 1969 edition in the Mark Twain Papers Series as well as in the following books: John S. Tuckey, *Mark Twain and Little Satan: The Writing of "The Mysterious Stranger"* (West Lafayette: Purdue University Studies, 1963); John S. Tuckey, *The Mysterious Stranger and the Critics* (Belmont: Wadsworth Publishing Co., 1968); Sholom J. Kahn, *Mark Twain's Mysterious Stranger: A Study of the Manuscript Texts* (Columbia: University of Missouri Press, 1978).

Robert H. Hirst
General Editor, Mark Twain Project
April 1982